CW01668607

Gordon Square

Tracy Martin-Summers

Michael Terence Publishing

First published in paperback by
Michael Terence Publishing in 2020
www.mtp.agency

ISBN 9781800940130

Prologue

"Dad, I can't find my shoes," came a tearful voice from the upstairs bedroom. Roberta took a second look under her bed, which housed all sorts of interesting and, according to Roberta, essential items. "Where are they?" she questioned, looking all around her room. She tossed to one side the remains of a half-eaten doughnut which she had secretly taken to bed last night, without permission. Her mother had strictly told her that she wasn't to have anything else to eat, as the previous evening she had made herself sick from eating too many marshmallows. Roberta wasn't very good at following instructions and seemed to be a law unto herself. Unlike her sister, two years her junior, who was a goody two shoes, Anika never did anything wrong. She seemed perfect in every way and was by far the favoured child, thought Roberta, glimpsing the tip of her black shiny, patent leather shoe. She pulled at the arm of her favourite teddy, Arthur, who was shielding the shoe from view and was pleased to see that they were both there. She scrambled from under the bed, shoes in hand, informing all who cared that she had located both.

There is a God, thought her father, eyeing the clock on the mantle which now showed 12.55pm. He placed his newspaper down on the coffee table and rose to his feet. "Well, perhaps if they can find their way onto your feet we can make a move," he shouted, exasperated by his eldest daughter's lack of organisational skills.

"I'm coming, I'm coming," yelled Roberta, doing up her final buckle and declaring herself ready at last. She raced down the staircase, two at a time and stood to attention at her father's feet. "Reporting for duty, Captain," she said, giggling.

A smile spread rapidly across her father's face. He couldn't help himself, Roberta always had a way of making him laugh, even when she was so annoying. "What on earth have you been doing up there?" he questioned. "No, don't tell me," he added, knowing that her explanation would take ages and they would be detained even further.

Roberta skipped her way up the garden path and stood patiently by the side of her father's car, while he locked the front door and made his way towards his black Cortina. He could just about make out the sound of the grandfather clock chiming in the hallway behind him, confirming once again that he was late picking his wife and daughter up from ballet. Anika was the talented one in this area. They had both joined the class but it soon became apparent that Roberta lacked any kind of grace in this art and was more suited to the football pitch than the theatrical world of ballet. Roberta was secretly glad that she hadn't been forced to pursue this Saturday afternoon pastime, which gave her more time to paint. She loved painting and hoped that one day her artwork would be admired by all in an art gallery in London and longed for the day she could outshine her sibling.

"Buckle up now," came the instruction from her father, as she climbed into the front seat beside him. She was only allowed to sit in the front when her mother wasn't with them, and she really enjoyed this privilege on a Saturday when they drove to the dance studio on Ryder Street. It was a fifteen-minute drive to the studio, so they were already late, as the class ended promptly at 1pm.

Her father started the ignition, shifted into drive and pulled away in his new automatic company car. He was a proud man, was held in high regard by all that knew him and was a total pushover when it came to his two daughters. Roberta started to fidget, reaching out for the controls on the dashboard. "Come on now," said her father gruffly, pushing her hand away with his left arm, "if you keep touching everything I will have to pull over and transfer you to the back seat." Roberta could never resist testing and poking everything that came in her direction and had decided that if she wasn't to become a famous artist she would be a scientist. She had told everyone this and often used it as an excuse to touch things that were no concern of hers.

They were soon pulling into Ryder Street, and Roberta could just about eye her mother who was standing slightly out of view behind an exceptionally overweight man wearing a black suit, fitting for a conductor of an orchestra, she thought. Anika was standing to her side practising her pirouette moves and neither seemed to look concerned about their lateness. Anika clocked sight of them first and started to run towards the car, as it was gracefully manoeuvred into a parking space conveniently four spaces away from where they were standing. Anika climbed into the back, fighting back her jealousy when she eyed Roberta in the front seat. She hated the fact that her older sister got to ride shotgun, when she always had to sit in the back. Roberta slowly undid the buckle of her seatbelt prolonging the time she was to spend in the front, knowing full well that this was going to upset Anika even further. "Come on now Roberta," said her father, knowing the reason behind his daughter's slow departure into the back. "Make way for your mother," he added, smiling as his beautiful wife opened the car door to aid her daughter's exit. "Sorry we're late love," he told her, dismissing his daughter's presence, making way for the love of his life.

"No worries," she assured him, we were late leaving the hall in any case, she told him. "Anika has been chosen for the leading role in a junior production of Cinderella," she told him.

Anika beamed from ear to ear, proud to have been given this distinguished role, as she shoved a pamphlet into Roberta's hand. "Look," she said, pointing to the name of the production that was to be the Christmas production December 1976. Joe smiled at his wife, thinking how stunning she looked in her fur coat, as her auburn locks framed her delicate features. He was the luckiest man on the planet, he thought to himself, as he pulled away from the pavement. Mary turned to look over her right shoulder at the girls, who were now sitting quietly in the back staring at the pamphlet. She knew that Roberta would be sulking at her sister's new-found stardom, and Anika, who was exceptionally sensitive was trying not to boast, albeit she wanted to shout it from the rooftops.

Joe glanced at his watch, noticing that they were now also late for their restaurant reservation. They always dined on a Saturday afternoon in an Italian restaurant called Gustavo and Roberta's. Roberta loved the fact that the restaurant, according to her, was named after her and mentioned this artificial fact every single week, without fail. Gustavo always reserved the seat by the window, overlooking the venetian courtyard and this was their special time together as a family. It didn't matter that they were a little late, time keeping was never really the family's strong point and Gustavo was fully aware of this and never made reference to it on their arrival.

"Buo pomeriggio mici piccolo," yelled Gustavo, approaching them as they walked through the front doors. He always referred to the girls as little ones, much to the annoyance of Roberta, who felt she was far too grown up for this form of greeting and that it reflected more on her younger sister who was seven.

"It's my birthday next month," she told him in an informative voice, "and I will be nine," she said, feeling that she wanted to get this point across.

"Well, well," said Gustavo, "from now on you will be young ladies, 'giovani donne," he told her, as he ushered them towards their usual table. Anika sniggered as he had included her in this reference and she knew that it had annoyed Roberta immensely, as she had a bright red face. Well at least it took her mind off the fact that the restaurant was called Roberta's, so they didn't have to listen to that nonsense yet again, she thought to herself. Gustavo shook her father's hand vigorously and then graced her mother's hand with a kiss. He always did this generous greeting which made them all feel like VIP's.

"Will you be having your very grown up birthday party here, Roberta?" questioned Gustao, smiling as he passed her a menu.

"No," she responded, "I'm having a disco at my house and all my friends are coming," and I'm getting a lava lamp for my birthday from Granny," she added, as if this was an extremely important point to add.

"You are an extremely lucky signorina," he told her, kissing the back of her hand like he did her mother's. Roberta liked this form of grown up greeting, she gave Anika a look of dismissal and then turned her attention to her lunch menu.

"I think I will have the tomato soup," she informed them all, smiling at her choice from the vast menu.

Anika scowled at her and then decided to say her piece. "I don't know why you bother to even look at the menu, Roberta, you choose tomato soup every single week, without fail," she told her, knowing full well that this was going to cause an argument.

"I do not," said Roberta, "last week I had oxtail," she informed her, in an annoyed tone.

"Girls, girls, can we stop this bickering at the dinner table please," said their father in an aggravated tone. "Everyone can have the food of their choice on a Saturday afternoon," he told them. Roberta nudged Anika while her father's attention was drawn to his menu. She was always pleased that on a Saturday they didn't have to abide by the usual rules of meat and two veg to ensure they got all their vitamins and that they could have anything they liked and that included tomato soup, if she so wished.

Anika chose spaghetti meatballs and her mother and father selected pasta carbonara. Gustavo looked across at Roberta eager to receive her choice of the day and smiled to himself when she said, "Tomato soup please, Gustavo, with a pinch of Italian herbs."

"Buon Appetito," he said, placed his notepad inside his apron pocket and made his way back to the kitchen in a bustling fashion.

Mary looked across at her husband as she placed her napkin on her lap. "Shall we go for a drive after lunch?" she suggested. "I rather fancy taking a look around the flea market in Dorchester Street. Margie West bought an antique table lamp for four pounds last week and I have to say I am so envious." She knew she would get her way even though it was a forty-five-minute drive to the next town. She fluttered her eyelashes and stroked the back of his neck, as she weaved her magic.

"Please, Daddy," said Anika, "please can we go, please, please, please," she said jumping up and down in her chair. Roberta sat in silence bemused by her younger sister and mother's conniving way in which they both manipulated her father into getting exactly what they wanted. She knew that her sister's pleas were merely because every time they went they both got a candy floss from the vendor who had a small cart on the corner of Dorchester Street and Melbourne Road. Her father's expression broke into a smile that lit up his whole face. She loved her father dearly, he was the best dad in the whole wide world.

"OK, OK," he said, admitting defeat and patting his wife's hand. "You win again," he said, jovially.

They ate their meal and chatted about their week and shared stories that had happened over the last seven days. This Saturday event was an important part of their lives and gave them all an opportunity to air their views and gave a good insight to what they were all up to day by day. Family time, there was nothing quite as special thought Joe, as he looked round the table at his beautiful family.

"Daddy, you should see my costume," said Anika, between mouthfuls. "It's pink," she said innocently, looking at his expression.

"Fancy that," said Roberta, unable to help her sarcasm.

"That's lovely, darling," said her father, scowling at Roberta but secretly enjoying his daughter's innocence.

"It's supposed to be pink, silly," said Roberta, "everyone knows Cinderella wears pink."

Anika looked at her mother for confirmation. "Historically yes, Cinderella's famous colour is pink but I guess it didn't have to be a foregone conclusion," her mother added. "Any reproduction can enhance or adapt things as they see fit for their production."

Anika gave Roberta a winning look and moved on to speak about Prince Charming.

"Who's got that part?" quizzed Roberta, suddenly curious.

"Billy Townshide," confirmed Anika, blushing. Billy Townshide was a popular boy, blonde, blue eyed and lots of girls in Anika's dance class, including her, had a crush on him. Roberta started to giggle and started pouting her lips in a kissing style. "Stop it, Roberta, you're always teasing me," said Anika, angrily.

"No, just showing you how to kiss a boy, as I believe, correct me if I am wrong, but I believe Prince Charming and Cinderella kiss at the end of the production," she informed her, smirking again.

"Oh, and you would know all about kissing," said Anika, standing up from her chair. "Daddy, please stop her from teasing me, I hate her," she said with a tear running down her cheek, "she always has to spoil things."

Anika sat on her father's lap, something she always did when Roberta was teasing her.

"Daddy's girl," said Roberta, mocking her younger sister again.

"Stop it right now, Roberta," said her father firmly.

"Yes, in fact," said her mother, "I am considering no candy floss for you." she added.

"Apologise to your sister now," said her father, wiping Anika's tears with his napkin.

"I'm sorry, Anika," she said gritting her teeth.

Anika returned to her chair with flushed cheeks and announced that she was full up and couldn't eat another mouthful. Joe settled the bill with Gustavo, while the girls went to the ladies' room and then they made their way out into the car park, waving and blowing kisses at Gustavo, shouting, "see you next week."

Anika, buckled up her seat belt firmly and began to read her Cinderella pamphlet again and Roberta sat staring out of the car window, wishing she hadn't caused such a fuss. She reached for Anika's hand without turning to look at her and was relieved when her younger sister's fingers wrapped around her own. Joe smiled as he caught sight of this gesture in his rear mirror and started up the engine.

"Right Mary," he said, turning to face his wife, "to Dorchester Market we shall go." They arrived forty-five minutes later and Joe was relieved to find a suitable parking space outside a chip shop that had closed for renovation. They were at the far end of the market, much to the girls' surprise, as they usually ended at this point.

"Does that mean we can have our candy floss now?" said Anika enthusiastically, "instead of later," she asked hopefully.

"Go on then," said her father, reaching into his pocket for some change, "but no more fighting girls. Let's have a lovely afternoon." Roberta chose green candy floss and Anika chose a traditional pink one. "There you go," said her father, handing the pink one to her, stating that it was especially for a young Cinderella that he knew.

Anika beamed and pulled a large piece of fluffy pink cotton-wool-like mixture from the wooden stick and put it in her mouth. It melted on her tongue, causing a fizzy sensation. "Yum, yum," she said smiling at Roberta.

Her mother combed the stalls looking for a table lamp equally as impressive as Margie West's and was just about to announce defeat when she spied the mother of all lamps on a stall run by a woman that looked as though she told fortunes for a living. "Just look at that Joe," she said, holding it up high like a trophy she had won in a marathon. "How unusual is that?" she said, returning it to the table, stepping back to admire its full beauty. Joe smiled to himself. His wife had a way to find something extravagant amongst a table of rubbish. "One man's junk is another man's treasure," she quoted, reading her husband's thoughts like a book. "Just look at it, Joe," she said again, holding it up once more for a further inspection. It appeared to be solid brass, ornate with features and had a small clock face featured in the centre of the body. Her mother was doing her best to sell it to her father, describing its anatomy in great detail. She finished her speech, defining the shade as fashionable and chic. Roberta thought it looked like a tea cosy but daren't say anything after her mother had gone to such lengths to secure approval.

"How much is it?" her mother asked, turning her attention to the gypsy-dressed seller, who was adorned with different coloured chiffon scarves. The seller was engrossed in trying to sell a cigarette lighter in the shape of a swan to an old man, who looked like a cross between Long John Silver and a cowboy, complete with eye patch and cowboy hat.

The seller knew she wasn't on to a winner, so was delighted when she realised that the auburn beauty was smitten with her lamp. "Five pounds twenty," she said, hesitantly, knowing full well that she had overpriced the item. Mary looked across at Joe, longingly.

It was an awful lot of money when you consider the average man's weekly wage was around thirty-three pounds.

Still, Joe was doing well and had just been promoted and his wage did exceed the norm. Four pounds sixty," he offered, "and not a penny more," he declared retrieving the lamp from his wife's hands and replacing it on the table.

"Very well," said the stall seller, glad to have made some money. It had been a quiet day and her total takings up until now had been three pounds eleven.

Mary squealed with delight, kissing both of Joe's cheeks in a French manner and held it up high like a true winner. "Just wait until Margie sees this," she said proudly.

Joe looked at his watch. It was almost 5.30pm and time they made tracks home. The sky was getting blacker by the second and he could tell they were in for a storm. "Right everyone let's make our way back through the market towards the car before the heavens open," he told them, feeling the first spit of rain on his forehead. They raced through the market at record speed, until they were in sight of their Cortina.

"Look," said Roberta, pointing up, "I saw a faint flash of light." It followed with a rumble of thunder and they all knew they had made it back to the car just in time. They clambered in and buckled up and soon they were on their way, weaving their way through the small market town.

After around twenty minutes they were deep into the mountain range that separated the quaint town of Ramchester from the City of Carlisle. The black sky looked threatening and the lanes were poorly lit. They continued on until eventually there was no street lighting at all. The rain was torrential, making driving almost impossible and the tyres were slipping and churning up the muddy pathway as they drove further and further into the mountains.

"Joe, perhaps we should turn back?" Mary suggested, growing more and more nervous the further they went. "You can barely see a foot in front of you and the wipers can't take the rain away quick enough," she added. Joe had already contemplated turning back and was battling with his conscious of leading them into disaster or turning back towards the market town.

"Dad, I'm scared," said Anika, starting to cry, curling up in a ball. She undid her seat belt to snuggle up to Roberta.

"Put that back on immediately," shouted their father in a tone of voice they had never heard before. "I mean it," he shouted, swerving the car and then regaining control. Roberta immediately assisted her sister back into the safety of her belt and they both held hands trembling.

"Dad I don't like it," said Roberta, echoing her little sister's earlier comment. "I can't turn round here," he announced, looking at his wife with a harrowing expression. "The lane is too small and we are on the edge of a mountain." Roberta started to sob. She had always loved driving round the mountain range in the daytime on a sunny afternoon. None of them had ever experienced how treacherous it could be in the dark in a torrential storm. The car continued to slip and the tyres quite clearly couldn't cope with the uphill climb.

"Joe, stop, let's sit it out," Mary suggested, trying to convince her husband that it was foolish to continue any further.

"OK," he agreed, "just around this corner is a wider area, where we could pull over and wait it out," he suggested.

They made it safely round the corner and Joe pulled the car in as far as he could, tucking them in against the mountain edge. He turned off the ignition and announced that they would wait it out until the storm passed. The relief flooded through them all in equal measure and Mary suggested the girls should amuse themselves with a game until the storm passed. They settled on a game of noughts and crosses with the aid of a torch their mother pulled from the glove box, and soon they were engrossed in their own little world again. The storm went on and on and there appeared to be no let up at all, until Joe was forced into turning off the headlights. He knew this was a dangerous move but his battery was running low, which would mean he would be unable to start his car again later when he needed to.

“Is that wise, Joe?” said Mary, envisaging the danger of no one seeing they were there.

“It’s a calculated risk, Mary, of us being able to restart the engine again when we need to,” he told her.

“But what if something comes the other way?” she questioned, growing nervous all over again.

“We are tucked in far to the inside edge,” he reassured her but had obviously considered this possibility himself. “Girls I’m going to need your torch,” he told them, grabbing it out of Roberta’s hand.

“But, Dad, I’m winning,” she told him crossly, trying to hold onto it tightly. “Roberta, I need to place it on the bonnet of the car so that a car coming towards us will see we are here,” he told her in a reasoning voice. She let go of the torch, sensing the danger of a car coming round the corner and not seeing they were there and started to panic all over again.

Joe stepped out of the car to position the the large square-shaped torch but was unable to place it where the wind wouldn’t blow it from its resting place, despite its weight. What can I use?, he thought, stepping away from the car and looking in all directions around him.

The rain was horrendous and was blowing him all over the place and he could see the girls faces peering out of the rear window. They looked petrified and he knew their safety was in his hands. He couldn’t stop shaking, could barely see a foot in front of him and considered this moment to be the most horrific he had experienced in his life to date. My God, what was that he could hear in the background, the wind and rain kept sweeping the sound away. He heard it again, it's a car, or a truck maybe, something was heading towards them in the darkness.

"No," he yelled, seeing the headlights heading towards them from around the ledge. He looked at the Cortina and then at what was heading towards them. It was big, far too big. It wasn't going to see them, there wasn't enough room. The noise of brakes attempting to stop, screeching like a howling fox. He couldn't get to them, he was too far away, the driver couldn't see him waving furiously, still holding the torch. He dropped to his knees as a rig, far too big for this mountain road, ploughed them off the road. It dragged them across to the edge of the ledge and then off the side turning over and over, as it bounced off the side of the mountain, a drop hundreds of feet below. Joe froze, unable to move momentarily, until the sound of the explosion ended his world. The world he loved – the family he had adored.

Then a high pitch scream echoed through the mountain range that sounded so horrific that Joe didn't realise it was coming from him. He knew they were dead but couldn't bring himself to move closer to the edge to see. What he could see was black smoke billowing up from below and the awful sound of burning and crackling and then a second explosion. He buried his head in his hands, he wanted to die. Why had he survived? he questioned. Then he refused to believe it and got to his feet. They might be alive, they might be alive, he thought, refusing to believe anything else could be possible. They might have been thrown free of the explosion, oh please, let them be alive. He staggered to the edge, searching, looking for his family thrown from the wreckage, perched safe on a ledge, oh please, please, please. He was shaking, soaking wet and desperate, his thought process completely disengaged. He clambered down the side of the mountain, slipping and sliding until he lost his footing and dropped several feet, hitting his head on a jagged rock piece and then falling and falling, tumbling through sharp bushes and trees which marked the landscape, until finally coming to rest hundreds of feet below in a stream. He lay there unconscious, bleeding profusely, totally unrecognisable, face half in the water.

He woke to the sensation of water lapping at his face and a faint voice in the distance. "I can see someone over there," came the voice, followed by more voices and the sound of trampling through woodland, squelching mud, torrential rain and more faint voices being carried by the wind. Was that a siren he could hear, it was hard to tell with the wind and rain. He tried to move but couldn't and then the reality of where he was and what had happened dawned on him. He lay there motionless, his surroundings illuminated by the blue circling lights. Don't let them find me, he thought, he wanted to die. He tried to turn his face fully down into the water but just couldn't move. He was helpless, possibly paralysed, he thought, he didn't care! He may as well be dead, he thought. He rolled his eyes to the right searching in the darkness. Could they still be alive? He considered the possibility. He remembered the explosion, how loud it had been and the billowing black smoke in the rain. The heavy rain may have extinguished the fire quickly, before it took hold he thought, he hoped. Every part of his body hurt but nothing compared to the loss, the total desperation, the uncertainty of not knowing for absolute certain. He tried again to move but the strain caused an unbearable pain right through his being and once again he lost consciousness.

His eyes flickered from the bright lights above. He closed them and then reopened them squinting. He must be dead, he thought, thank God he didn't have to go on alone without his family. Are those the lights that you see when you're dead, showing you the way to whatever's next? he wondered. What was that? he questioned himself. He could hear beeping. What was that beeping?

One

"Despite your professional analysis of this situation, Doctor Gyllensvan, what is your gut feeling? You mention in your summary 'neutrality of attitude', can you be more specific?" Mike stood back up from the sofa, where he had just sat down and walked towards the window. He paused momentarily, before adjusting the venetian blind, just wide enough to glance at the city below and to lighten the room, ever so slightly. The darkness was overbearing. He had noticed on the two previous occasions he had interviewed the doctor that his surgery was depressing, cut off. Yes, that was a good description, cut off, he decided. He had previously wondered why the blinds were always in the closed position and a lamp, just giving off an amber glow was what presented itself. The room was stifling, overbearingly hot and was in desperate need of some air, albeit from the smoggy cold city outside.

He looked directly at the doctor. "To tell you the truth, Doc, I'm not big on all this medical stuff but I'm puzzled! It's been three weeks now since we found the girl, you must have a little bit more to give me than this. Shows no sign of any emotional attachment to anything at all, you state here in your daily observation report. Human interaction, almost impossible, so forming any type of patient-doctor relationship has proved non-existent. Can you be more specific? You must have achieved… learned something over the last few weeks?" Mike sat back down, agitated that they were no further forward than the night he and his partner had brought her in. He crossed his legs and shuffled the papers and then dismissed them to the floor. "Give me something, Doc, you must be able to give me something?"

Doctor Gyllensvan rose to his feet and stepped away from his desk, glancing towards the now opened blinds. He adjusted them slightly, dimming the room once again and sat back down behind his desk. "There is nothing, nothing I can add at this time to what I have already detailed in my report," he said, defending his summary. He looked perplexed, bewildered to the point of exhaustion.

Mike inhaled and paused. He considered the doctor's task and then once again grew frustrated at the wait. Three weeks he had waited, wondering, surmising, coming up with unimaginable reasons for finding a girl, age unknown, in the depths of a blisteringly cold winter's night in Gordon Square. He had been unable to concentrate on anything else since he found her. Sleep deprivation had taken a back seat compared to the sheer desperation he felt in discovering the truth. "How old do you think she is?" he questioned, picking the papers up from the floor and shuffling them back into some sort of order. He stared at the date on the bottom right-hand corner of the report, 2019. "You would think we would be advanced enough in this era to be able to ascertain more than we have," he thought out loud.

"Difficult to determine at this stage," the doctor responded, "as I specialise in mental health, but having had no breakthrough at all as to her mindset, physiological evaluation has been somewhat impossible. I have been unable to enter into any kind of two-way conversation with her at all and have based my report purely on her physical appearance and unresponsive cognitive demeanour. She is lethargic, disinterested, non-compliant and, in my opinion, would benefit from holistic nursing. My gut feeling was your initial question, detective, well my gut feeling is that this girl has undergone some sort of physical and mental trauma, so emotionally disturbing that she is in shock and will need professional ongoing support to bring her back."

"Bring her back?" questioned Mike, standing up once again.

"Yes, bring her back from the place her mind is now taking solace, time out. I feel her mind has slipped away, somewhere dark and unreachable and it may take months if not years to restore, if at all."

"That's quite a gut feeling, Doc," said Mike running his eyes briefly over the summary of her physical evaluation before walking towards the door. "Her initial medical assessment, undertaken by a Doctor Leeson in A&E, indicated severe malnutrition, hair loss, poor personal hygiene, body odour, greasy hair/skin, excrement, it's hardly likely she's slipped somewhere unreachable," said Mike, once again wondering what type of pathological trauma this young girl may have experienced, albeit there was no evidence of any sign of physical restraints but there were markings of some historical abuse, he noticed. "I'll be in touch, Doc," said Mike turning the oversized brass handle on the door and nodding at him. "Thank you for your time," he said, and slipped out into the hallway. He felt uneasy once again as he made his way down the corridor and back out into the foyer, haunted by the possibilities, the unimaginable horror that this young girl lay victim to, had endured, which had finally broken her. What brought her here, he wondered, what brought her to him. He found her that night and now he found it impossible to let go. He wasn't going to let go, he was going to find out the truth.

He looked across the foyer at his partner. She was flirting with the desk clerk, who in turn looked equally enchanted, drawn in by her magnetic beauty and voluptuous figure. He was clearly smitten and was capturing her contact details into his iPhone. Yep, she's done it again, thought Mike smiling. Like a lamb to the slaughter, he considered. Mel had a way about her and was without a doubt a head turner and had left a string of heart-broken lovers behind her over the years. She wore her heart on her sleeve, was honest, trustworthy but had difficulty with commitment. She caught sight of Mike in her peripheral vision and knew he was watching her. She adjusted the front of her all-too-low blouse and swept her blond hair back away from her face as she stepped away from the desk. "Thank you for your help," she uttered, pretending to be engaged in some sort of professional discussion, "you have been most helpful." She shook his hand.

"I'm sure he has," said Mike in a teasing voice, as they walked towards the reception doors.

"Leave it," said Mel, with a wink. "Just a little Saturday evening entertainment," she informed him.

"Well be careful," said Mike as they made their way down the hospital steps, "I don't think this city can take any more male broken hearts," he told her, laughing.

Mike stopped in his tracks, midway across the car park. "What the hell?" His car, his pride and joy was displaying a car-park sign with the wording 'reserved' on it, with the metal post deposited right through his windscreen, resting between the steering wheel and his newly-upholstered leather seats. His alarm was intermittently sounding every ten seconds and a crowd of people had gathered at the scene. Mike pushed past the spectators, making his way to the front. "What the fuck?" he glanced across at Mel, who was trying to disperse the crowd that were continuing to gather round the vehicle. There was blood speckled across the windscreen with a bloody handprint on the car bonnet. The trail of blood continued down the passenger side door and onto the floor where two men were engaged in a scuffle.

Mike attempted to separate them by pulling on the collar of the leather jacket worn by the man who, quite clearly, had the upper hand. The man swung a punch in Mike's direction, catching him across the bridge of his nose and sending him spinning into the side of his car door.

"Stop it," shouted Mel, "stop it," as she raced over to Mike, helping him back up onto his feet and steadying him. The two men continued swinging punches at one another until two hospital security guards intervened, separating them with force. Another was calling for reinforcements with the aid of a walkie-talkie and within minutes hospital police had taken control of the situation.

Mike watched as the two guards assisted with the restraining of the two men, who were now being forcefully encouraged into the back of a hospital police vehicle.

Mike looked back across at his beloved Morgan and then lowered his aching head into his hands. Why him? He thought, raising his head once again. Why hadn't they had their scuffle further along, away from his pride and joy. Of all the days to decide to take it for a spin. He nearly hadn't, pausing as he unlocked his trusty old van, smiling across at his work of art. It had taken years to restore it, painstaking years of investing every spare penny he had and hundreds of man-hours until it had reached perfection. Something made him close the van door that morning and stroll towards the Morgan, smiling. What's the point of owning it if I don't make use of it? he had reasoned, as he climbed behind the wheel. Now he stood in front of it, blood dripping from his nose, staring at the shattered windscreen. He reached for the post, wrapping his fingers firmly around it until he had a good enough grip to retrieve it from its resting point, flinging it to the floor in anger. Mel put her hand on his shoulder in an attempt to console him. "Let's get you seen first, before we deal with the car," she advised him, passing him a screwed-up tissue from her pocket. She knew what the car meant to him. It had been left to him in his father's will and she knew he had spent every available hour restoring it. "Come on," she repeated, guiding him back inside. They made their way back into reception, following the signs towards A&E. Two reception booths were manned, with a queue five or six deep, and a third displaying a 'closed' sign. Typical thought Mel, as they took their place in the queue behind a man who smelled like he hadn't washed in a decade.

"Let's leave it," said Mike, agitated by the thought of spending all afternoon in A&E.

He turned to leave but Mel, once again, intervened. "We can't leave it Mike, look at you! You resemble a pug. Quite clearly it's broken, so if you don't want to look like someone who's spent years in the ring having the living daylights beaten out of you, we had better remain in the queue and wait our turn. Go and sit down," she instructed, pointing to the only vacant chair in the waiting area. "I'll wait it out and call you when it's our turn," she continued. Too tired to argue, he eyed up the vacant seat and wedged himself between a man who kept shouting out obscenities and a little boy who was perched on his mother's lap, whimpering.

Two hours forty-five minutes later, a nurse came bustling out, holding a clipboard. She glanced up briefly and then called, "Mike Brugge." Finally, thought Mike, rising to his feet, his head now pounding and his face totally unrecognisable.

He turned to face Mel, "Shan't be long," he informed her, as if he was totally in control of the situation and would govern the time frame.

"Sure," said Mel, smiling to herself. Why did he always assume he was in charge? He followed the nurse through the double doors and into the first cubicle and took his position on the stretcher bed.

"So, what happened to you then?" asked the nurse, holding his chin and turning his face both right and then left. She felt the bridge of his nose, tweaking it from side to side during her assessment. Mike winced, pushing her hand away. "Well it's definitely broken," said the nurse, stepping back away from him.

"Tell me something I don't know, Nurse Brown," he said, glancing at the name badge pinned to her apron.

"So how did you do it?" she questioned a second time.

"Two lunatics assaulted me outside," he informed her.

"And why did they do that?" she queried.

"Look, Nurse Brown, I know you're only doing your job but so was I. I was here visiting Doctor Gyllensvan. Not as a patient," he added, "he was assisting me with a case I am working on. After which, I was returning to my car and two lunatics were fighting and had put a signpost through my windscreen. One of them was obviously using it as a weapon, aiming it at the other but my car came between them. I tried to intervene and one of them clomped me."

Nurse Brown retrieved a surgical wipe from her trolley to clean the area and then placed a cold compress on to help with the swelling. "Hold that for a moment," she instructed. "I'm afraid you will need to wait for the swelling to go down and then I recommend manipulation under anaesthetic. I am going to prescribe some painkillers, which you will need to take four-hourly and you will need to continue with the cold compresses." she added. "Your nose will need to be manipulated within the next fourteen days for the best end result." she informed him. "Now I need to place some gauze inside your nostrils and some surgical tape for support, so please try to relax a little while I do this."

"Manipulation under anaesthetic," said Mike, "is that really necessary?" he asked her, wincing once again from the pain of having gauge stuffed inside his nostrils.

"If you want to look like your old regular self, then yes," said the nurse, helping him to his feet. Mike resigned himself to the fact that this was his best option, as he glimpsed himself in the reflection of window. He left the casualty bay and then made his way out to the waiting area where Mel was pacing up and down shouting into her mobile.

"What's up?" he gestured to her with a frown, as he screwed up the prescription offering regular paracetamol and threw it aside.

"My landlord," she said, mimicking someone attempting to strangle someone, as she ended the call. "He's refusing to fix my heating until I catch up with my rent and I just can't do it right now and it's so bloody cold," she told him.

"How behind are you?" Mike asked, wondering if he could help and then recalling his beloved Morgan and how much that was now going to cost. Hoping that the insurance would sort that, he repeated. "How behind are you Mel?"

"Two months," she said, with a sigh. "Two months totalling £2,000."

"Two grand, you mean to say you pay a grand a month for that studio that you can't swing a cat in."

"My cat's very happy there," she said, trying to bring a smile to his swollen face. "And anyway, it includes bills," she told him, attempting to justify the exorbitant expense, so that she didn't look like she was a total pushover and had some control of her finances.

Who am I kidding, she thought to herself and why am I even attempting to hide the fact that my landlord is ripping me off and it would actually be three grand next week. "Just not managing as well as usual," she told him, "but I will sort it. Just a blip," she added.

"Two grand's not a blip, Mel, is it?"

"Let me help. Perhaps if we pay some, he will at least sort the heating for you," he offered, nudging her arm.

"Hey, don't try to distract the attention from you," she said, nudging him back, "you're just as strapped. What did the nurse say anyway? Are you going to get your 007 good looks back or are you going to resemble a pug from now on?" she asked, giggling.

"Well it's broken, obviously," he said, wincing as he touched it. "Got to be manipulated, whatever that entails," he told her, as they walked back through the car park towards the car.

"Well we can't drive that," said Mel, reaching for her phone again, staring at the shattered windscreen. "I'll call a cab," she added, before Mike had the chance to speak.

"Yes, you go and I'll wait for the recovery truck, Mel, it will probably take hours anyway," he told her, "no point us both being here."

"Hey, you're in no fit state to be hanging about here, Mike, look at you, you're a wreck," she told him.

"Thanks for that, Mel, you've made me feel tip top," he said smiling and then wincing again from the pain.

"I'll call my brother and he can tow us back and you can call someone out tomorrow," she offered. "And anyway, it's freezing," she added. Mike stood motionless staring at his car while Mel called her brother who happened to be conveniently in and had a tow rope. "It's all sorted," she claimed, walking back towards him with a satisfied look on her face. "He will be here before you know it," she claimed.

Mike studied the extent of the shattered windscreen declaring that there was just enough clearance to see through it and decided Mel had made the right call after all. "Thanks, Mel, I really appreciate your help," he said putting his arm around her as a friendly gesture. "You're right, I'm a wreck and my head's killing me," he told her, as he sat down on a nearby wall.

Mel sat down next to him, finding the wall rather chilly through her jeans. Shuffling from side to side, she asked, "So what did Dr Gyllensvan say anyway?" she quizzed, curious as to whether there had been any breakthrough and whether they were any further forward.

"Well, the scary thing about it all is the fact that she's not communicating at all," said Mike. "Completely non-compliant to the extent of not even talking."

"Maybe she can't talk," said Mel. "Have you considered the fact that she might be mute?" she suggested, standing up and brushing her hand across her backside.

"No, I hadn't considered that possibility," he said, standing up wondering if Mel had hit the nail on the head.

"Do you think Dr Gyllensvan has?" she continued, pacing back and forth looking out for her brother.

"Didn't see anything in his report," he said, aggravated that he hadn't thought of that while he was in the doctor's office.

"Well maybe that's worth exploring," said Mel, suddenly waving furiously to attract her brother's attention, who had just driven into the car park in a rusty old transit van.

"Hey, Pete, thanks for being a lifesaver," she yelled in an all-too-loud voice, as he climbed out of his van. Pete reached forward to shake Mike's hand as he approached them, acknowledging his sister's welcome with a nod and then turned his attention to the Morgan.

"So, who have you been upsetting?" he asked, assessing the damage and then opening the door at the rear of his van to retrieve a tow rope.

"No one," said Mike. "It wouldn't be so bad if it did have something to do with me but it was a case of being parked in the wrong spot at the wrong time. A completely fucking pointless act," he told him, sitting back down on the wall to tie the lace of his trainer.

"Yeah, two guys were fighting," continued Mel, attempting an explanation that she was now too cold and fed up to go into detail about.

"Two idiots," added Mike, "that, thankfully, to my satisfaction have been arrested and may face assault charges, together with criminal damage, if I get a spare minute to press charges," he told him.

"OK," said Pete, understanding immediately that he was really pissed off and in pain and that now was not the time for a lengthy blow-by-blow account of the situation. "I assume the car will start?" asked Pete, as he walked around to the other side.

"Yes, just not fit to drive legally with the smashed screen, so it needs towing."

"Right, reverse the car out, Mike," Pete instructed, moving things along, so that they could all get the hell out of there. Someone else had pulled into the space in front, restricting access and had parked so close they were almost sharing the space.

Mike nodded, opening the driver's side door to climb in. "Thanks, Pete, I'm in your debt," he told him, switching on the ignition and positioning the car so that the tow rope could be secured and then switched it off again. Mel jumped in the transit van beside her brother and they slowly made their way out of the car park. Mike switched on the radio in an attempt to lighten his mood and smiled to himself as the tune playing referred to car trouble.

"Thanks, Pete," said Mike, shaking his hand once again, "I'm really grateful for your help," he told him as he climbed out of the Morgan, which was now back in its parking space, where it had sat for the last four years during its restoration. Mike waved across at Mel. "See you in the morning, Mel," he shouted, climbing the steps to his first-floor flat, where he had lived for the last eight years. As he reached the top and turned the corner, he could see there was a parcel on his doorstep, leaning up against the front door. He reached down to retrieve it, recognising immediately it was the emblem for the front of his car bonnet. The final piece to complete the restoration he thought, sighing to himself, well that's not going to happen now anytime soon, he considered, tossing it on the hallway table along with his keys.

He stared momentarily at the kettle and then decided he needed something stronger, much stronger. He poured himself a glass of wine and slumped down on the sofa, flicking channels until he settled on a soap that really needed no concentration whatsoever. His face ached and his head throbbed and he knew that the most sensible thing to do would be to take some paracetamol and have an early night. Instead he downed the wine and then reached for another. He picked up his mobile and stared at the screen until he located his insurance company number to make the call. He didn't really feel like running through all the details now, so was secretly pleased when he heard the out-of-hours recorded message asking him to leave his contact details for a call back. He sat thinking, sliding further and further into the dark space, he was familiar with and poured yet another glass of wine and then another. He changed position on the sofa and stared up at the ceiling, thoughts darting from one thing to another, finally settling on the girl who had stumbled into his world three weeks ago in Gordon Square. Where had she come from, he wondered? Why won't she communicate with anyone, and what the hell happened to her he thought, as sleep overtook him and the glass fell to the floor.

He had a restless night, waking over and over in a hot sweat. Dreams that were a mix of his current and past life, together with the girl he had found, only this time she was dead in the boot of his Morgan. He sat on the sofa rubbing his head, staring at the two empty wine bottles and the glass on the floor. He stared down at his foot which felt damp and strange, realising that his foot was resting in spilt wine that had sunk into the pile of the carpet. Nice, he thought, standing up and then steadying himself from the rush he suddenly felt. Why hadn't he just gone to bed like any normal person? he considered, as he made his way to the bathroom to pee. It burnt like mad and he knew that he was seriously dehydrated. He also knew that he had been due at the station almost two hours earlier and that there would be trouble ahead.

His mobile phone rang and he could see it was Mel. He could also see that he had missed fifteen calls from her. Fuck, fuck, fuck. "Morning Mel," he stuttered, trying to sound as normal as possible, as he sat on the edge of his bed. "Yep Yep, I know it's 10.30, Mel, I just had some stuff to sort but I'm on my way now," he told her, hanging up before she could respond. He staggered back to the bathroom and put his head under the cold tap, shaking it from side to side like a sheep dog, then regretting it immediately from the pain that caused. He starred in the mirror, just long enough to comb his hair, as the reflection was somewhat disturbing. He brushed his teeth swiftly, sprayed some deodorant and reached for a polo shirt from the clothes horse. God, I feel crap, he thought, swallowing a paracetamol, which he washed down with some milk directly from the bottle. He opened the cupboard, needing something to help soak up the wine but was greeted with half a loaf of wholemeal bread that had turned green and a half-eaten box of wafer-thin mints. I need looking after, he considered, as he slammed his front door shut and raced down the stairs.

He stared at the Morgan and then climbed into his van, turning on the ignition and fumbling with the volume control on the radio. It was belting out a classical number, far too early in the morning as far as he was concerned when all he needed was his sunglasses, which were somewhere in the glove box. He continued to rummage with one hand as he steered the van out from its parking space, until thankfully he eyed them on the floor of the passenger footwell. Hallelujah, he said out loud, squinting from the sun. Hallelujah, fucking hallelujah.

Mel was waiting for him in the car park as he pulled into the space next to her Golf. "Where the hell have you been?" she yelled, as he climbed out of his van. "Christ, you look like shit," she told him, before he could answer her first question. "Dhillon's having a hissy fit, as we were supposed to have been part of a briefing this morning to do with the Gordon's Square girl, which incidentally, he postponed until your arrival. He's up there now pacing back and forth, yelling at everyone he comes into contact with," she informed him. Mike looked up at the window of Dhillon's office, knowing he was in for more than a briefing. Chief Inspector Lawrence Dhillon, a tough detective, fair, but you didn't want to get on his wrong side. He hated lateness more than anything. Punctuality was key with him and if you were more than a few minutes late, you paid a high price. Mike headed towards the station door, with Mel in tow, wondering how much this morning's delay was going to cost him.

He pulled open the door hesitantly, wishing he could turn back round, and forced his way forward with Mel still chirping in the background.

"Well?" said Mel, still waiting for him to say something.

"Well, if you would give me half a second to answer, Mel," he told her, stopping in front of the vending machine, while reaching into his jean's pocket for some change, "I'll tell you." He selected black coffee with extra sugar and turned to face her. "In fact, there's nothing really to tell," he said, walking towards his desk, "I had a few wines, overslept and that's it in a nutshell." He sat down, opened his desk draw, searching for a random sugar sachet and slammed it shut. "I'm never late, I'm always punctual and Dhillon knows that. Surely you told him what happened yesterday at the hospital," he said, agitated that he was about to go into battle, with an aching head, when he felt too crap to put up a good defensive argument.

"Yes, of course I did," said Mel, sitting down at her desk, directly opposite, hoping that she had done enough that morning to counter Dhillon's forthcoming attack. "I explained to him that you had been assaulted and had spent most of yesterday afternoon in A&E," she told him. "Anyway, he only has to take one look at you to know that we're not spinning a line, Pugsy," she said with a half-smile.

"Very funny," he said, taking a slurp of his coffee and wincing. Everything about him hurt.

"Brugge, Bailey in my office NOW," shouted Inspector Dhillon from across the other side of the office. They stood up simultaneously to order and headed towards the inspector's office. "Close the door," he instructed, sitting back down behind his desk. "Where are we at with the Gordon Square girl?" he asked, not mentioning the lateness but instead going straight in with what he wanted to know. They both sat down on the two chairs directly in front of his desk, relieved that he had decided to bypass the punctuality issue.

"Not very far, I'm afraid," answered Mike reluctantly. He was hoping to be a lot further along after his visit to Doctor Gyllensvan, and was frustrated, to say the least, about having nothing further to go on.

"She's non-communicative, in fact she's not speaking at all," said Mike.

"We don't even know if she can speak," added Mel, remembering her earlier suggestion that she might even be mute.

"Do we have anything, a name perhaps?" asked the inspector, standing up as if he was about to walk straight through his desk.

"No, not even a name," said Mike, staring up at him from his seated position, feeling vulnerable as he towered over him. "We are referring to her as Jane Gordon for the purpose of documenting our findings," he informed him and we are now backtracking through missing person records, as you would expect. The problem we have," continued Mike, "is that we have nothing at all to go on. We don't know her ethnic origin or her age, albeit she looks somewhere between fifteen and twenty-five, and is Caucasian, but she could be much younger," he added. "She is so malnourished, it's difficult to determine if she's even gone through puberty."

"Although," interrupted Mel, "she could be older, there are lines around her eyes but I had wondered, considered even, if they were caused through squinting. She's so pale she may have been kept in the dark and then exposed to light, a form of torture," she said.

"She squints continually, actually," added Mike, thinking back to the night they found her. "She was shielding her eyes and cowering the night we brought her in."

"How did she end up in Gordon Square?" asked Inspector Dhillon.

"Maybe she was always there," said Mike, considering the possibility out loud.

"Do some house-to-house enquiries," the inspector instructed, knowing full well that that was where they started. "Again," he said, reading their minds. "You may have missed something," he added.

Mike rose to his feet, his mind in overdrive. Those houses did have basements, he pondered! "Yes, we will do some more research into who owns or rents there, what their history is and see if any have cause for a search warrant," said Mike. He headed towards the door as the inspector gave the usual signal that the meeting had been concluded.

"Not you, Mike, sit back down," he instructed. "Close the door behind you, Mel," he told her, as she rose to her feet. Mel left the room, pulling the door to, just enough so she could stand outside and listen. "All the way, Mel," said Dhillon. "All the way so it clicks, so that you are unable to eavesdrop from behind the wall," he said with a smirk! He turned his attention back to Mike, as Mel closed the door firmly, feeling embarrassed at having been caught. Mike waited for the long overdue ear-bashing about his lateness that morning, having thought he had escaped it, when Dhillon surprised him with a totally unexpected offer.

"There's a position going down at the headquarters in South Wales. It's a DI role," he told him. "It's from immediate effect and I would like to put you forward, subject to tying up all the leads on the Jane Gordon case first," he continued. "I don't want to lose you from my team but you have been headhunted and I don't feel I can stand in the way of a promotion, not one with as many prospects as this," he added. "You will be in vice, leading a team in the world of gambling, narcotics, prostitution, human trafficking, etc., you know the score and what it entails."

Mike had worked in vice before. He was good at it but it had its pressures, it had been the downfall of his marriage, or at least one of the reasons behind its decline, and his eventual divorce. It was hard going, emotional and sometimes painful. It also meant long hours and going undercover. Could he do that again, he considered. He had no one to answer to, no one to come home to, no one to nag him anymore. What was keeping him here anyway, he thought? His job had become his world, he hardly saw his daughter and felt he was a big disappointment to her. Maybe this would be just the thing, leading a team. Something that would make her proud of him once again. The cogs were turning as his thoughts darted from one to another. He rose to his feet, realising that he had remained quiet since the offer.

"Something to consider," he said walking towards the door. "Give me time to mull it over," he told him, as he reached for the door handle.

"Don't take too long," the inspector warned, "they need an answer… oh, and Mike, don't be late on my shift again!"

"What was that about?" asked Mel, eager to be filled in with all the details. She had already decided that it wasn't anything to do with this lateness that morning, as he wouldn't have told her to close the door behind her. Inspector Dhillon was known for having no qualms whatsoever about embarrassing anyone in front of others. He often gave people a grilling with an audience. It was his specialty, his signature. "Well come on, spill the beans," she told him, eager to hear the big secret. She perched on the edge of his desk, crossing her legs and staring down at her red shoes. "Come on, tell me," she begged him.

"I've been offered a senior detective role," he reluctantly told her. He had wanted to keep it to himself, until he had made a decision but he knew that she would just keep on and on until he told her.

"A senior detective role," she quizzed! "Where, here?" she asked, not giving him the opportunity to answer. She adjusted her seating position and stared directly at him. "Are you moving to another station?" she asked, again not giving him the chance to reply.

"It's in South Wales," he finally said, giving more away than he wanted to at this stage. "In vice," he added, standing up and moving away from her overbearing intrusion to his personal space.

"Vice, but for Pete's sake, Mike, it nearly ruined you before, she reminded him.

"No Mel, it ruined my marriage, it didn't ruin me and in any case there is no marriage anymore," he argued. "It's just me now and I need something, something more than this," he told her, as if he had already made up his mind to go.

"But what about the case, the Jane Gordon case?" she asked him, with a worried expression.

"If I do decide to go, I'll tie that up first," he told her, hoping that that would bring a close to all the questions. Mel sat back down at her desk, as if she was going to quiz him more but she didn't, she sat there quietly, contemplating, worrying. She didn't want him to go. He was her best friend. She hadn't really realised that until just now.

"Right let's move on with the case at hand," said Mike, putting his personal circumstances on the back boiler for the time being. "What do we know about the people that live in Gordon Square?" he said. "Let's track back through property sites on the net and see when houses were sold or rented, etc., to get some sort of idea," he continued.

"Idea on what exactly?" asked Mel.

"Well, who bought what and when," he told her, "we can then research where they came from and if there was any history that went before."

"Before?" questioned Mel.

"Yes, let's take each household and research the owner's history, their past, whether they have been in prison, any mental health issues, etc., see if anything has been flagged."

"If we judged everyone by that method, even I would be a suspect," she told him, laughing. "Mike, we don't even know if she came from Gordon Square, she could have staggered there from a neighbouring road or even been abandoned there."

"Abandoned?" quizzed Mike.

"Yeah, by someone who had got fed up with her, perhaps someone looking for new prey," she told him.

"God, this really is a needle in a haystack, there are so many possibilities," he said running his fingers through his hair.

The desk phone rang and Mike stared at it, as if he didn't know what to do with it. He answered it on the fourth ring and then slammed it down as if it had bitten him.

"What?" said Mel, meaning 'well who was it', what did they want gesture. "They've found another girl," said Mike.

"Exactly the same set of circumstances, Mel," he told her.

"What, in Gordon Square or somewhere else?" she asked.

"I'm not sure yet," he said, regretting hanging up so quickly, without gathering more information. "But she's in the same age group, blonde, not speaking, lethargic, dirty. There's two of them, Mel, two of them," he repeated, as if he couldn't quite believe it unless he said it twice. He grabbed his jacket from the back of his chair, making it wobble and gave the 'let's get out of here order', as he made his way back out of the station door towards his van.

"Well, where are we going?" shouted Mel, rushing to catch up with him and dropping her handbag in the process. She gathered up her possessions and replaced the lid on her new red lipstick that had rolled underneath the magazine rack in reception. She was confused as to how Mike knew where to go.

"Where are we going?" she repeated, as she made her way out of the door into the car park towards Mike's van.

"They've taken her to the same hospital for evaluation," he told her, climbing into the driver's seat and turning on the ignition. Mel jumped in beside him, fumbling with her seat belt in haste and zipping up her handbag, before he drove off without her. She draped her coat across her in an attempt to keep out the cold, as Mike seemed to have no time to waste.

"Slow down, Mike, she's hardly going anywhere, is she?" she reasoned as he sped out of the car park like the Sweeney.

"I know, but this could be a breakthrough, Mel, we might be able to communicate with her." Mike was desperate to know where Jane came from, it had consumed him totally over the last three weeks and he felt certain that he would get some answers now and no one was going to stop him.

They identified themselves at the hospital reception desk and were asked to wait to one side while the receptionist made some enquiries. Mike was pacing up and down like an expectant father, waiting to hear if he had a son or a daughter, when a nurse wearing a crisp light-blue uniform and a badge identifying herself as Nurse Wilson approached them. She indicated with a gesture for them to follow her through to an office where they were greeted by Doctor Leeson.

"Take a seat, please," Doctor Leeson instructed, nodding towards the two seats set beside his desk. He was an oversized man in all directions and was almost as wide as he was tall. His curly hair and under-groomed eyebrows made him look cartoon-like. He almost didn't look real, like he was a caricature of himself.

He opened a file and read from his notes, a scene almost identical to the night they had found Jane. He detailed his findings exactly, as he had that night, three weeks prior, which made Mike feel like he was reliving the same evening, in groundhog mode. "Are they related?" asked Mike, wondering if this would be the case. "Were they sisters?" he wondered out loud, curiously.

"Their appearance tells me almost certainly," the doctor responded, "but blood tests will confirm if this is the case," he added, rising to his feet. He opened the office door and gestured for them to follow him down to one of the consulting rooms where the unidentified Ms Gordon was being examined.

She sat perched on the bed staring at the wall with her back facing them. She had dirty blond hair, looked frail and there was the same odour of neglect, identical to the first girl. She sat motionless, just like Jane, as if she was a mannequin, unreal, not of this world. Mike walked around the bed alongside Doctor Leeson and gasped as the girl raised her head.

"Oh my God," said Mike, with a look of sheer horror, "they are twins, twins," he repeated, taking another look. "Are they twins?" he asked, turning to face the doctor for confirmation.

"We think so," said Doctor Leeson, sisters at the very least, he told him. Mike stepped back unable to take in what he was seeing, it had never occurred to him over the last three weeks that there might be more than one casualty in this nightmare of a situation. I mean why would you even consider that the ordeal might extend to two victims!

"Has she attempted to communicate at all since she was brought in?" Mel asked, moving in for a closer inspection.

"No, nothing at all, not even a gesture," answered the doctor. "I dropped one of my medical instruments earlier, which crashed to the floor making me jump out of my skin. She didn't even flinch," he told them, recalling the moment.

"I think they are deaf mute," said Mel, bringing her earlier conclusion to the table.

"Yes, we are already testing that theory," Doctor Leeson replied, "but we are slightly handicapped with her unresponsive cognitive behaviour. We are totally reliant on test results, as opposed to communicative findings. It's like performing an eye test on someone who is unable to confirm which symbol is clearer," he continued, "you become reliant on science, such as pupil dilation, a light technique, similar to the method used for babies. In the case of the twins, we are trying to test without being too invasive, due to their vulnerable status," he told them. "It's going to take time, patience, lots of patience I'm afraid. We are not going to solve this overnight, I am going to run some further tests tomorrow morning," he informed them, "and then I am going to hand her over to Doctor Gyllensvan." He gestured towards the door, indicating that the meeting was drawing to a close, scribbled a brief note on the notice board above the bed and then ushered them out of the room.

"Thank you for your time this evening, Doctor Leeson," said Mike, as they walked back up the corridor. Doctor Leeson extended his hand to Mike, nodded at Mel and then moved on to his next patient, an over excitable pensioner, who was convinced she was Queen Victoria.

Mike's stomach let out a loud rumble, as he glanced at his watch on the way back to the car park. "I need some food, Mel," he said, eyeing up the burger van parked on the edge of the grass verge outside the physiotherapy unit. He watched as the man at the front of the queue decided between ketchup or mustard as the topping of choice on his giant hotdog, which made Mike's mouth water. He reached into his jacket pocket for his wallet and pulled out his last £10 note and joined the back of the queue, inhaling the smell of fried onions in the air. It was still two days until payday so this was a foolish move but he didn't care, he just needed food. The blackboard stand perched alongside the van showed an exorbitant price list, a ridiculous price for junk food, considered Mike, but the smell had won him over. "Four pounds fifty for a hotdog," he exclaimed, "daylight robbery!" he told the girl serving. Mike managed to negotiate two hotdogs for £5 from the young blond, who was flirting with him, while her co-worker was having a cigarette out back. Mike strolled back over towards Mel, smiling from his never-ending charm and handed the second hotdog to Mel, confirming that he still had his good looks, wit and mesmerising allure, despite his injuries.

"How come you're flashing the cash so close to payday?" she asked, in a teasing jovial way, as she bit into the hotdog with enthusiasm. "A hotdog's hardly flashing the cash, Mel. You obviously haven't been out for a while, or have your recent dates been convincing you that this is fine dining?" he said, nudging her with a smirk.

Mel wiped the ketchup from her chin with the transparent cheap napkin that Mike had issued her with, scowled at him and then gave him a wink. "My dates of late have come in all forms," she claimed giggling.

"Tell," said Mike, moving in closer, as if this was top secret and might be overheard.

"Well, you remember that guy I told you about who rescued me by the side of the road, when I had a flat tyre?" said Mel, continuing to giggle.

"Yeah," said Mike, trying to recall the incident and wishing he'd been paying more attention at the time.

"Well, you remember I said how good looking he was and that he had such delicate features, including the most amazing eyelashes?"

she said starting to giggle again and then almost choking. She composed herself to deliver the punchline, when Mike's phone rang.

"Damn," said Mike, reaching into his pocket to the sound of church bells, a ringtone that irritated the hell out of him but kept defaulting every time he attempted to change it. "Just as it gets interesting," he said, standing up from his van bonnet to take the call.

Mike paced up and down listening intently and then gestured that it was his insurance company returning his earlier call. He had left them a voicemail and now he had a young-sounding girl, clearly reading from a script, asking him numerous questions. Mel watched him with interest, amused by his answers, pre-empting the questions he was being asked. She giggled when she heard him say, "Is that question really relevant? How can you ask me that when I explained that two men were fighting near my car and shoved a sign post through my windscreen?" he continued. "How can you ask me if it was my fault, for God's sake, I didn't even know them! No, I wasn't driving," he answered. "I have already told you I was approaching my car when I saw them fighting by the side of my car, no I didn't actually see them put it through my screen but it didn't get there on its own," he said, running his fingers through his hair and gripping it tightly. Mel could tell he was getting angry as the caller was clearly running through a question sheet, most of which wasn't relevant. "Look," he said, feeling the anger rising through him, "I think it would be best if we continue this conversation later, I'm far too busy right now," he added. He ended the call abruptly, replacing the phone in his right-hand pocket and continued to pace, obviously needing to take a few minutes to compose himself.

He turned to face Mel, about to offload when he thought better of it. "Cheer me up, Mel, continue with your tale before I explode," he told her, unlocking his van, after searching in all his jacket pockets for the keys.

Mel started to giggle again, as she climbed into the passenger side, trying to remember where she had left off. "Well, we were having dinner," she continued, "and it was all very romantic, candles and all, when the question came up about marriage. It turned out he had been married and had two small children but had recently divorced. I asked if the children lived with their mother and he said 'yes'. I then asked if he got to see them regularly and he said, 'yes, every day'. We continued to chat and I said he was lucky to see them so often, as children often live with their mother and that's when he dropped the bomb shell," she told him, still laughing.

"I know what you're going to say," Mike teased. "He was the mother, or should I say 'she' was the mother," he said, joining in with the laughter.

"Yes, would you believe it?" she said, recalling the moment. "Apparently, she had decided to be true to herself and that she wasn't going to live a lie any longer."

"Fair play," said Mike, thinking it must be awful to have to live a lie.

"Yes, I totally agree, and after chatting with him/her all evening his storey was desperately sad. However, I did tell him that it wasn't fair to date someone without them knowing his true gender, as in fact that was just another lie. It ended with no tears anyway," she told him, "but it just makes me smile when I think of how else I may have discovered the truth…" she said, giving him a wink.

"Indeed, that could have been awkward, although you never know you might have enjoyed it, they say a change is as good as a rest," he said, teasing her again.

"Don't you go there," she said, nudging him again, as he steered the van out of the car park.

"Twins, or at least sisters," said Mike, turning his attention back to the case at hand again. "This really changes things, Mel," he said, moving into second gear, as he turned the corner into Weaver Street.

Mel looked across at him, wondering what he was thinking. "Go on," she said, eager for him to share his thoughts.

"Well, think about how long they may have been missing. Twins would really flare up in the news, wouldn't they?" he asked. "I mean, can you remember reading about twins going missing?" he said, trying to think back over the years.

"Well, I guess it would depend on how many years we are talking about," she said, trying to think back over all the cases she had been part of, and historical news, prior to her joining the force. "They could have been abducted as small children and then, of course, it would effectively be at an age when we wouldn't have been interested in the news, as we would have been too young ourselves," she added. "I mean, I went from toys to boys and didn't really get interested in anything like that until much later," she added.

Mike stopped the car suddenly pulling into a layby. "I think that's it, Mel, this is not a recent thing, we need to track back over the last decade or even further than that," he told her. I don't think they've seen the light of day for years."

Two

They drove back to the station in silence. An eerie silence, the only thing separating them from their personal thoughts was the sound of Derek Nimbel doing his midweek quiz show on the radio. Mel reached out to change channels. She hated Derek Nimbel's quiz, she thought it sounded false and wondered how many people tuned into it, if any. She kept pressing the auto-tune button, searching and searching until Mike brushed her hand away, as he moved swiftly into his usual parking space. "We're here now, Mel, no point messing with it," he told her. "It returns to that channel every time I start up the engine anyway," he told her.

"What is it with you?" she questioned, "it's the same with your mobile ringtone. Are you magnetic or something?" she said, laughing.

"Only with women," he said, grinning as he opened the car door to exit.

Mel looked up at Dhillon's office window. She could see he was standing with his back to it, with his phone to his left ear. She watched for a few moments until he repositioned, looking directly at her. She closed the van door, wondering how their next meet would pan out. They didn't really have much more to tell him, other than the fact that there were now two Jane Gordans, both of whom appeared mute, and again nothing more to go on. Mike followed her glance towards the office above. "Yeah, wonder what his reactions are going to be now that there are two," he quizzed.

"He's going to be a total nightmare," she told him, following him into the station. Mike took the station steps two at a time, as usual, swinging open the door and standing to one side to allow Mel to enter first.

"Thank you, my prince," she said, smiling.

"Coffee?" he asked, stopping in front of the vending machine. It was a standing joke between them that Mike never made it past the vending machine when he entered the station without selecting a coffee.

"No, I'll pass this time, thanks," she told him, leaning against the wall. She watched as he made his usual selection, with extra sugar, amused by the fact that, after all these years, he still had to fish in his pocket for his readers to select his choice. You would think by now he would know which button to press blindfolded, she thought to herself.

Mel glanced across at the large station clock on the wall and was surprised it read 4.05pm already. "So which one of us is going to type up today's findings?" she questioned, hoping it was her. Mike made his way across to his desk and opened his drawer.

"Toss you for it," he said, reaching for his lucky fifty pence piece. "You going somewhere?" he suddenly questioned, as he watched her expression change at his suggestion.

"Quite the opposite, actually," she answered without looking at him. She had wanted to delay her return home to her apartment that evening, as her landlord was making himself a total nuisance and was beginning to make her feel really uncomfortable with his sleazy suggestions. Mike could tell something wasn't right.

"You mean the city is safe this evening without you," he giggled, secretly concerned that there was more to it.

"Very funny," she said, not joining in with their usual banter.

"Tell you what," he told her, "why don't we do the report between us and then we go for something to eat," he suggested. Mel accepted the offer with over the top enthusiasm and switched on her PC to start. Mike instinctively knew that something wasn't right. He had worked with Mel for years and they had seen each other through all sorts of problems, including the breakdown of his marriage. She never wanted to stay late, ever. There was always something she needed to do, somewhere she needed to be. He paused, exhaled and was about to quiz her when he decided not to run with it now but would raise the subject again later, over dinner.

Mel started the report and Mike added his piece bit by bit, pacing up and down, as he recalled the day's events. His thoughts then turned to his earlier suggestion about going for something to eat as he made his way to the gents. He reached into his pocket for his wallet. He knew there was nothing in there but checked again, in case there was a hidden note in the lining. He had exactly £5.50 in his pocket and perhaps a bit of copper. Not exactly the result you wanted when you had just offered to take someone to dinner. He wandered back to his desk and watched as Mel taped furiously at her keyboard. "Mel, I'm actually a bit strapped financially at the moment," he said, feeling a little embarrassed at backtracking.

"Aren't we all," she responded, looking up from her PC.

"Tonight's dinner," he continued, "do you mind if it's a frozen pepperoni pizza from my freezer?" he suggested, hoping that this feeble offering would suffice.

Mel smiled across at him. "It's my favourite kind," she said. "Absolutely perfect," she added.

"Good," said Mike, relieved. "If my memory serves me right, I think I have a couple of beers in the fridge too," he added.

"Oh, you really know how to spoil a girl," Mel said, in a teasing voice.

Mike grinned, pleased that he had managed to pull it off and stood behind Mel's shoulder reading her version of events. Satisfied that she had managed to correctly report on things as they stood to date, he decided that while they had earlier referred to them as the Jane Gordon girls, the second girl needed her own identity.

"They will progress with their recovery at different rates and will need to be reported on individually," Mike told her.

"Yes, I had already considered calling her Sally for the time being," Mel suggested, "until we discover their true names."

"Ideal," said Mike. "OK, let's wrap it up and go," he suggested, "it's nearly 6pm already."

Mel looked across the office to see who was left. Karen Williams was working away tirelessly in the corner, PA to Dhillon, who really put in some hours, albeit more for the love of the job than anything else. Then there was William, known to all as Billy and his partner Benny. They were still wandering around aimlessly. Mel smiled inwardly to herself. If only they knew they were called 'The Flower Pot Men' behind their backs. She got to her feet, content that she had put in enough hours for one day and decided to check out alongside Mike. After all a pepperoni pizza was waiting for her.

Mel climbed in into her Golf, parked next to Mike's and tailed his car out of the car park towards his flat. It was a short drive and much more convenient than the thirty-five-minute drive she had each morning in rush-hour traffic. She pulled in at the off-licence two streets from his apartment and took a look in her purse. Mike thought he was strapped, she thought to herself, tipping the contents out on the passenger seat. A ten pence piece rolled off the seat into the footwell. Oh no you don't little fella, you're needed tonight, every last one of you, she thought, counting her change. She scraped together £2.20 and sighed. Hardly worth stopping for, she thought. She gathered it up, thinking that's probably two more beers than they would have otherwise and climbed out of the car to see what she could harvest. She pushed open the off-licence door which let out a jingle, indicating to the shop keeper that he had a customer.

A small man with a bald head and long moustache stepped out from the back, smiling. "Evening, Miss," he said, standing to attention ready to serve. Mel opened the door to the fridge, eyeing up the beers, wondering what was the cheapest.

"Evening," she said as she scooped two unknown beers from the front line of the fridge that were priced 99p each. She placed her change on the counter, embarrassed by her modest purchase and turned to face the door.

"Pleasant evening," said the shopkeeper, still smiling.

"You too," she said, closing the door behind her. "Last of the big spenders," said Mel, out loud, as she climbed back behind the wheel of her car.

She arrived outside Mike's apartment a few minutes later and parked directly behind his Morgan. She sighed to herself, wondering how soon he would be able to fix it, gathered the two beers and made her way up the steps immediately opposite. Mike had left the front door slightly ajar and Mel let herself in, calling out that she came bearing gifts. Mike smiled, as she put the two beers down on the counter top.

"A totally unknown brand," she advised him, "but it was by far the cheapest in the shop and probably totally disgusting," she said laughing.

"Beggars can't be choosers," he said reaching for the bottle opener and removing both tops with ease. Mel smiled as the tops ricocheted to the other side of the kitchen and then laughed again as Mike made no attempt to retrieve them from the place they had fallen. He handed one to Mel, took a swig of his own and declared it fit for purpose.

It was a cosy apartment, the kitchen part separated from the front room by the aid of a small breakfast bar, which housed two stools.

Mel took up residence on the nearest stool facing inwards to the kitchen, so that she could face Mike, as he attempted to retrieve a pizza from the depths of his freezer.

"So, tell me, Mel," said Mike, uncertain how to approach the subject, "but forgive me if I've got the wrong end of the stick but you seemed to be reluctant to go home this evening?" he questioned, without looking at her. He pulled the pizza from its box and unwrapped the cellophane, which kept sticking to his fingers, and then searched for a suitable baking tray from his cupboards. It was a large pizza and it took three attempts before he found one large enough to fit and then switched the oven on to heat. He sat down opposite her, waiting for an answer, staring directly at her as if about to interrogate her.

Mel sighed, she didn't really want to talk about it tonight but she knew Mike wouldn't give up unless she told him something. "It's just my landlord," she told him, feeling disgusted at a sleazy suggestion he made to her last month about clearing her debts. "I mentioned it before," she told him. "Remember? I said I'm a little behind with the rent and that he's chasing me for it. That's all, it's nothing more than that. No psychopath boyfriends hiding in the closet, I promise," she added, with a smile.

"Yeah, but it's a bit more than a little behind, though, Mel isn't it?" he questioned. "You said two grand earlier."

"Well, it will be three grand on Friday and I just haven't got it," she told him. "As fast as my wages hit the bank, they're swallowed by the overdraft and I just go round in a circle."

"Bloody hell, Mel," said Mike, as he caught sight of the light going out on the oven. He stood up, reached for the pizza and slung it in the oven with ease. "Can Pete help you out a bit until you get back on your feet?" he questioned.

"No, Pete's got his own problems and three kids to feed," she said, sighing.

"Where does he live?" questioned Mike. "I know he is fairly local but where exactly?"

"Pete lives on the Highland Estate. You know, the mobile-home park on Clarendon road," she told him. Mike nodded, he knew it well, a rough place, run down and definitely in need of a council-money injection. "The van's bursting at the seams, definitely no room for me and he has no spare funds to talk of," she told him. "His work is hit and miss and his misses, Clare works all hour's God sends," she said, thinking about how the kids are often left to roam. "My sole family unit," she said sighing again. Mel's parents had died when they were small children.

Mike thought how sad it was that she really didn't have anyone. No other family members, no husband or children of her own, she was totally dependent on herself. No wonder she was a tough cookie, thought Mike, standing up to check on the pizza. Mike knew they had been orphaned as children but I guess he thought she had some extended family somewhere, but no one… that really was tough. "So, what will you do?" he questioned further. "I can give you a little, Mel but I don't think my small injection will make that much difference really," he told her. "Three grand, Mel," he repeated, shaking his head.

"Mike, I don't want to talk about it any more tonight, please. It's so depressing, I need you to cheer me up and discussing my finances isn't gonna hit the spot." she told him, raising her bottle and clinking it against his.

"OK, OK," he said, slicing the pizza into six pieces and passing her some. "I was just worried, that's all, still worried actually," he said, with an expression on his face that told her he wasn't going to leave it there.

"Have you heard from Laura recently?" she questioned.

"Not as much as I would like," he said, moving from the counter to the sofa. He slouched down and put his feet up on the coffee table and took another bite. The uni she got into is in Wales, so a lot further away than originally planned."

"Guess the offer Dhillon made about moving to South Wales could help you with the geographical thing," she said, attempting to smile. She really hoped he wouldn't go but with his daughter now living down there, that's even more of a reason to go, she considered. She was losing her best friend and soon she would have no one at all. A gloomy feeling swept over her and Mike could see that she wasn't in a good place.

"Hey," he said, "come over here and help me choose a film to put on," he beckoned. Mike had an impressive DVD collection, it was another way of avoiding subscription packages to TV and broadband providers and keeping his costs down to a minimum.

Mel smiled as she ran her finger across the spines of his vast collection. "Hey, what about this?" she suggested, pulling out a copy of an old timeless movie they had both probably watched numerous times over the years. "It's got all the old greats in it and the scene where he chases her into the attic gets me every time, especially where…"

"OK, don't remind me then, or there will be no point watching it," Mike interjected. "I had forgotten that bit," he said, laughing at her choice and desire to describe each scene, "I haven't actually seen that one for years," he added.

Mel joined him on the sofa and soon they were both lost in the world of fiction, which they both needed to ease their stress levels. Mike watched with interest as Mel interacted with the film, jumping at all the predictable scenes and hiding her face behind his cushion. She finally let out a scream that made even Mike jump. He started laughing. "I really don't know how you can be so spoked when you have already seen the film," he told her. "You knew that bit was coming," he said laughing.

"I told you," she said giggling, it gets me every time. Mel sat watching the closing credits with interest. She always did this, which amused Mike greatly. Every film they watched together Mel never moved until the very last word came up on the screen. Mike had never asked her why, but he liked this little quirk about her character. Perhaps it was about getting value for money, or was she delaying her way back into reality?

Mel was sprawled out at one end of the sofa, looking much more content than she had earlier. "Thanks, Mike, I really appreciate your company tonight, especially your gourmet cooking," she said, smirking.

"My pleasure," he said, getting to his feet, enjoying her sarcasm. He secretly knew that if she had gone home, she probably wouldn't have had anything to eat at all. "It was lovely to have someone to share the evening with," he told her. It was lonely living there by himself and he couldn't quite get used to his own company after a busy family life. "Am I throwing you a duvet or are you heading home?" he questioned.

"I'd better head back," she told him. "I don't want to arrive at work in yesterday's clothes," she added.

"Yeah, The Flower Pot Men will be on to you like bees to a honey pot," he told her, laughing.

"Indeed," she said, rising to her feet. "Goodnight, my bestie," she said to him, kissing him on both cheeks gently, as his face looked so bruised and tender, she moved towards the front door.

"See you in the morning," Mike responded, closing the door behind her. He flopped back down on the sofa and was soon out for the count.

Mel arrived back at her studio apartment and let out a sigh of relief. Niko, who owned the kebab shop below and was also her landlord, had closed for the evening and the place was in darkness. She now didn't have to endure any more rent collection proposals and could make her way up to her apartment without going into battle. She had just got to the third step, when she glimpsed him stepping out from the shadows. "Kaló apógevma, Miss Mel," came the voice stepping out from the darkness. Fuck, thought Mel, there's just no getting away from this jerk.

Mel stopped in her tracks, turning towards him, sickened by the very sight of him. "Evening," she said gruffly. "Am I to take it that you are lurking in the shadows waiting for me or are you terrorising some other poor woman in the darkness?" she said sarcastically.

"Only those who owe me money," he said sharply.

Niko owned the whole block and was a very wealthy man but no one liked him. He was greasy, smelt, and had a sordid way about him. No wonder he was single Mel thought, smelling him from where she was standing. He had an evil face, one only a mother could love, she thought, taking two more steps towards her apartment.

"Not so quick, my little beauty," came his slimy, seedy voice as he caught hold of her hand on the banister rail. He retained his grip and moved onto the second step. Mel pulled her hand away sharply, making him wobble slightly and moved up two more steps.

"Feisty little mover aren't you," he said, enjoying the fact that he was making her nervous.

"Fuck off," she told him.

"Oh, I intend to," he said, "all over your face," he said laughing.

"You're a sick bastard, a sad little evil man, with no friends," she told him moving further up the staircase.

"Well you're going to be a poor, lonely, homeless person by the end of the week if I don't get my money," he said angrily. "Remember my proposal, Mel," he said, turning round and making his way down the two stairs he had climbed. "Fuck me and your debt will be cleared," he said laughing, as he walked into the darkness.

"Never," she shouted loudly, "not even if my life depended on it." Tears stung to her eyes. What the fuck was she going to do? She thought, climbing the final few stairs to the terrace above. Her front door was set between two others all leading from the terrace above the kebab shop. She stood fumbling with her keys, struggling with the broken lock and rushed inside, closing the door firmly behind her. She dropped to her knees, leaning back against the door and cried. How was she going to get out of this mess? Where would she go? She had no money, no family, she was desperate. She reached out to touch the radiator, stone bloody cold. Yes, she was freezing as well. Mel sat in the same position, leaning against the door for most of the night. She was too scared to put a light on in case he came back for a second dose. She stared up at the clock which said 5.30am. She had sat there for so many hours she was completely numb. She had decided that she was going to see her bank manager as soon as the bank opened and had sent Mike a text, informing him that she would be a little late that morning and not to worry.

She showered in cold water, hating every moment of the experience, cleaned her teeth and sat in front of her dressing table, staring at her reflection. She put on a little mascara, ran a light bit of blusher across both cheeks and then put on a nude colour lipstick. She started to brush her hair, which was slightly greasy but the thought of extending her head under a cold shower hose, as well as her body was more than she could stand that morning. Instead she sprayed it with dry shampoo and put it up in a ponytail. What should she wear to see the bank manager? she questioned, opening up her wardrobe door and sliding the coat hangers to one side. She needed to go straight to the station afterwards, so didn't want to make it too over the top as she had to work wearing it as well. She chose black jeans, a cream blouse and a fake Burberry style jacket. She stood staring at her reflection in her mirror for ages, content with her choice. How the fuck did she get into this mess? she thought, battling with her conscience. She had to find a way out. She made her way into the kitchen and switched on the kettle. She had two tea bags and a spoonful of coffee as her only possible option. She opened the fridge and smelt the milk which had gone out of date days before. Black coffee it is then, she thought to herself, knowing that black tea wasn't an option for her. She sat at her kitchen table watching the clock tick round to 8.45.

Her bank was on the corner of Temple Street, one street from her apartment but despite this she decided to take her car, so she didn't have to return to her apartment later when the kebab shop was open. This was, in fact, a bloody nuisance as she would then need change to park her car on one of the meters. She knew it was a toss up between seeing that wanker again or getting a fine. What the hell she thought, she was up to her neck in debt anyway and the thought of seeing that sleazy sex-seeking negotiator was more than she could bare. She pulled away in her car and then noticed that the final space at the end of her road was available. It was far too far away from the shop for Niko to see her later and was a stone's throw from the bank. Perfect, she thought, climbing out of her car, someone must be looking down on me today.

She stood outside the bank knowing it would be opening its doors in the next few moments but conscious in case Niko saw her. She felt so relieved when she heard the clerk opening the front doors, she took all three steps at once. "Good morning," said the young fresh-faced clerk smiling, as she pulled open the large vault like doors.

"Good morning," said Mel, relieved to be inside. She eyed the three stations at the counter, two of which were manned, the third still had the closed sign wedged against the window. "I haven't got an appointment," she told the girl, who was now turning a wheel on the back of the ATM machine, "but I was hoping to see someone about a loan."

"Take a seat, Miss…?"

"Oh, my name Melanie Bailey," she told her, filling in the gap.

"Take a seat, Miss Bailey and I will see what I can do," she said, pointing to the small seating area, which had five seats and a small round table stacked with brochures. Mel sat down, fidgeting until she decided to sit on her hands before she had no nails left. What was she going to tell him – that he was her last resort before basically being raped?

"Miss Bailey," came a male voice from behind the screen, "this way please," he added.

Mel looked up and saw a man, extremely professional looking in a navy-blue suit. He looked to be in his mid-forties, had a kind face, the sort you would be proud to take home to meet your parents, if you had any, of course, she thought.

"Take a seat," he said, pointing to the chair beside his desk. "I'm Mr Stevens," he informed her.

For the second time that morning, Mel sat down to order and stared at what could be her saviour.

"What can I do for you this morning?" he questioned, with a bright smile.

Mel cleared her throat, crossed her legs and decided to get straight to the point. "I would like to apply for a loan," she told him, smiling.

"You can make an application online," he told her, not looking up from his PC.

"Yes, I know that," she said, changing positions on her chair, "but I am in a hurry. You see, I have fallen behind with my rent, three months actually," she added, "and I am finding it extremely difficult to catch up, I am also into my overdraft, which means that as soon as I'm paid it gets swallowed up and the cycle starts again."

"Can I have your bank account number, Miss Bailey or your bank card?" he gestured, holding out his hand. Mel reached into her jacket pocket and handed it across to him, nervously.

Mr Stevens tapped in her details and stood staring at the screen for ages. "Yes, you have been in your overdraft for some time," he said, glancing up at her.

"Yes, I realise that Mr Stevens, which is why I'm here. As you can see," she said standing up and walking towards the window, "I am two thousand pounds overdrawn and I have a landlord breathing down my neck for three grand rent arrears. However," she said, giving it her best shot, "I am employed full time, I am a police officer and therefore could be considered a pillar of the community. I work extremely hard, haven't had any time off work for over six years, with the exception of this morning, and know that once I get this loan, hopefully get this loan," she rephrased, "I will be back on track. You can obtain work and personal reference on me," she told him, "I can give you all the details immediately," she said, feeling desperation setting in again.

Mr Stevens looked across at where she was standing. "Miss Bailey, or can I call you Melanie?" he said, reaching for his calculator, "I am sure there is something we can do for you," he told her, glancing over at her again to gain eye contact. "Please sit down so that we can run through the details and work out some figures," he said, gesturing towards the seat by his side.

Melanie sat back down revealed. "Really?" she said. "You mean you can help me?" she added, unable to believe she qualified for a loan. "Thank you so much," she said, shuffling about on her chair. "How much will it cost me?" she said, wondering how this was going to be calculated and managed.

"Right," said Mr Stevens, "I suggest a five-year loan for the sum of five thousand pounds."

Melanie looked at him in amazement, "Five thousand pounds," she repeated.

"Yes, three thousand to settle your rent arrears, and two thousand to clear your overdraft. Now with interest at today's rates, your repayment plan would be set at one hundred and fifty per month for five years."

Melanie jumped up unable to contain her overwhelming feeling of gratefulness and almost hugged him. "Oh my God," she said really. Just over one hundred pounds a month for five years. She could manage that, as she had no other debts. She had been saved. She would show that little turd that he would never get her, ever.

Mr Stevens ran through some questions, which seemed to take forever, quoted terms and conditions over and over and then printed the papers for her to sign. Melanie thanked him profusely and made her way out of his office feeling so much lighter now that the weight of her financial status had been lifted from her shoulders. She nodded at the clerk who opened the door earlier that morning and was about to leave, when she stopped in her tracks. She turned around to face the clerk again with a question and walked back towards her. "I need to see Mr Stevens again," she asked, suddenly panicking.

"I'm afraid he has another client in with him now," she told her, pointing towards his office door, which was just closing behind a small black-haired woman.

"But I need to see him, I have another question," she said, shaking.

"Can I help at all?" said the clerk, in a polite, professional voice.

"Yes, hopefully," said Mel, moving closer to the window. "I have just secured a five-year loan, if I give you my details can you tell me when the funds will be available," she asked eagerly. Mel passed her bank card over the counter, trembling.

The clerk swiftly entered her details and confirmed smiling that the funds would be available first thing Monday morning.

Mel walked out of the bank in a daze. Her hands were trembling as she tried to locate her car keys from her handbag. She turned the corner cautiously, looking as far up the road as she could see and then quickly unlocked her car. It will be OK, she said to herself. I will let him know that he can have the whole bloody lot first thing Monday morning. It will be OK, she kept repeating to herself.

She drove back to the station with a sinking feeling and also feeling like she was metamorphosing into a parrot, as she kept repeating the words 'it will be all right' over and over, out loud. She parked her vehicle next to Mike's, as she did every single day and slowly made her way into the station. She was still dazed, not really sure if she had hit the jackpot or not. It felt like all her lottery numbers had just come in but she wasn't quite certain if she had renewed her subscription. She sat down quietly at her desk and then looked around. With the exception of Karen and the new girl, Tina, there was absolutely no one else around. She opened up her PC and stared at her calendar, wondering if she had missed anything, when the door to the meeting room down the hallway opened and she could hear everyone coming up the hallway, talking nineteen to the dozen. She could hear Mike giving out instructions, presumably to Bill, Benny and Paul who were also working on the case, and then they all filed into the room.

"Morning Mel," said Mike, sitting down at his desk opposite. "Did you get everything sorted?" he asked, in a caring voice.

"Sort of," said Mel. "I'm sure it will be all right," she told him. God here I go again she thought, I'm turning into a goddamn parrot.

"What do you mean 'sort of'," said Mike, standing up and perching on the edge of her desk.

"Well, I went to the bank, like I said in my text, and sorted a loan," she told him.

"And…" said Mike, trying to see what the problem might be.

"Well, thankfully, I have managed to sort a loan that will sort out all my problems but, and this is where the 'sort of' comes in to play, the cash won't be available until Monday morning," she told him.

"Well, surely the little fuckwit can wait until Monday," said Mike, returning to his chair.

"Yeah, hopefully," said Mel, wondering if she should tell Mike about his 'indecent proposal'. "Let's hope so," she said, saying 'it will be all right' over and over in her head.

"So, how was this morning's briefing?" she asked him, turning her attention back to the Jane Gordon case.

"Well, basically it was bringing everyone up to speed about the second girl," he told her. "Dhillon's still chirping on about house-to-house enquiries, which I have now given over to the flower pot duo and I want Paul to concentrate on finding out who owns or rents property in Gordon Square and surrounding area.

"And us?" questioned Mel, wondering what the day had to offer.

"We're going back to the hospital as the blood results are back – just before the briefing a call came in from Doctor Leeson," Mike informed her.

"And?" said Mel, "didn't he give you the results over the phone?"

"Well, he said he had solved a few questions and that we might want to drop by to discuss his findings but also he is having a session with her again at twelve, and thought we might want to sit in on it."

"Interesting," said Mel, she certainly didn't want to miss the session with the girl, Sally. She looked at her watch. It was 11.30am, she had missed so much of the morning already. She pulled on her jacket, wrapped her cream scarf around her neck and put her fashionable, but over the top, hat on.

Mike smiled across at her. "You look very smart this morning," he told her. "All dressed up with nowhere to go," he said, smiling.

"I did have somewhere to go," she said laughing. "I had an impromptu meeting with my bank manager and now I have an extremely pressing interview with a top physician."

"Get you," said Mike, pulling his leather jacket off the back of his chair, laughing. His jacket was his trademark, no matter what the weather. Mel wasn't even sure if he owned a coat.

"Have you eaten this morning Mel?" he questioned, as if he was her father.

"Nope, not yet," she answered. "To be honest, I don't really have an appetite at the moment," she said, recalling the night before.

Mike was worried about her, there was more to this than she was letting on he thought. He decided he was going to keep a close eye on her for the time being. She needed looking after. They made their way to the hospital in silence, both consumed by their own thoughts.

Doctor Leeson was waiting for them on arrival and the receptionist bustled them through to his office without even confirming their names. She had remembered them from yesterday and was obviously as curious as they were about the girl.

"Has she said anything yet?" she asked, as they made their way along the corridor.

"Not that we're aware of," said Mike, wondering if there had been any development in this area. The receptionist knocked on Doctor Leeson's door and opened it, without waiting for a response.

Doctor Leeson rose to his feet, as if taken by surprise. "Good Afternoon," he said, looking up at the clock on the wall. He gestured to the two seats by his desk and opened his file. They both nodded as an acknowledgement and sat facing him. "OK," he said, shuffling his papers, "what have we found out?" he said, perusing his findings. Mike and Mel sat patiently, looking at one another. They felt like they were waiting for A Level results and kept fidgeting, like teenagers.

"Right, let's start with the bloods," he said, staring at the phlebotomy results. "I can tell you with absolute certainty that they are sisters, however, not twins. We have carried out full zygosity DNA testing to establish whether they were identical or fraternal twins and I have to say I was completely taken by surprise when the results confirmed that they were neither, however, all the cell samples taken from them confirm that they do share both parents, which explains to their genetic likeness," he continued.

"But they look like twins," interrupted Mike, staring at the doctor for answers.

"Yes, theoretically it is possible to inherit almost exactly the same set of genes as one's sibling. This is what has happened here," he told them.

"Do you know how old they are?" questioned Mel, looking at Mike in amazement. She had been so sure they were twins.

"I have compared the first girl's results with girl two and have analysed their bloods for their biological age."

"God, can you do that nowadays?" said Mike, thinking how much science has advanced.

"Indeed we can," said Doctor Leeson.

"And?" said Mel, eager to know.

"Well, we have been studying the enzyme changes which develop between childhood and adulthood and can conclude that girl one is approximately eighteen and girl two is sixteen, or thereabouts."

"Why didn't Doctor Gyllensvan know the first girl's age, when I interviewed him?" he asked, his inquisitiveness getting the better of him.

"Doctor Gyllensvan studies mental health," he told him.

"Yes, but girl one has been in his care for the last three weeks!" he added. "I don't understand why this information didn't get through to him," Mike queried.

"Well, we have only just carried out the sibling DNA testing and the enzyme testing was carried out at the same time, this all costs thousands of pounds and our hospital budget is under extreme pressure and we have to make decisions, some of which may not be to your liking," he told them firmly, defending his hospital principles. "We have to distribute where the need is greatest to save lives," he added. "Now, are you ready to sit in on today's session?" he asked in an authoritative tone.

Doctor Leeson rose to his feet and asked them to follow him. "This will be our last session here," he informed them. "She will be moving over into Doctor Gyllensvan's care this afternoon," he said, closing his office door behind them.

"Will we be in the room, when you question and examine her, Doctor?" asked Mike, wondering what this might do to contribute to her already fragile status.

"No, indeed not," said the doctor. "Only me and Nurse Wilson will be present with the patient, you will be behind a one-way window," he told them.

They took up their position in a small viewing room opposite a one-way mirror, facing a light airy room with an artificial view of the beautiful countryside. This was obviously to give the illusion of a wonderful sunny afternoon to help boost morale, thought Mike, taking it all in. To the left was a medical style bed, complete with bedside cabinet, and centre stage stood a small four-seater table with chairs. The room was decorated in light blue and lemon and looked to Mike that it had been specifically designed to help a patient relax and feel happy. It was obviously in use as there appeared to be some personal effects, such as a dressing gown, slippers and a puzzle on the table.

Doctor Leeson explained that this was one of five rooms designed for patient study cases. "We place patients with specific problems in these viewing rooms so that we can analyse their behaviour patterns," he told them informatively.

"Well, where is she now?" asked Mel curiously.

"Nurse Wilson will be bringing her in shortly," he told her. "All these rooms have toilets and hand basins adjoined but none have full shower or bath facilities. These rooms are for patients with severe problems that need to bathe in strictly supervised conditions. Some in harnesses for their own safety," he told them. "We have one bathroom, which is fully equipped, for these five rooms, as the room requires specialist equipment, expensive specialist equipment," he added, before Mike queried yet another hospital policy.

"She will be here shortly, as Nurse Wilson and her team have been dealing with her personal hygiene this morning," he told them.

Doctor Leeson explained how the session would be conducted and then sat making notes while Mel and Mike watched on in silence.

Mike suddenly asked, "Has she eaten anything since she's been here?"

"Very little," said Doctor Leeson, "mainly dry bread."

"She's so thin," said Mel, "so malnourished, you would think she would be shovelling it in." She was thinking how she could eat a whole pack of Jaffa Cakes in less than ten minutes, when she was bored.

The door opened into the room and Nurse Wilson, a small middle-aged auxiliary nurse, and Sally entered. Sally was wearing a brightly coloured pink tracksuit and looked clean and tidy. Her hair had been washed and dried and could now be classed as a honey blond. She looked pale, gaunt with extreme shadows under her eyes, exhausted from her ordeal. She was still squinting and Mike could see, she was trembling violently. Nurse Wilson sat her at the table and joined her on the chair opposite. She nodded to the auxiliary nurse that she could leave and then she gave the thumbs up. Doctor Leeson rose to his feet, acknowledging that this was his signal to enter the room.

They watched intently as Doctor Leeson entered the room. They noted that Sally was totally non-responsive and didn't even try to elude from his presence. She merely sat there, motionless, devoid of any communication, exactly like Jane.

"What happened to them, Mel? What could have happened that was so bad, it removes you from your very being, your soul," he asked. "To me it looks like their soul has been destroyed, discarded, removed, there's just a shell." he told her, staring at the child in disbelief.

"Do you think they may have been part of one of those cults?" she questioned. Suddenly bringing in a whole new line of investigation.

"I think we may need to explore that possibility, Mel. Could be witchcraft, sacrificial nonsense, who knows? but we need to explore everything."

Doctor Leeson sat down at the table with a large notebook. He scribbled notes as he ran through some obligatory questions, despite knowing full well they would remain unanswered.

"Stupid, if you ask me," Mel stated. "What's the point of asking her that, knowing full well she is not going to answer."

"He has to start somewhere," said Mike. "He has to try and build a picture. Perhaps she may physically react to something, which could indicate her feelings towards certain things." Mel looked vacantly at him. Mike went on to elaborate, "for example, certain things, or items may provoke a reaction that might indicate something. These doctors know what they're doing, Mel, they are trained in this field, this is their thing."

"Yeah, perhaps," said Mel unconvinced.

Doctor Leeson suddenly raised his arm to point at the mural, which totally surprised them all. Sally jumped up, backed away from the table and cowered in the corner of the room. She was devoid of any verbal communication and didn't even so much as make a whimper but her head was buried in her hands and she was totally still.

What happened there, thought Mike, standing up to move closer to the window. "Look Mel, she's not even trembling any more, she's totally still. She's gone inside herself again," he said. "That's what she does – they do," he corrected. "They are removing themselves completely from the situation."

The session lasted another fifteen minutes and then Nurse Wilson helped her over to the bed. Sally went willingly, or so it appeared, guided by the nurse who gently positioned her into the sleeping position and covered her over with a blue duvet. She lay there staring, eyes wide open.

"Why are her eyes open?" Mike questioned out loud.

They left the hospital in silence, walking towards the car. This case was really getting to them and was taking its toll. Mike stopped at the van and looked over at Mel, who was waiting for the door latch to pop up. "OK, let's go back and see what everyone's managed to uncover and see what we can build on this case today," he told her. "Then," he said, "we can think about what we are going to eat later." Mike felt adamant that he was going to keep an eye on her until she had paid off her sleazy landlord, as it was obviously troubling her.

"Oh, I've got a date tonight," she told him. "You know, the security guard from the hospital foyer."

"Wow, that was quick work," said Mike, pleased that she wasn't going to be spending her time by herself at her apartment. "When did he call?" he asked inquisitively.

"He sent a text while we were in the viewing gallery and I have just accepted," she told him.

"Slick work," he said, climbing into the driver's seat. Mike buckled up his seat belt, adjusted the radio from its default setting and selected reverse. What an afternoon, he thought, once again wondering what had been the girl's plight.

Mel seemed back to her usual self at the station, leaving Mike to do the daily report. She was obviously in a hurry to get back so that she had sufficient time to get ready for her date.

"Where's he taking you?" questioned Mike, grinning, as Mel reached for her jacket.

"Not sure yet," she responded, "but he's picking me up from my apartment at seven o'clock," she said, with her usual glow.

"Is that wise, Mel?" he questioned, "you don't even know him properly? Why did you give him your address?" he asked her nervously.

"Oh, stop it, big brother, It will be fine." she said, wrapping her scarf around her neck, smiling. She rose to her feet, gave him a peck on the cheek and was gone.

Mike sat there staring into space for a few minutes and then turned his attention back to the report. It was going to be a long evening, as there was lots to cover. He also needed to have quick catch-up with the lads to see what they had unearthed from their research. He looked across at Paul who had been given the task of investigating who had bought or rented property over the last decade, to see if he was on target. He was deep in conversation with someone on the phone, as Mike tuned into his tones. Mike decided to see what he had uncovered, so that he could start pinning things together. He stood behind him momentarily, as Paul compiled the findings from his call onto his notes and then quizzed him thoroughly. Paul never came to the point quickly, he had a way about him that prolonged the most simplistic of things. After about ten minutes Mike's head was reeling. "OK," he said, "that's good work Paul." Mike decided he needed to go, he needed a drink, so staged an early exit.

Mel had made it safely into her apartment without any intervention from Niko and was busy deciding what to wear. She really needed to wash her hair but couldn't face a cold shower that included her long blonde locks, as this would prolong the agony beyond bearable. She decided she would manage a quick shower but would boil the kettle for her hair. She chose some music, suitable for her state of mind and carried the kettle into the bathroom. "What a fucking performance," she said out loud, gasping as the poured the third jug over her head. If that wanker doesn't sort my heating out soon, I'll… she didn't really know what she would do but it felt good letting off steam. She wrapped her hair in a towel and sat down at her dressing table, staring at her reflection. She was an extremely attractive woman with all her assets in the right places but Mel never saw it that way. She was always dieting, trying to change things that were, in fact, perfect as they were. She let out a sigh, tipping the contents of her make-up bag onto her dressing table. She needed a more seductive look, she thought, this evening, rather than the boring, sensible look that she adopted on a work day.

"Let the transformation commence," she said out loud, and then joined in with the song that was playing. She always got ready to music. It made her feel good. She chose a ruby-red lipstick, black eye liner and decided to put on her false lashes. She brushed her cheeks with some light bronze blusher and then sealed her look with some dusting powder. She removed the towel from her hair and gave it a quick comb. "What are we going to do with that this evening," she said to herself, holding it up seductively. She tipped her head upside down and roughly dried it and then took another look at herself in the mirror. Yes, an updo tonight, she thought. Let's go for some sophistication. She gathered some pins and set to work, leaving some pieces down, until she felt happy with her appearance. She chose some delicate dangle earrings that Mike had given to her last year for her birthday, smiling to herself, when she thought of him. She had strong feelings for him, brotherly, best-friend-feelings and she knew with absolute certainty that she didn't want him to go to South Wales.

She was just fastening her black dress when the doorbell rang. It made a silly noise that she had always intended to change but had never got round to it. She knew the tune would play five times before it stopped and was real annoying. Mel glanced over at the clock on her bedside table. It was 6.30, boy, he's eager, she thought, stepping into her high heels, hopping as she went. She looked up the staircase to see if she could recognise the image from behind the frosted-glass front door and stepped up onto the first step. Mel's studio was an odd design yet trendy. As you came through the front door there was a glass balcony with a staircase leading down to her studio. Her kitchen and dining area were open-plan with an L-shape turn, slightly separating her sleeping quarters from the rest. She had a small shower room, just off of this section. She did love her little studio, especially the fact that it had bi-folding doors which looked out over a tiny terrace, just large enough for a bistro table and chairs. She made her way up the staircase, feeling nervous about her date. Should she invite him in? she considered. She had no wine, or should she grab her coat from the hook by the front door and step straight out?

She had just released the latch on the door when it swung open with real force. It crashed into her face, spinning her backwards against the balcony edge.

"My, my, don't we look real pretty this evening my little seductive slut?" he said, grabbing hold of her throat and lifting her off the floor. "There was no need to dress up for me," he said, sarcastically, pushing her to the floor and kicking the door shut behind him.

"I've got your money," she told him, tears running down her face.

"Show me," he said, dragging her by the hair towards the top of the staircase.

"I haven't got it here now," she said, sobbing, "but I will have it first thing Monday morning."

"Mel, I've just about had it up to here with all your excuses," he said articulating with his hand to his throat.

"But I've sorted it," she said, wiping the blood from her nose with the back of her hand, "I've sorted it," she repeated between sobs.

Niko stood towering over her, enjoying the power, dragging her back up off the floor. She was balancing right at the top of the staircase, as she could feel the edge of the top stair with the tip of her toe. A creepy smile spread over Niko's face. "OK, shall I believe you this time, or not?" he said, dangling her with one hand. "Nope, don't think so," he said, loosening his grip. "I think you need to pay me by some other means," he said, pushing her backwards with force. Mel tried to grab the banister but it was just out of reach, then Niko kicked her in the chest, the force sent her reeling to the bottom.

She lay there crumpled, broken, petrified as to what would come next. She had never been so frightened in her life. "Please no," she said, trembling as he towered over her once more.

Niko let out an eerie laugh as he stood with one leg each side of her broken body. "'You will never have me', I believe were your parting words yesterday, my little slut," he told her. "Well I think you might be a tad wrong there," he said, ripping her black dress open from the neck, exposing the entire length of her body. He unbuttoned his trousers, salivating as he stared at her half-naked body in her black lace panties. Mel let out a scream, which Niko muffled with his hand across her mouth. Mel bit into it, desperate to escape his grasp, making Niko let go momentarily. This angered him to the extent that he punched Mel so hard she lost consciousness.

She woke to the sound of the front door closing and the sound of Niko's creepy whistle as he left her apartment. She could barely move, she ached in every part of her body and thought her leg may be broken. She reached down between her legs, her knickers were gone, her legs spread wide. Tears ran down her face, she knew she'd been raped, she could smell the semen all over her.

Three

Mike was sitting at the bar on a stool next to a man who wouldn't stop jabbering. Every few seconds he cried out, articulating with his fists, as he watched the boxing match on the large plasma screen TV set across the corner of the bar. Mike had chosen the wrong spot, he needed peace and quiet and was lost in his own thoughts. He wanted a quiet beer by himself and had chosen this bar, as it was usually quiet. It was payday, every bar would be rammed tonight, he thought, as he moved to a less crowded section. He stared at his phone, willing it to ring. He wanted to know how Mel was getting on. He should have made her promise to call him to confirm, he thought, angry that he hadn't suggested it to her earlier. He swigged his beer and placed the bottle down on the table. "Friday night and all alone," he said out loud for all to hear. He blushed, embarrassed by his sudden outburst and then gestured to the barman to bring him another bottle. He knew that the third bottle would put him over the limit but he was only two streets away from home, staggering distance, he thought.

Should he call her just to make sure, he battled. He sat staring at his phone wishing she would call him. He didn't want her to think he was stalking her for Christ's sake. For fuck's sake, he thought to himself, let's just give her a quick call to make sure the guy's genuine and not some weirdo. He downed another mouthful and then searched for her number. It was the last number he had dialled, the only other number being his insurance company. I'm a sad fuck, he thought listening to the phone ring over and over.

Mel was lying by the foot of her stairs, struggling to move. She could hear her phone ringing on the coffee table. She raised herself up to a sitting position and tried dragging herself along the floor.

She felt for certain her leg was broken and every part of her hurt. She was halfway between the foot of the stairs and the coffee table when her door bell went. Mel stopped momentarily and froze. Had Niko come back for more. She started to sob all over again, trembling. She suddenly realised that it was probably Brian, her date for the evening. What was the time, she wondered? How long had she been unconscious? She stared up at the clock on the wall. It was two minutes to seven. It would be Brian, she knew it would be but she didn't call out. She needed to make it to the coffee table so she could call him to check that it was him standing on the other side of the doorway.

Her mobile rang again over and over until she eventually got to it. She could see it was Mike's name on the front screen. "Mike," she said crying, "help me, please help me, I've been raped."

Mike jumped to his feet, knocking over his beer, as he scrambled out from the corner booth. "Mel, where are you? Are you at home?" he questioned, trembling as he searched in his jacket for his keys.

"Yes," she said, crying, "please hurry."

Mike climbed into his van knowing that he might be slightly over the limit but his best friend needed him. "That fucking bastard," he shouted out, referring to her date that evening. He drove like a lunatic over to her apartment, the thirty-five-minute drive taking forever. He swerved to a halt outside the kebab shop and took the stairs three at a time. He could see a man peering through the letterbox calling out her name, over and over. He grabbed the collar of the man's jacket roughly, dragging him away from the door. "What the fuck have you done to her?" he screamed violently.

"Steady on, man," the burly man said, rising to his feet and shaking Mike off. "I've only just got here." He told him, "but something's not right, as I can hear her crying but she won't come to the door."

"Mel, open the door, it's me, Mike, open the fucking door." Mike stood back from the door and charged at it. He did it again and again until the lock started to buckle. Brian stood there like a limp lettuce wondering what the fuck he had got himself into when the door suddenly gave way. Mike raced down the stairs, shouting for him to call an ambulance.

He stopped at the foot of the stairs and dropped to his knees. "Oh, Mel, who did this to you?" Tears sprung to his eyes as he composed himself and made his way over to her. He cradled her in his arms. "Who did it, Mel, who did it?"

She looked up at him, one eye completely swollen shut. Blood was streaming from a gash above her left eyebrow and from her nose and her face was swelling up by the minute. He pulled her open dress across her to cover her modesty and asked her again. "Mel, tell me who did this?"

"It was Niko," she said, blood running out of her mouth. "It was Niko," she repeated, in a whisper.

A rage came over Mike like he had never experienced in his life. He knew he was going to kill the bastard, it was just a matter of when.

Brian had slowly made his way down the staircase in total disbelief. "The ambulance and police are on their way," he confirmed in a shaky voice.

Mike wrapped a throw around Mel's shoulders and cradled her until the ambulance arrived.

Mike sat holding her hand in the ambulance as they blue-lighted their way to Holden City Central. Mike could see Mel was in agony, as she winced with each turn the ambulance took. A drip had been placed in her right arm and she was being questioned by a medic. They were also administering strong pain relief, which Mike could see was making her slur.

Mike felt helpless, unable to know what to do to help and was totally reliant on the medics for their support. He held onto Mel's hand like both their lives depended on it. He felt sick to the pit of his stomach, imagining what Mel had been through, with no one to help her. A tear trickled down his cheek, as he saw her wince in pain again, as she tried to get comfortable on the stretcher. It was more than he could bear and he knew that, once he had got her to the hospital, he was going to find that bastard and it wasn't going to be pretty.

The ambulance came to a halt outside the A&E entrance and the rear doors were opened. A team of medics transferred Mel onto another stretcher and raced her inside the hospital, along a corridor into an assessment area. Mike followed in pursuit before being stopped short of the double doors by a nurse.

"I'm afraid you're going to have to wait here, Sir," came an instruction from a nurse pulling at his arm, preventing him from entering.

Mike stopped, turning to face the nurse. "But I need to stay with her," he told her, "I'm all she has," he added, suddenly realising that he actually needed to be with her, as well.

"We will keep you fully informed," said the nurse, guiding him over to the seating area. "I will need to ask you some questions Mr…?" She reached for her note book in her pocket.

"Oh, Mike Brugge," said Mike. "My names Mike Brugge."

"What is your relationship to the patient?" asked the nurse, looking up from her note book.

"We are police officers." said Mike, starting to tremble again. "She is my partner," he added, "but also my best friend and I really need to get in there," he told her, getting to his feet and heading towards the door.

The nurse once more stopped him in his tracks. "Mike," she said, guiding him back to his chair, "you will be of more help to her if you could explain to me what has happened to her."

"She's been raped," said Mike, putting his head in his hands. "By some psychopath," he said, shaking violently.

"Do you know who by?" asked the nurse, taking his hand in hers.

"Yes, I do," said Mike, shaking her off and getting to his feet again, "her landlord, her sleazy landlord, and all because she owed him rent," he said gesticulating with his hands towards the ceiling, as if he just couldn't believe it himself.

"So, this wasn't to do with your job, in the line of duty, so to speak?" queried the nurse again, scribbling furiously on her note book.

"No, it wasn't," he told her, "completely unrelated. This has nothing to do with the force at all, I'm here as her friend, in the capacity of a friend," he added, realising that she was actually more than a friend. Mel meant so much to him. They had been partners for over ten years and she played an important role in his world.

The nurse looked up from her notes. "Can I ask what happened to your face? were you attacked too?" she questioned.

"No, no," he stuttered, my injuries relate to another incident," he told her. "Hazards of the job, nothing to do with this," he reassured her, thinking what this must look like.

The doors swung open and a doctor stepped out looking directly at them. "Nurse Ryan, you're needed in here," he told her, holding the door ajar for her to enter.

She closed her notebook and rose to her feet. "I will talk to you later, Mike, and I will keep you fully up to speed. She's in good hands," she reassured him, as the door swung closed behind her.

Mike rose to his feet, deciding he needed a coffee. Or at least he needed something. Something to hold in his hands. What he really needed was a drink, a stiff drink he thought.

He walked back into reception in search of a vending machine when he saw two of his police colleagues standing at the reception desk. The officer to the left, Jim, was engaged in conversation with the receptionist but Dave caught sight of him as he entered.

"Mike, are you OK mate?" he said, walking towards him, with a concerned look. "How's Mel doing?" he asked, not knowing the full extent of things.

"Not good," said Mike, feeling a rage run through him. "Not good," he repeated. He sat down, trembling. He couldn't stop trembling, his whole body felt out of control. He felt for the first time in his life like he could actually kill someone.

"We were called to the scene." Dave informed him, "but the ambulance was just pulling away as we got there, so we are just starting to piece things together now," he added.

"Yes, what can you tell us?" asked Jim, sitting down on the chair to his left. "Her fucking landlord, that's what's happened," said Mike, jumping to his feet. "She was behind on her rent, so he beat her up," he told them. "Then he raped her and left her unconscious. She could have died," he said, starting to pace back and forth. He threw her down the stairs, I think her leg is probably broken," he said, recalling what that Mel had told the medic in the ambulance. "She black and blue," he said, looking directly at Dave.

"I want a full team round there now," Mike instructed, feeling the rage run through him again. "The kebab shop on Kingsbury Rise, just off of Temple Street. Guy's name is Niko. Don't know his last name," he added, "or his home address but he owns the whole block, so one of the residences will have his address, any one of the residences will have it," he added. "Knock on all the doors," he told them, "and when you've got him, call me, before you take him to the station, got it," he said, glaring at them both.

Dave put his hand on his shoulder. He knew exactly what he meant and nodded in acknowledgement. "Got it," he said looking over at Jim. Dave and Jim left immediately, knowing that Mike meant now, and headed out through the main hospital entrance.

Mike sat there momentarily until he recalled his earlier thoughts about finding a coffee. He reached into his pocket for some change, eyeing the coffee machine in the corner of the waiting area and put on his glasses. He selected his usual then returned to the seating area outside the assessment area doors and waited. It felt like forever before the doors opened and a doctor stepped outside. Mike rose to his feet, eager for some information.

"Mr Brugge," the doctor questioned, walking towards him.

"Yes?" said Mike, longing for some information.

"Your partner…" the doctor started to say.

"Friend," interrupted Mike, "best friend, partner, everything actually," he said, starting to tremble again. "How's she doing, Doc?"

"She is strong, very strong actually," he told him. "A strong-willed woman. But the strength of it is, she's been through a horrendous ordeal. She's been beaten, raped and left unconscious. Her injuries have resulted in severe concussion, bruising to the brain, known as contusion. She has neck sprain, together with a broken leg and a hairline fracture to her left wrist. She has multiple bruising, both to her face, chest and inner thighs. She has some internal bruising as well."

Mike buried his head in his hands again while the doctor continued. "We have dealt with her physical injuries and settled her for the evening, while we await test results." the doctor told him.

Mike lifted his head and stared at the doctor. "Test results?" queried Mike, looking at the doctor, vacantly. "Yes, yes, of course," he said, suddenly recalling his years on vice, where he dealt with prostitutes, rape victims, on a continual loop.

"We have to carry out a sexual assault forensic exam," the doctor continued. "This is for the safety of Mel regarding any sexual disease but also with regards to DNA specimens for evidence. We have also provided EC protection."

"What's that?" questioned Mike.

"Morning after pill," said the doctor, "emergency contraception."

"Can I see her please, Doc? I really need to see her," he begged, pulling at his hair.

"They are just waiting for a porter to take her up to the ward now, so you can see her shortly," he told him. "But she is very drowsy, so don't expect too much this evening," he said, heading back into the assessment room. "Please, take a seat in reception and we will send for you shortly," he instructed.

Mike made his way back to reception and paced back and forth until a nurse came bustling out calling his name. "Mr Brugge, please follow me," she said, heading towards the lift. She pressed the button and waited, silently unengaging. She looked young, inexperienced but Mike couldn't care less if an alien was taking him to see Mel. The lift doors opened and the nurse selected level 5 and then headed towards Byron ward. She swiped her pass on the door and stepped aside for him to enter and then turned into the first room on the right-hand side. Mike stopped unable to take in what he saw. Mel was lying there in a neck brace, her head bandaged with multiple bruises everywhere. Her leg was in plaster, suspended from the bed in a hoist and her left wrist was in a support bandage. Mike was unable to take his eyes off her, to the extent that he didn't even notice the nurse leaving the room. He slowly walked towards her and stood by the side of her bed. Tears rolled down his face as he reached for her hand. "I will get him, Mel, I promise you, I will get him," he told her.

He sat holding her hand for hours, torturing himself about not calling her earlier. The reality of it was, it probably would have made no difference at all, as Nikko was obviously a sadistic bastard and could have assaulted her at any time, he reasoned. But he wanted to protect her and he wasn't there and it really riled him that he had not acted on his instinct. He saw the signs, he knew something wasn't right. Especially when she was reluctant to go home the other evening. Why didn't he just tell her she could stay with him until she caught up with her rent arrears, at least it was warm. The more he thought about it, the more it angered him. The thought also occurred to him that if she had no heating due to the faulty boiler, she would have had no hot water either. God she must have been showering in freezing cold water. He sank deeper and deeper, feeling he had failed her as a friend, the guilt and anguish getting the better of him. He sat staring at her, willing her to wake up, so he could tell her how much he cared and that when she was discharged, she was to come home with him and he would look after her. Mike looked up to the sound of faint knocking on the door.

The nurse from earlier popped her head round advising that it was time he went. "Visiting time finished hours ago," she told him, "and I need to carry out some observation tests," she added. She suddenly saw the expression on his face change. "Are you OK, Sir?" she questioned in a kind voice.

"Yes, yes," he repeated, getting to his feet. It suddenly occurred to him that he didn't want to leave her alone until they had located Niko. What if he came to the hospital, he thought to himself, torturing himself still further.

Mike found himself interrogating the young nurse about their security procedures in the hospital, until he realised that he was probably overreacting. Niko was unlikely to show up here, he reasoned, as he was probably in hiding. Mike reached for his jacket from the back of his chair and then kissed Mel on the hand gently. "I will be back in the morning," he said in a whisper, so as not to wake her. He nodded at the nurse, backing out of the room, so that he could look at her for a little longer and quietly closed the door.

Mike sat outside the hospital entrance, waiting for a cab. He knew he didn't want to go home, he wanted to find Niko. He needed to find him before he was handed over officially to the force. He rose to his feet and started to pace back and forth. "Where the hell is this cab," he spoke out loud, scanning the car park entrance. Each time a car came in, he willed it to be his cab, disappointed each time as the car parked and the owner made their way to the pay and display machine in the far corner. Friday night, he considered, one of the busiest nights of the week, he could be here ages, he reasoned. He sat back down on the wall and stared at a young girl sniffling, perched a few feet away from him. She was shaking violently, to the extent that she was unable to retrieve a cigarette from the pack. She fumbled over and over until Mike decided to intervene. "Let me help you with that," he said, moving towards her to assist.

She looked up, tears streaming down her pretty face and then looked back down at the cigarette pack. She raised her head again, "Thank you," she said, in a whisper, trembling as she passed the box over to him. Mike retrieved a cigarette from the box and passed it to her. "Help yourself," she said, reaching in her pocket for her lighter.

Mike paused at the offer. He desperately wanted one, he needed one, he needed something to do with his hands. It had been exactly two years and three months since his last one and it had been an agonising time during the withdrawal process. He knew he had been a total nightmare to be around and had promised himself and Mel that he wouldn't put himself – or anyone else – through that again. He watched as the girl exhaled and made herself more comfortable on the wall as she stared up at the night sky. The old familiar smell of tobacco beckoning him like a dangerous friend. "Thank you," he said, putting one in his mouth and reaching for her lighter, before considering it any further. He sat back down next to her on the wall, silently, staring out into space. He briefly wondered what her story might be as he scanned her over-exaggerated appearance of someone trying to look extravagant but not quite pulling it off. His thoughts then turned back to Mel, lying helplessly in bed, her leg suspended in a hoist, covered in bruises, emotionally damaged beyond belief. He sighed, took another drag of his cigarette, wondering where the hell Niko was and whether his colleagues had had any luck locating him.

He glanced at his watch again, he had been waiting twenty-five minutes already. Where the fuck was this cab, he thought, getting to his feet? He watched as the girl made her way back into the hospital entrance and then watched as another set of headlights entered the car park. Hey, this could be it, he thought, as the car stopped a few feet away from where he was standing. He motioned to the driver, as the car window slowly opened and nodded as he opened the rear door to climb in. "Kingsbury Rise please, just off Temple Street," he directed the driver.

He pulled his mobile from his jacket pocket and searched for Dave's details. He needed to know if they had made any progress in finding the sick bastard. Agitated that he didn't appear to have it, he searched for Jim's. "Thank fuck," he said out loud, selecting his number, not caring what the cab driver thought of his language. The phone rang over and over and then went to answer phone. He left a brief message for him to call back and sat back and waited. The cab made its way swiftly through the Friday night traffic, pausing momentarily for a gaggle of women dressed in pink, holding up the traffic on a crossing. They were singing loudly, the worse for drink and were holding up the bride-to-be, who's veil had slipped over her face. "Oh, to be carefree," thought Mike, enjoying briefly the sight of a group of women on a hen night, taking his thoughts for a split second away from the nightmare he was in. The cab finally pulled into Kingsbury Rise and Mike gave instructions where to stop. "Pull over here, mate," he said, reaching for his wallet and pulling out a fiver.

Eight pounds twenty," said the driver, staring at the five pound note he had just been handed. Mike reached into his pocket for some change, thank God it was payday, he thought to himself. If this had been yesterday, he would have been walking back to Mel's. He settled his bill reluctantly, and climbed out of the cab and stared across at his van. It was parked with the driver side wheel perched up on the kerb, at an angle. He recalled the earlier events where he had swerved to a halt, scrambling out of the car desperate to get to Mel and then the thought occurred to him. His keys, where were his keys? He went through his jacket pockets at record speed, relieved when he felt them in the inside pocket. Relief flooded over him, as he walked over to his van. That's all he needed he thought, turning the key in the lock as the fob was broken, climbing behind the wheel.

He was just about to start the ignition, when his phone let out its usual annoying tune. "Jim, thanks for getting back to me mate, you found the sick bastard?" he asked, knowing the answer before he asked the question. He waited for Jim to prove him wrong, he wanted to get his hands on him now. He could taste it.

"No not yet, Mike, sorry but I promise you, we are on it," he told him. "We've located his home address. Sad little fucker has all that money, owns the whole block, yet lives like a pauper. Lives on Mount Pleasant, Melbourne Towers, number 23, but I assure you there ain't nothing pleasant about it."

Mike pulled at his hair, he often did this out of despair. "OK, mate, thanks for the address. Keep on it, I want surveillance on his home address, shop, anywhere he's likely to go, including family and put an APB alert out on him, but Jim, Jim you listening? I want him first, got it?"

"Got it, Mike, I understand."

He hung up and threw the phone onto the passenger seat. At least he now knew where he was heading, 23 Melbourne Towers.

He knew Niko wouldn't be there but he wanted to see it. He wanted to see where the little fuckwit lived. He reversed slowly out from between two cars that had parked after him and headed towards Melbourne Towers. Why on earth was he living in a run-down council block? he questioned himself. Mount Pleasant was a nasty area, full of drug addicts and prostitutes and the crime rate was exceptionally high. If you had any sense you would give it a wide berth, let alone live there, thought Mike, pulling at his hair again. Something's not right, he thought, something's not right, he repeated to himself. It just doesn't add up. He pulled outside Melbourne Towers ten minutes later and looked up. "What a shithole," he said out loud, looking around at the rundown, almost uninhabitable council block.

He parked behind an old fiesta, 03 plate, with a missing wing mirror and no wheels. Well that gives me great confidence, he thought as he double checked he had locked his van before proceeding further. He walked a few yards past an overflowing skip full of broken furniture items, turning the corner towards the front entrance. In the porch section of the entrance was an old navy sofa with a young, probably past her prime, woman offering her services.

"Ello mister," she said, straightening her skirt and trying her best to look seductive. "Are you looking for a little loving?" she questioned, with a cackling laugh.

Mike looked across at her, unable to decide if he felt sorry for her desperate state or was just repulsed by her very being. "Not tonight, Josephine," he said, pulling open the front door of the building and stepping inside. He pressed the button for the lift and waited. Nothing, he thought, pressing the button over and over. He glanced down at the floor and saw a sign written on an old piece of cardboard which read 'out of order' with a cross through it. Next to the cross was a crude picture of a penis and an overly large set of balls. Lovely, thought Mike, such a high class of residency. He took the stairs two at a time, assuming that number 23 was probably on the first level. "Bingo," he said out loud, eyeing the door in the corner with the number 23 on, the 3 hanging downwards, like a W. He stopped short of the doorway and stared. He looked through the letterbox to see if there were any lights on, nothing, as expected. He wanted to charge the door and force his way in but he was a police officer, he reminded himself. He stepped back and looked up and down the hallway. "For fuck's sake, who am I kidding," he said. Two of the neighbouring doors were hanging off the hinges and one was propped up against the opening. This was hell on earth, even the police steered clear of this area, he thought. He turned the handle just in case the twat forgot to lock it. It opened, swung right open, hit the wall and bounced back for another go. A cat screeched and ran past, scaring the living daylights out of him. "Jesus," he said regaining his composure. He stepped into the hallway, which was bare of any inhabitants. The smell, however, was repugnant. Something lived here, he thought, something repulsive, rodent-like, he considered. How fitting.

He continued his way, holding his hand over his nose and mouth, gagging. The smell was so overwhelming that he had to pull his jumper up over his lower face to make it more tolerable. To the right was the front room. A hideous looking red velour sofa stood to the right with a coffee table directly in front. The table contained two overflowing ashtrays, a tobacco tin, four empty beer bottles and two girlie mags. What a creep, thought Mike, looking at the open page of a girl about to be degraded by four men in masks, holding an Alsatian dog. The only other furniture item was a portable TV perched on a stall in the corner of the room. He turned towards the bedroom, almost feeling reluctant to proceed any further. He pushed the door open and stepped back, the smell was overpowering. It was a mix of sweat, severe body odour, mixed with semen, totally foul. repulsive, beyond belief. He left the room swiftly and entered the kitchen, again unable to believe that a person could live like this. He glanced at the room swiftly, taking in the overflowing dishes spread across the sink and drainer, moving down towards the bin that was resting on its side, the contents of which cascaded over the entire length of the room. To think the guy owns a kebab shop, he thought, trying to recall if he had ever eaten there.

On the kitchen windowsill was a photo in a brown frame. Mike moved closer to see who it was. Could that be him, he wondered to himself? He had never met him but needed to know what he looked like. There, staring back at him, was a picture of a greasy-haired man, possibly late fifties, sixty maybe he considered, with a quiff and stubble. He was wearing a black leather jacket and had his arm around an older woman dressed in an apron with a tight looking bun on her head, presumably his mother. Mike stepped forward to grasp the frame so that he could move it under the dim light, a bulb hanging from the ceiling without a shade. What an ugly, evil-looking bloke, he thought, unable to take his eyes off of his smug expression. He threw the frame to the floor and made his way back up the hallway. He stopped at the door and turned around for a final look. Something's not right here, he considered. This is not the life of a man who owns an entire block of apartments.

He needed to sleep, he thought, as he made his way back down the stairs and out towards his van. If he didn't, he would be no good to anyone tomorrow, he decided, but how was he going to switch off from this horror of a situation, he wondered. He started the ignition and slowly moved away from the block, heading back out of the estate towards the main road. He stopped at the corner of Eastern Street, eyeing a 24 hour off-licence, battling with his conscience. He knew he shouldn't but he needed something to knock him out, stone cold. A slippery road, he argued with his inner self, as he found himself requesting a bottle of scotch and unsurprisingly twenty of his old faithful's. He picked up the cigarette packet hesitantly from the counter and added a lighter to his order, nodded at the shopkeeper and stepped back out into the night. He needed to get home, he needed a scotch and he desperately needed a cigarette.

It was 12.45pm when he finally stepped back through his front door. He could feel the anger growing deeper and deeper with every step he took. He paused as he closed the door, eyeing the Morgan emblem on the side table. I had thought that was a bad day, but this, this really blows everything else out the window, he thought to himself. He removed his jacket and dropped it to the floor and headed straight to the kitchen cupboard to retrieve a glass. He poured himself a large scotch and then searched for something to use as an ashtray, finally settling on an old saucer.

He sat down on the edge of the sofa, took a swig of scotch and unwrapped the cigarette box. This is it, he said to himself, knowing if he lit up another cigarette there would be no turning back. He played with the lighter for a few seconds longer, lit the cigarette and slouched back, inhaling the smoke. He knew he would have to answer to Dhillon again tomorrow morning but he was heading straight back up the hospital and nothing was going to stop him. He wanted to be there before she woke and nothing was going to get in the way of that. He poured another scotch, feeling himself starting to untense and lit another cigarette. This was going to be a long night.

He woke to the sound of church bells chiming in the distance, then realised that it was his mobile on the breakfast bar. Confused for a moment he started to recall the events of the previous evening, before making his way over to retrieve his phone. He glanced at the kitchen clock, hoping it was still early enough to reach the hospital before Mel woke and then looked down at the name flashing on the screen. It was Dhillon. God fancy having to start the day with him, he thought, scratching his head and swiping right on his phone. "Morning, Sir," he said, trying not to yawn as he spoke, pulling a stool from under the bar to sit on. Dhillon didn't draw breath, asking question after question, grilling him about every single detail, until Mike stopped him in his tracks.

"Sir, Sir," he interrupted again. "I'm going to make my way up to the hospital again now and then I will be along to the station afterwards with more details. Sir, it's been a long night but I will be there as quickly as I can but I need to see Mel first," he told him, ending the call before Dhillon could say anything else.

He sat there motionless for a while, feeling the effects of the scotch and tobacco from the previous evening and then decided on a shower to freshen himself up. He ached everywhere and his neck felt crooked and crunchy and his nose still felt very tender. That's what happens when you get pissed and fall asleep on the sofa he told himself, stretching his arms up over his head. He turned on the shower and looked at himself in the mirror, deciding he didn't have time for a shave. This was going to be a cat's lick and a promise, he said to himself, pulling his polo shirt off over his head. He kicked off his jeans and stepped into the shower, standing motionless, with his eyes closed, as the water cascaded over him. He felt dreadful – but not as dreadful as Mel feels – he said, suddenly putting things into perspective. He dried himself briskly, cleaned his teeth and dressed in record speed. He needed to get there before she woke.

It took ages to get to the hospital, probably one of the worst days to tackle the traffic, he considered. It was late November and the world and his wife seemed to be on the roads, presumably preparing for Christmas, he decided. He never did any shopping until the week beforehand and his one trip to the shops each year was always with Mel, or at least it had been for the last eight years, since the breakdown of his marriage. He thought about Mel's road to recovery and decided that she must spend Christmas with him this year, he wasn't having her spending it alone. "Finally," he said out loud, indicating to turn into the hospital car park and pulling into what was probably the only vacant space in the entire car park. God, that was a stroke of luck, he thought, searching for change for the pay and display machine. He stood behind two elderly women that were trying to put together sufficient funds to park for the minimum period. They appeared to be ten pence short and were turning out all their pockets, in search of a coin. Mike was just about to offer his assistance, when the woman in the bright-red headscarf shouted, "Edna I have one, my dear, slipped into the lining it did," she said smiling with a look of victory. She pushed the coin in the slot, retrieved her ticket and headed back to her vehicle, arm in arm with her companion, giggling. Mike studied the parking options and then decided to pay for two hours. Dhillon was breathing down his neck and he now felt divided. He had so many things to cover. He wanted to be there for Mel. He wanted to take care of her during her recovery. He still needed to investigate the ongoing saga of the Jane and Sally Gordan case but more than anything he wanted to track down Niko. One thing at a time, he reasoned with himself as he entered the hospital reception.

He made his way up to level 5, recalling his journey in the lift with the young nurse the previous day and studied the ward names on the lift chart. Deciding on Byron, he stopped short of the doors and rang the bell. The bell sounded over and over until eventually a nurse returned to the desk station and released the latch, without even looking up. The doors opened towards him and he stepped forward into the corridor without anyone intervening. 'Security at its best', thought Mike, angry that he was able to get through to Mel's room without even so much as being asked who he was. He confirmed the name on the door, Melanie Bailey, which had been scribbled in a black felt pen on a dry-wipe board, just underneath the door window and he peeped in to see if she was awake. Relieved to see that she was still sleeping, he slipped in and sat down quietly on the wing-back chair next to her bed.

He sat staring at her for ages, unable to believe the sight that was before him. Her swollen eyes were now completely black and the bruising had really come to the forefront overnight. He wondered if she had woken at all during the night and whether her ordeal had caused any nightmares or confusion at all, considering the head trauma. He leant forward, as if he needed to hear her breath and then sat back in his chair sickened at what she had been through and what Niko had done to her. He reached out and stroked her hand and then he took it in his. Tears welled up in his eyes again and anger began to take over. "I will find him, Mel, I will find him," he said in a whisper. "I won't let him get away with this, promise you." He reached into his jacket in search of something to wipe his eyes, then settled on his sleeve instead.

He sat there for about fifteen minutes, torturing himself over and over until the door opened and a slightly framed nurse bustled in to do Mel's observations.

"Good morning," she said in an over-loud voice, pulling the curtains aside in one clean swoop. The light flooded the room, making even Mike shield his eyes momentarily, as he adjusted his seating position.

"Morning," said Mike, thinking there was nothing good about it, as he looked back across at Mel.

"Has she woken at all yet?" asked the nurse in a bright breezy voice, as she straightened the bed covers and removed the thermometer from its resting place.

"Not as far as I'm aware," said Mike, thinking he should be asking her this question. "I haven't been here long," he told her. "Around fifteen minutes," he added. "I have to say, though, I was a little surprised that I could walk straight in here," he said, waiting for her reaction. "I mean, I walked straight in, without so much as anyone questioning who I was," he continued.

"All our ward doors are secured and opened by a control panel at the nurse's station," she said in a positive voice.

"Yes, I realise how I got here but what I am trying to say is that no one questioned who I was. I merely rang the bell and a nurse released the switch without so much as looking up," he told her.

He stood up and walked towards the window, agitated by the lack of security and turned to face the nurse again. He watched as she removed the thermometer from under Mel's arm and recorded her findings on the clip chart, returning it to the hanging position at the foot of the bed.

"Well, this is a hospital, Sir, not a high-level security prison," she said with a smile.

"Indeed," said Mike, wondering if the nurse had been briefed on exactly what had happened to Mel. He sat back down in the chair and watched as the nurse took her blood pressure, wondering if the pressure of the device might cause her to stir.

"Do you know if she woke at all during the night?" he questioned, deciding to quiz her further.

"I came on duty at 6am this morning, Sir, but from what I understand from the night staff she has had a peaceful night, waking only twice. She has a head trauma," she added, "and that can cause a concussed state of sleep," she told him.

"But I always thought you shouldn't sleep if you had a head injury," said Mike, remembering when he had fallen out of a tree as a child, his mother wouldn't let him sleep for several hours.

"We do tend to wake children every few hours with head traumas but adults we tend to rely on observational tests. However, Melanie woke naturally twice and was coherent on both occasions," she told him. All the signs are good, Sir, please don't worry," she said in an almost innocent voice, devoid of the full extent to which Mel's injuries were sustained.

"Thank you, nurse," he said, deciding he would be better off talking to a doctor. "Can I see the doctor responsible for her please?" he asked, wondering what time this would be possible.

"The doctor will be doing his rounds this morning at 11.00am prompt," she informed him. "He starts at the far end, usually, so I would envisage him reaching Melanie after midday," she added.

Mike looked at his watch as the nurse prepared to leave and decided that he would have sufficient time to get back to the station, brief Dhillon, check on any updates from Dave and Jim regarding Niko and get back before midday. He desperately needed to speak to the doctor so that he knew how best to deal with Mel's recovery. He was going to be in charge of that, he decided. He kissed Mel's hand and stood at her side a few moments longer and then made his way back out into the corridor. Deciding there was very little he could do about security and assessing the likelihood of Niko showing his face, he headed back to the car park, juggling the order of things he needed to do by priority.

By the time he reached the station, Dhillon had already gathered everyone in the briefing room and was about to enlighten them all on last night's events. Mike could hear everyone's banter, as he selected his usual coffee and made his way down the corridor to join them.

"Just in time," said Dhillon, beckoning him over towards him, with a look of relief on his face. Mike nodded and leaned back against the desk next to Dhillon, facing the rest of his team and listened as Dhillon covered the events of the previous evening, relayed to him earlier by phone. Mike looked across at Jim and then Dave, hoping that by now they may have unearthed something but by the expression on their faces and the questions they were asking it appeared that they were no further forward. Mike drank his coffee in silence waiting for Dhillon to hand the stage over to him, sickened as he listened to Dhillon describe Mel's rape and brutal attack to the entire team.

Dhillon gave the usual signal to Mike to take over the briefing and Mike bought them all up to speed with regard to his hospital visit that morning. "Mel's had a relatively peaceful night, according to the nurse this morning," Mike told them all, "but she does have a contusion which is bruising to the brain. This may take some time to heal and, from what I understand, she will need complete rest to recover from her multiple injuries. I plan to take her home with me when the time comes, as she has no immediate family in a position to help her," he told them.

"Now, in the meantime we need to find Niko. Jim, Dave I want you out there, leave no stone unturned," he instructed. "I want that little bastard found. The hospital has carried out a full SOEC, so they will have the physical evidence for you to run him through the database. I want to know if he has raped before." He gave the order for them to go now, immediately. "Karen find out who Niko's family are, where they come from, who he's related to. Find out if he has any brothers, sisters, is he an only child. I want everything on him so we can track him down. Tina get on to the land registry and see who owns the kebab shop, together with the surrounding properties. I can't believe for one second that they belong to him. He lives like a pig," he said, growing angrier by the second. "Paul, Billy and Ben I want you to carry on your research into the Jane and Sally Gordon case, as we can't afford to take our eyes off that. Someone out there knows something. Two girls can't just come out into the midnight air from nowhere," he told them. "Now, we know they are sisters, so where did they come from, who are their parents? I want every missing person listed checked against this over the last fifteen years. My gut feeling tells me they came from the Square or the immediate surrounding area. Bring us back something," he instructed with over exaggerated gestures.

Dhillon watched as Mike gave instructions to everyone. This was usually Dhillon's role but he was taking a step back, he knew Mike needed to lead this. He could see this had affected Mike deeply and that Mel had been his partner for over a decade and he knew that he wouldn't rest until Niko was behind bars. He gave the nod in confirmation that they had all been given their tasks and dismissed everyone from the room.

"Mike, hold back a second," he said loudly, calling him back over. "I know this is personal to you, but I need you to keep a professional head on it, OK?" he said, staring directly at him.

"Yep, Sir, I will," he answered not looking at him, knowing full well that if he got his hands on Niko, it wouldn't be professional. "I will," he repeated, looking up and staring at him with eyes ice cold.

"She's one of ours," he said, patting Mike on the shoulder. "She's one of our own, and we will do everything in our power," he confirmed, leaving Mike by himself, as he headed back to his office.

Mike sat for a few moments to gather his thoughts. He had so much to do. The last three weeks had been torture, dealing with what was then one girl but now there were two. They had been starved, neglected, mentally tortured and lord knows what else they had endured, and now there was Mel, raped, battered, abused. What was happening to the world, so many evil people capable of such horrendous acts. He was going to get the person who had done this to the girls and he was going to find Niko. He knew without a shadow of a doubt that he would not rest until he had solved both cases.

He looked at his watch, it was almost 11.30am and he needed to head back to the hospital. Fuck, the day was half-gone already and he had achieved nothing at all, he thought, as he raced out of the room back down to his office. He stopped briefly at his desk, eyeing the orange flashing light on his answer phone. He looked at his watch again, sighed and flicked the switch to listen to his messages. The first message was from Doctor Leeson confirming that Sally Gordon was being transferred at 2pm to Doctor Gyllensvan's department. The second was from Doctor Gyllensvan's secretary informing him that at 4.30pm they were going to reintroduce the girls to each other, and that it would be advantageous if he was present. He knew he couldn't miss that. He rose to his feet, briefed Paul about the Gordon girls and then rushed out of the office. He needed to get back to the hospital.

Four

He arrived shortly after noon, praying that the doctor hadn't yet reached Mel's room. The journey had been horrendous with the Saturday afternoon chaos. The roads were jammed with shoppers preparing for the season ahead and it took a further ten minutes to locate a parking space. Finally, he thought, ringing the buzzer outside the ward doors, drawing breath. He had run up five flights, after eyeing up a hoard of visitors at the north-side lifts and two porters transferring a patient on a stretcher bed on the opposite side. He had no time to waste, he'd thought as he bent forwards panting trying to contain a stitch. He rang the buzzer again, peering through the window, as he watched a team of doctors enter Mel's room. Oh no, he's going to miss them he thought, as he buzzed again and banged on the window, attracting the attention of a visitor, collecting water from a machine just outside Mel's door. The latch let out a clicking sound and the doors slowly opened towards him. Mike didn't wait for them to fully extend but squeezed in through the smallest gap, as they made their journey to the fully opened position. "Thanks," he shouted to the little grey-haired woman as she made her way gracefully back down the corridor.

Mike entered the room like a tornado firing questions at the doctor, before introducing himself. He paused, realising how he was conducting himself, apologised, and then went full throttle again. The doctor was accompanied by three others, presumably doctors or at least high up the medical chain, each of whom had a clipboard and was busily scribbling notes. Mike sat down, put his head in his hands and then looked across at the doctor to start again. "Sorry, Doctor, let me start again, my name is Detective Sergeant Mike Brugge and I am the partner of Mel, Detective Constable Melanie Bailey, from Holden Crime Investigation Department. I am also her personal friend and probably as close to a next of kin as you will get at this moment in time, with the exception of her brother. Unfortunately, I do not have a contact number for her brother, Pete, but I do have a partial address. We may have to wait until Mel wakes before gathering any more info on him. What I can tell you," he continued, was that my partner was raped and abused by her landlord and we currently have an APB out on him."

He paused, turning his attention back to Mel, grasping her hand in his. "How is she doing? Her head injuries, can you tell if there will be any lasting damage?" he questioned, his eyes filling with tears again.

The doctor put down his notes on the edge of the bed and held his hands in a grasp in front of him. He smiled a warm, friendly smile at Mike and started to reassure him that the internal head injuries were being carefully monitored and that everything pointed to a full recovery. "All her vital signs are normal and there is no evidence of brain damage," he confirmed. "Your friend had a lucky escape," he told him, picking up his clipboard again.

"Well, I wouldn't call it lucky exactly, Doc, she's been raped and beaten half to death," said Mike, feeling agitated at the doctor's lack of acknowledgement of exactly what had happened here.

"What I mean to say is, physically she will recover," said the doctor. "I see cases where brain damage is so severe, it can affect the cranial nerve, which can affect facial nerves, affecting everything from chewing, smelling, etc. A blow to the head can cause retinal detachment, retardation, coordination issues with motor skills and at worst, complete paralysis both mentally and physically. So yes, in terms of what could have been, we are hoping for a full recovery. Emotionally, however, that is a completely different story," he told him.

Mike rose to his feet again to shake the doctor's hand. "I'm sorry, I didn't mean to imply that you were underplaying her condition, Doc, I guess I'm still in shock at what had happened to her and I'm panicking about the long-term effect this is going to have on her life," said Mike.

"I fully understand the emotional turmoil you must be in, Mike," said the doctor, "we will do our best to deal with her physical needs to restore her to health and we will also organise counselling to deal with the emotional side of this." The doctor turned to leave, nodding at his team to follow.

"Doctor, when can I take her home?" he asked eagerly.

"Let's review that in a few days when we can be more accurate with our assessment," the doctor told him.

"Doctor, can I take a note of your name please," said Mike, suddenly realising that in his haste on arrival, he didn't acknowledge his introduction.

"I'm Doctor Richards," he told him, nodding again and heading out of the door with his crew in tow.

Mike sat back down staring once more at Mel and then turning to look out of the window There was no view at all, just another brick building, so close you could probably touch it. The building, however, was much lower, so the sun just managed to peep over the top brightening the room first thing in the morning. By the afternoon the light had completely gone and the room was totally reliant on artificial light. He didn't know what to do with himself as he fidgeted in his chair and then paced up and down. He really hated hospitals. He continued to sit there willing her to wake up, wishing that things had been different. He looked at his watch, thinking it was probably time for her next set of observations when there was a light knock at the door.

A large African woman in her mid-forties entered the room with a tray of food, laying it to rest on the table near the foot of the bed. "Hello," she said smiling, "and how are we doing today?" she asked in a pleasant tone. She looked non-medical, possibly auxiliary as she was wearing a light-coloured lilac uniform and was serving lunch to all the patients. She had obviously been instructed to observe any notes above the bed-head in terms of whether they were nil by mouth or had any allergies or dietary requirements, as she took great pains to read all the notes above the headboard before serving. Content that there were no specific instructions, she unveiled a sandwich, small pot of yogurt and a carton of juice.

"Seeing as she's sleeping, I will leave it here for when she wakes," the auxiliary nurse told him. "Can I get you a cuppa?" she offered, smiling once again.

"Yeah, that would be great," said Mike, taking her up on her offer. "Milk with three sugars please," he said, placing his order. She bustled out of the room, reappearing a few minutes later with a cup of tea in a polystyrene cup.

"Here you go," she said, passing it over to him. She reached into her apron pocket and pulled out a small packet of biscuits and three sugar sachets. "To keep your sugar levels up," she said with a wink, slipping them into his hand.

"Thanks," said Mike, appreciating the gesture.

"You look like you've been in the wars too," she said, studying his bruised face and swollen nose.

"Yes, it's not been our week," he said, trying to be more friendly.

"Well, if there's anything else you need I will be around outside," she told him.

"What's your name?" Mike suddenly asked, feeling he may need it later.

"Daisy," she said, a smile spreading over her round, friendly face.

"Daisy, I'm going to have to leave shortly but will you keep an eye on my friend for me. She has been through a terrible ordeal and I'm worried that when she wakes she may be in shock and need settling and reassuring that she's safe. Can you keep popping in on her, please? I know you must be very busy, but I would be extremely grateful if you could watch over her for me."

"I'm on duty until 6pm, so I can certainly keep an eye on her until then," she confirmed to him, in a friendly manner.

"Thank you so much, Daisy, I will try my best to get back around six." Content that she was now in safer hands, he finished his tea and made his way back down to reception.

He returned to his van, noting that he was just back in the nick of time, before his parking ticket expired. He had two minutes to go and could see a traffic warden making her way towards his van. She had presumably been watching his van noting he had very limited time left and then turned on her heels heading back towards the other end of the car park. "Yes, you're not clocking up any commission on me lady," he said, out loud to himself, as he steered his van out of its parking space. He stopped just short of the entrance deciding to give Jim a call before he went any further. He selected his number and waited while it rang over and over, before going to voicemail, yet again. "He never answers his bloody phone, that bloke," said Mike, suddenly pausing mid-speech, as it beeped ready for him to leave a message. "Jim, call me back when you pick this up. I want to know where you're at, whether you've found anything out," he said in an angry tone. He ended the call and then threw the phone onto the passenger seat. He looked at his watch and then selected first gear, debating his next move. He decided to head to the kebab shop to find out a little more about the infamous Niko.

He pulled into Kingsbury Rise at 2.45pm, noting the time on the clock above the bank doors on the corner of Temple Street. That was Mel's bank, he thought to himself. A lot of good that visit did her, he thought as he pulled into a parking space on the corner of her road. Well, the sick bastard is going to be three grand short now because he won't be needing it where he's heading and that's gonna cost him a hell of a lot more than money. That's going to cost him his freedom, his sanity and hopefully his arse, he thought, thinking about how he would be tolerated by the inmates in Wexworth Scrubs. That is, of course, if there is anything left to send to prison once I get a hold of him, he considered.

He locked his van and started to walk up Kingsbury Rise, looking around at the area itself. It was a nice road, lots of trendy shops, even the kebab shop was an 'eat-in' restaurant, not just your usual take out. Why the hell is he living in squalor if he owns all this, he thought. He stopped directly in front of the shop and looked up. There were three apartments directly above the shop itself and, from what Mel had told him, his estate extended the entire block. He walked inside and stood by the small take-out section counter, behind a man who was choosing his salad toppings in a very finickity fashion.

"Is Niko around?" he asked the tall greasy-haired man who appeared to be the only one serving.

"Haven't seen him since yesterday evening," replied the man as he wrapped the kebab in white paper and handed it to the customer. Four pounds eighty-five, please, mate," he said, holding his hand out to receive the customers money. "Tell you what, though, he must be very popular as you're the third person here today looking for him," he said, as he gave the customer change from a £5 pound note.

Mike waited a few moments for the customer to leave the shop and then went on to question further. "Does Niko own this shop and the surrounding apartments?" Mike asked.

"You would think he owns the block and everyone in it, the way he carries on," said the man, wiping his hands on his stripy apron. "But to tell you the truth, I'm not entirely sure. He obviously must have some sort of stake in it," he went on to say. "How much, no one knows," he added. "Why the interest?" he asked, as he wiped down the preparation area and tossed the cloth to one side.

"Just curious," said Mike, not wanting to reveal his identity, just yet. "Just looking at renting, possibly buying something round here," he said, hoping to throw him off the scent.

"Well if you want my opinion, you'd steer clear of Niko. Nasty bastard," he said, looking over his shoulder, obviously not wanting anyone to overhear him.

He looked as if he was going to elaborate a bit more but thought better of it. He turned around and started slicing off kebab meat into a pile and Mike knew the questioning had come to a close. "Well, thank you for your time, you've been very helpful," said Mike, turning to leave. He stopped and turned. "If he does come by, would you please let me know," he said, scribbling his number on the back of a discarded paper napkin and passing it to him. "It's very important that I get to see him," Mike added as he turned to leave.

"Yeah, I'll add it to my address book," said the man sarcastically, "along with all the others," he added. Mike realised that the man had obviously got a bit nervous and understandably so, if Niko was as notorious as described. He nodded, opened the door and stepped out onto the street. What was Niko's game, Mike wondered, as he made his way back down the street towards his van.

He still felt rough from the evening before and really needed something quick to eat before making his way to see Doctor Gyllensvan. He had been eyeing the kebab skewers, while questioning the guy but remembering the state of Niko's flat he knew that was not an option. He stopped outside the bakers and decided to settle for a sausage roll instead. He stared at the cakes in the window, spotting his favourite iced bun with the cherry in its centre. Today, however, it didn't seem so inviting, as he spotted Mel's favourite coconut slice, by itself on a tray at the end of the counter. He pushed open the door and stepped inside, feeling the warmth as he stepped in from the chilling wind outside.

"Hot sausage roll please, love," he said, reaching in his pocket for some change, as he approached the counter. He was the only one there, with the exception of a young woman with a small child of around three, who was desperately trying to choose which cake to select. Mike popped his pound coin on the counter and smiled to himself as he watched the little girl select the coconut slice. "Great choice," he said, smiling as he opened the door and stepped back out into the cold.

He sat back behind the wheel of his van and took a big bite of the oversized roll. Wow that's hot, he said to himself, enjoying the fact that it had just come out of the oven and was freshly baked. He considered making a cigarette his next course and then decided better of it. Nope he wasn't going there, he thought, brushing the pastry flakes from his jeans. He knew he was weak when he was under the influence but nothing was going to interfere with his investigation today. He started the ignition, waited a few minutes for the windscreen to clear and then headed back towards the hospital to see Doctor Gyllensvan. God, I seem to be spending more time at the hospital than at the station over the last few days, he thought. Perhaps I should buy one of those weekly parking tickets he had seen advertised in the reception foyer. Would be much cheaper, he considered, wondering if he had any more pound coins in his pocket.

The hospital car park was heaving, not a space to be found, thought Mike as he drove round and round in the hope that someone would leave. It was almost 4pm and he wanted to see Doctor Gyllesvan before he sat in on the session where the sisters were reintroduced. He was just about to claim defeat and head over to the multi-storey when a small grey haired woman came out from the reception area and headed over to her car. Mike remembered her from earlier, she was the one that let him into the ward when he was running late that morning. Now here she was again about to grace him with a parking space. "My guardian angel," said Mike out loud, as he reversed swiftly into the now empty space.

He made his way round to the psychiatric block where Doctor Gyllesvan's depressing dark office was and entered by the side door. He stopped at the lift, pressed the green button and waited. He pressed again, growing frustrated and then finally decided to take the stairs. He walked around the corner towards the reception area and stopped dead in his tracks at the bottom of the staircase. He could see Brian sitting behind the desk, motionless, staring into space. He suddenly felt sorry for the guy. To think he had only met Mel the other day and had innocently arranged a date, which ended up being hell on earth. He stood staring for a few more moments wondering what must be going through his mind and then took the stairs two at a time.

He reached the third level and paused for breath. God, I'm getting too old for this shit, he said to himself, panting as he held onto his waist and lent forward. He opened the door and turned right, and then right again, pausing at the desk, just outside the doctor's office. He waited a few moments until the clerk caught his attention, who then gestured for him to take a seat, while she finished the call she was on. "Sorry about that," she said, rising to her feet, as if she had done something wrong in her delay to tend to his needs. "Been a busy day," she added, returning her headset to its cradle. "How can I help?" she said, retaking her seat.

"I'm due to see Doctor Gyllesvan at four-thirty to take part in a session but I was hoping to catch him prior to it, I have a few things to discuss first," he added, "that would be beneficial to my investigation." The clerk smiled and looked down at her desk diary and confirmed that there was a small ten-minute window at 4.15.

"Can I take your name, please?" she asked, smiling.

"Detective Sergeant Mike Brugge from Holden CID," he told her, as he changed seats to face the window. Mike watched as the clerk typed a message to the doctor on her screen and then waited for a response. A minute or two later, the door flew open and Doctor Gyllensvan gestured for him to come in.

"Glad you could make the session," said the doctor, extending his hand out to Mike. Mike shook it vigorously, delighted that he would get a few minutes of the doctor's time, before the girl's session. "Take a seat," said the doctor, nodding towards the chair by the window. Mike sat down, bemused, yet again, how dark it was in there, with just the amber glow of his desk lamp. How did he work like this, he thought, looking at the blinds in the closed position?

"You look like you've been in the wars yourself," said the doctor, referring to his blackened eyes and crooked nose.

"Yes, I encountered a couple of yobs outside here the other day," said Mike, recalling the events from two days prior. "But my car took the brunt of it," he said, eager to steer the conversation back to the topic of the girls. "So, now we have two girls, Doctor, siblings. Both traumatised from the same ordeal," he said, moving the topic back on track. "Can you tell me how things are progressing with the first girl? Incidentally for the purposes of our investigation we are referring to the first girl as Jane and the second as Sally. We are also using the name Gordon as their surname, where they were both found, Gordon Square," said Mike.

Doctor Gyllesvan rose to his feet and walked towards the window, opened the blinds slightly and turned to face Mike. "Jane is still non-compliant, motionless and withdrawn. She doesn't interact at all to the extent that she is being spoon fed, to avoid anxiety levels, which seem to accelerate around food," the doctor told him. "We have observed her eating like an animal on all fours, if food is left unattended," said the doctor.

"Has she spoken yet, Doctor?" Mike asked, curiously.

"No, not as yet but she seems to trust the nurse that has been assigned to her," the doctor advised. "If anyone else enters the room she goes to the corner and cowers down but over the last few days she has stopped this activity when the nurse enters. This is the only milestone we have to offer," he added.

"What does she do all day?" Mike asked, wondering what it was they were observing.

"She stares into space or cowers in the corner," said the doctor. "It's going to be a long way back to recovery, if she makes it," he added. "We have spent the last hour observing her sibling since her transfer and concluded the same findings. Putting them together has its risks, but I see no other way forward than rehabilitating them together," he told him. "They will share the same observation room and will be observed and monitored around the clock." The doctor looked at his watch and motioned towards the door. "We need to make our way down to the observation centre now, Mike, where I have a team of experts ready and waiting," he informed. He opened the door and gestured for Mike to follow.

They made their way down to the observation centre, which appeared to be housed in the basement area of the hospital. They had descended five levels in the lift, followed by a further flight of stairs and, by Mike's calculation, they were now three levels below ground. Mike followed the doctor along a short corridor which opened up into a wide-open space. There was a small nurse's station to the right, manned currently by a security guard and a nurse, the only other occupant was a cleaner mopping the floor, whistling to himself. There were a series of doors on the same side as the nurse's station, presumably offices or stores and a set of double doors to the left and a further set at the far end.

The doctor nodded at the nurse and smiled. "Good afternoon, Julie. Let me introduce you to Detective Sergeant Mike Brugge," he said, smiling. "He will be working with me on the new sibling case, so you will see a lot more of him over the coming weeks," he told her. Mike shook hands and smiled, thinking how sullen and grey the young nurse looked. He wondered momentarily if it was the effects of working below ground, or worse, working with patients that were severely troubled or even insane, he thought.

Julie smiled at Mike and welcomed him to the observation suite. "Welcome to Isaac ward," she said, rising to her feet. Mike wondered if it had been named after Isaac Newton, who appeared to study everything scientific, including psychology and then confirmed his theory when he eyed Newton Ward above the doors at the far end. "Follow me, please," she instructed, moving towards Isaac ward. She stopped short of the doors and typed a long access code into a keypad followed by fingerprint recognition.

"Security is very tight here," Doctor Gyllensvan informed him, as he watched Mike's reaction as they entered through the doors. "Some of our patients are extremely dangerous and pose a high risk to safety," he added. Mike shivered suddenly, curious if not slightly anxious at being so close to possible psychopaths as they continued to make their way through into Isaac ward.

They entered a long corridor with doors either side, which stretched as far as the eye could see. The nearest door was a small kitchen area, which was next to a room marked 'staff room'. On the opposite side to the kitchen was a bathroom, full of high-tech equipment, hoists and restraints and Mike guessed this was a similar set up to the observation suite where Sally had been held by Doctor Leeson. As they walked along the corridor Mike noted each door had a patient's name on and the ward appeared in full occupancy. So many troubled people, thought Mike to himself, as they stopped at the door where Jane was being held. Mike watched as the doctor removed the word Doe from the name Jane and replaced it with Gordon and then typed a code on the keypad. They waited for a few seconds and then he held his thumb, followed by his forefinger on the finger recognition panel. The door then slid to one side. They entered a small observation room, exactly as he had experienced with Sally. Four chairs positioned theatre-style had been placed adjacent a large viewing window, two of which had laptop pads specifically for the observation staff to record their findings.

Doctor Gyllensvan pointed to one of the chairs without a laptop and asked him to take a seat. The chair to his right, fitted with a laptop was already occupied by a nurse on the 24-hour observation team, who was busy typing her findings. Mike wondered what she might be typing, seeing as Jane was lying on her bed motionless. The room was similar to Sally's with the exception that you could tell she had been in occupancy much longer, as there appeared to be more personal effects. There was a large mock window to one side which projected a daylight image of a pretty garden on a summer's day. Mike noted it must be a recording, as it appeared live but was devoid of any living image, so as to avoid anxiety. You could see the gentle breeze blowing the leaves in the trees, giving a really relaxing feel to the room. It had been designed so that the light image dimmed as night time came and eventually went into full darkness to represent night time. Doctor Gyllensvan explained it was linked to a timer so was representative of real time. As a result, the room was brightly lit and looked cheerful and fun. The decor was pale green and yellow. Shades, specifically chosen to relieve stress, and the room was furnished simply with a bed, complete with bed rail to prevent falling, a table centre stage with four chairs, a small wardrobe and an ottoman for storage. Two of the walls had fixed shelving where a selection of carefully chosen books had been placed, together with some ornate objects, presumably to provoke a reaction or obtain some sort of interest to the patient.

Jane was lying on the bed facing the window, completely still with her eyes wide open. She was wearing a light blue tracksuit and looked warm and groomed. She did, however, look extremely stiff, almost unreal, like a waxwork and looked introverted, completely withdrawn into herself. Mike studied her face with interest, waiting for her to blink. Doctor Gyllensvan interrupted his curiosity, pulling him back to the conversation at hand, going on to explain Jane's daily routine. "Currently, Jane has no routine that she instigates herself and is therefore guided through daily processes. Every single part of her day is artificially prompted, encouraged and spurred by the nurse's intervention," the doctor told him. "We have, however, noted that there appears to be a form of bonding between her and Nurse Somers, Julie," he added, giving her her less formal title and making her seem less sterile. "Jane no longer cowers in the corner of the room when Julie enters, which, in relation to other nursing staff, is a major milestone. As such, Julie is now her main key worker and deals with most of her requirements and personal needs, within the constraints of her working hours of course." The doctor advised.

Mike watched on with interest, wondering how a young girl could remain so still and lifeless to the extent that her soul appeared to have been removed from her physical being.

"Introducing her to her sister," said the doctor, should in theory provoke a reaction of some sort but I am at a loss as to predict the outcome, in light of the severity of the situation," the doctor told him. The doctor nodded at Julie who then promptly left the viewing room and then reappeared through a door leading into Jane's room. The door was directly opposite Jane's bed, so could be viewed by Jane without her having to move. "Note how she doesn't even flinch when Julie enters the room and continues to lay there motionless," the doctor pointed out, as he stood up from his chair and moved closer to the window.

Julie pulled a chair from the table and placed it next to the bedside. She made herself comfortable and then spoke in a soft voice to Jane. "Note there is no physical interaction, such as holding her hand or stroking her face," the doctor stated as he retook his chair. "That provokes a distressing reaction, so at present this is completely off limits," he informed him.

"Good afternoon, Jane," said Julie, holding her own hands in a grasp, so as to remember not to reach out to her by mistake.

Mike looked across at the doctor, "Jane?" he queried, "you're calling her Jane to her face?" he continued to question.

"Yes, as in Jane Doe," the doctor advised. "We have to give her a name, an identity of sorts, while she is in our care or it makes it impossible to interact or engage with her," said the doctor. Mike watched on with interest as Julie continued to communicate with her.

"As explained to you during our earlier discussions," said Julie, "we are continuing to investigate what happened to you, so that we can help you with your recovery and are really pleased to tell you that we now have your sister in our care," Julie told her. She waited for a reaction but, as expected, Jane continued to lay there motionless as Julie went on to explain further. Mike rose from his chair and moved closer to the window, in an attempt not to miss any type of reaction, a blink, a tear, anything at all.

"As you can see," said the doctor, looking across at him. "We continue to engage with Jane, ensuring that we inform her every step of the way about what we are doing to help her rehabilitation, what the police are doing to catch the perpetrator, etc. We have to make the assumption that she understands what we are telling her in the hope that we will eventually have a breakthrough," he said.

"It is not to our advantage to presume mental retardment at this stage and have to assume that her condition has resulted from severe trauma," the doctor advised.

Mike continued to watch in silence, totally captivated by the experience, marvelling at Julie's commitment in explaining what was about to happen next. "I am going to go and collect your sister now, so that you can be together," Julie told her. "It would be really helpful to know her name," Julie encouraged, "but I will leave you to decide, while I go and get her," she said standing up from her chair. Julie stood momentarily at the foot of the bed and then made the decision to replace the chair at the table.

"Why did she put the chair back?" Mike asked. "Surely it would be better to sit Sally directly in front of her, so that she could see her?"

"Because we have to stretch the possible outcome to its maximum," said the doctor. "We have to assume Jane's desperate need to see her sister will supersede her demand for non-engagement or compliance and that she might leave the bed and take a seat at the table," the doctor told him. "This will also give us an insight as to whether she can understand what we are telling her, her mental capacity, absorption of the facts," said Doctor Gyllensvan, explaining how leading the patient subconsciously has major advantages. Mike watched as Julie spoke to Jane once more in a really gentle tone, explaining that she would be back in a few moments and if she would like to get up to greet her sister that it would be really good.

"There you go," said the doctor. "The seed has been planted and now we wait," he instructed, as Julie left the room. They watched on in silence, willing something to happen, hoping that her sister's presence might be the breakthrough they had been waiting for.

"Look, she's moving," said Mike, rising to his feet, in case he might miss something if he stayed seated. Jane had turned from her side, flat onto her back and was now staring at the ceiling, she then sat up moved the bed rail slightly and swung her legs over the side of the bed and stared towards the window image. Doctor Glyllensvann was now making contact with Nurse Somers via his message bleeper, asking her to delay re-entry, until he gives the signal.

Mike watched on, willing Jane to step down from her bed. "Go on Jane," he said to himself, as he watched her push the bed rail completely out of the way and stand on her feet. She stood motionless, staring at the table and then chose the chair facing the door, directly by the side of her bed. "Oh my God, she's doing what you predicted," said Mike.

"Yes, the need, desire to see her sister has moved to the forefront," the doctor advised, as he checked the nurse was recording each detail with exact accuracy. "This proves she understands what we are saying to her, which gives purpose to everything we have done towards her rehabilitation to date," he told him, in a satisfying, almost relieved tone. He then reached for his bleeper and gave the signal for Julie Somers to re-enter the room.

Mike waited with bated breath, wondering what the girl's reactions would be. He wondered if they might speak, would they cry? Would they hug? How was this going to be played out? he wondered as he sat back down. He watched transfixed as the door knob turned and the door slowly opened. Mike could barely breathe and his hands were clenched so tightly, his nails were digging into him. He released his grasp and put his hand up to his head, pulling at his hair until he realised it hurt. He rose to his feet once more, totally captivated by the moment, as Sally walked in, ushered by Julie. He watched hypnotised, as Sally was guided to the seat immediately opposite Jane and asked to sit down. Mike didn't know who to concentrate on first, as he switched his attention from one to the other, like a game of tennis, frightened he might miss a vital reaction from either of them, totally captivated by the moment. It was like time stood still, had in fact been removed from real time, was he breathing Mike asked himself? He was standing motionless, just like the girls had been. He leaned against the glass window watching every move with scrutiny until, slowly, a tear rolled down Jane's cheek and she rose to her feet. She walked round the table to where her younger sister sat and knelt down beside her chair. Sally let out a wail, which turned into a piercing shrill and then settled into a heartfelt sob. Jane wrapped her arms around her younger sister and Sally held onto her like she might never let her go and then they rocked back and forth. Jane then rose her head up and stared at the ceiling and then a deadly scream came from within, harrowing and tormenting. They both sat cradled together, locked in their heart-wrenching torment, pain so excruciating that only they knew why.

The screaming turned into wailing and then into gentle sobs, until eventually both girls grew quiet, returning to their original soulless status. Julie spoke once more in a very gentle tone, explaining that she was going to guide them back over to the bed. She gave them a detailed description on how this was going to be achieved, as she watched them both climb up onto the bed. They cradled one another in the spooning position and Julie covered them over with a duvet, pulling the bed rail back down into position. She went on to explain to them that she was going to leave the room for a while so that they could get reacquainted but would be back later on with their supper. She dimmed the lighting to a soft amber glow and quietly left the room.

Mike turned to face the doctor who appeared to be in the same spellbound state, as he concluded that, as harrowing as that had been, it proved that they understood what was being asked of them, that they weren't deaf or mute and now the true road to recovery could commence.

Five

Mike spent the next twenty minutes wrapping things up with the doctor and it was agreed that he could sit in on another session with the girls on Monday afternoon. This was going to be a tough investigation and needed to run side by side with Niko's, thought Mike, as he made his way back down to his van, prioritising what needed to be done next. He looked at his watch, which now read 5.45pm and decided to head back to the station to see where things were at.

He parked in his usual spot and stared at the empty parking space next to his – Mel's space – her blue golf should be there and she should be by his side, where she had been for the last ten years. He paused for breath, the sudden emotion taking over him and overwhelming his very being. He stared up at the night sky, giving himself a shake and moved on into the station. He was exhausted emotionally and physically and felt his loyalties being pulled in all directions. He stopped at the vending machine, searched through all his pockets for his glasses and then located them on his head. Plonker, he thought, giving his pockets a second rummage for some coins. He selected his usual and made his way through to his desk, where Paul had decided to take up residency.

"Hello, mate, and to what do I owe this visit?" he said, nudging him off his chair.

"Evening, Mike, I was looking for your last hand-written notes on the Gordon case. You left the other evening without transferring them electronically," he told him. Mike thought back to the evening he threw in the towel and headed off down the pub, without typing his report. Mel's date night, which turned into a rape night. He tossed his notes over to Paul and asked where they were at, running his hands through his hair.

"Well, Ben and Bill have been continuing with their door-to-door enquiries and have been interviewing residents in and around the Square," he told him. "One of the occupants was very helpful, Mrs Turner from number 25, on the Square itself invited them in for coffee. You know the scene, little old dear, nothing better to do and needed the company. Well, while they didn't uncover anything to do with the case, as such, she did let them have a look round her house. We wanted to get the general layout to see if it was possible to hide two girls for such a long period of time without raising suspicion."

"And?" said Mike, wishing he would get to the point.

"Well, the houses stretch over four floors, as expected, and all have a basement area. Most houses along that stretch are owned by several occupants, as they have been made into flats, but Tina tells me from her research at the land registry that some are wholly owned and these are the ones we are now concentrating on," he said.

"Did she unearth anything at the land registry regarding Niko's empire?" Mike asked, remembering his specific instructions to her.

"Yes, she's been uncovering all sorts and Niko's not what or who he appears to be," he said, as he perched on the edge of Mel's desk.

"Enlighten me," he said, rising to his feet.

"Niko's a form of errand boy or should I say, man, as the guy's around sixty," Paul told him. "We're still trying to establish where he fits into things and who he's related to but what I can tell you is, he doesn't own Mel's flat or the neighbouring properties and that's for certain."

"Well, who the hell does?" questioned Mike.

"The properties are registered to Seabourne Investments," Paul told him.

"And they are who?" questioned Mike, growing more and more aggravated by the second. Why would someone rape someone because they were behind with the rent if they didn't even own the property, thought Mike? It just didn't make sense.

"Yeah, well, that's where we're digging now because Seabourne Investments seem to be some sort of tax front. It just gets deeper and deeper," said Paul. "How's Mel doing Mike?" he asked, knowing that this was really personal to him.

"Still asleep when I left her earlier but I will be heading back there later," he told him.

He patted Paul on the back and moved on round to the briefing room, where Karen and Dhillon were talking.

"Hey, Mike, how's Mel doing?"

"Asleep," he repeated, standing in front of the briefing wall. He stared at Niko's photo with hatred and then across at the Gordon girls. He recalled the events from earlier and turned to face the others. "I sat in on a session with the Gordon girls this afternoon," he told them. "They have been reintroduced," he added.

"How did that pan out?" asked Karen, curiously. Dhillon leant back against a desk and waited to be filled in on all the latest events and Mike regaled the whole afternoon in great detail.

"They are not retarded, deaf or dumb and that we have witnessed today," he said, drawing breath after a long and detailed account, "but they have been through an ordeal beyond our comprehension," he told them. "I now feel that once Nurse Somers gains their full trust and starts conversing with them, we may have some chance of finding out where they have come from. Until they start talking, we need to concentrate on finding Niko," he said. "Two separate cases, I know, but with Niko we aren't handicapped by two silent victims," he said, as he searched through his pockets for a hanky.

"Karen, can you type up everything I have told you this evening so that everyone is fully up to speed as to where we are at with the Gordon girls, as I need to get back to the hospital," he told them. Karen nodded, gathered her paperwork and left the room. "How's Jim and Dave doing?" Mike asked, agitated by the lack of feedback.

"They are trying to trace Niko's family tree and have gone to interview a neighbour at Mount Pleasant who, I might add, seems quite willing to speak for a backhander of course," said Dhillon.

"Good, that's something at least. They might be able to give us some family names and addresses, so that we can work out how he fits into things," he said, wondering if that woman in the photograph was his mother. Perhaps he was adopted, but how the fuck did he end up an errand boy, he thought to himself, as he walked slowly out of the room. He wandered back over to his desk, exhausted and sat down briefly. He looked across at Mel's desk opposite and wondered what she would do. She was always good with ideas, solutions. She had a way of solving problems and dealing with difficult situations. Together they were a team, by himself he didn't feel complete. He was beginning to wonder if she was, in fact, his other half, his better half. He rose to his feet and walked over to the window, staring down at the empty parking space. He was going to get that bastard and he was going to pay dearly. He gathered his jacket from the back of his chair and claimed his keys from the edge of his desk and shouted good evening to anyone who was left.

Walking back to his van he suddenly felt anxious about Mel waking and him not being there and this made him accelerate from his slow saunter. He fumbled with his keys and climbed in behind the wheel and, once more, set off back to the hospital. Daisy had long since gone home, he considered, and now he wouldn't be able to get any information about how the afternoon had gone. Damn, he really wanted to speak to her before she clocked off. It was Saturday night, pitch black and the world and its wife appeared to be out in force. The journey back to the hospital was lengthy, painful and totally frustrating. It took twenty minutes longer than usual and the only let up was the empty parking space not far from the front entrance sitting there waiting for him. Thankful for this small mercy, he clambered out of his van and headed back up to Byron ward, feeling the effects of the cold, wintery night in his bones.

He waited patiently for someone to release the doors, as he pressed the buzzer for a second time and then turned right towards Mel's room. He stopped short of the door and peered in through the window, wondering what he might see. Would she be sitting up, awake and able to talk or would she still be asleep? He wasn't sure what he would prefer. He wanted her to be awake as this would show improvement but with this came reality. She would have to face what had happened to her and this would be a difficult situation to witness, painful for them both. He entered the room quietly as he could see that Mel was laying down on her side, facing the window. He gently moved round to the other side of the bed so that he could sit in the wingback chair facing her. Her eyes were closed and he sat down, almost relieved, feeling like a coward who couldn't face having to deal with her emotions, should she wake. His eyes were then drawn to a small white envelope marked for the attention of 'Mike' propped up against a water jug on the bedside table that had been pushed over to the corner of the room. Mike rose to his feet wondering if it might be from Daisy and hoped that she had some good news for him. He sat back down and tore the side of the envelope open with the edge of his key and slid out the note.

Dear Mike,

Sorry I couldn't wait any longer for you but I have some news for you regarding Mel. Mel woke up twice during the course of the afternoon. Once very briefly for a sip of water and then resettled shortly after. The second time was around 5pm when she stayed awake for around half an hour. We had a little chat and she took a few bites from her sandwich and a few sips of juice. She did ask for you and I told her that you had been there and that you were coming back this evening. Her message to you was that she wants you to wake her when you arrive, as she doesn't want to miss you again.

Best wishes

Daisy.

Mike read the note again and then pushed it inside his jacket pocket, as he sat staring at Mel. He lent forward and stoked her face very gently whispering her name. "Mel, it's me, Mike, I'm here for you Mel," he said, a tear rolling down his face. He felt so nervous he could feel his hand tremble against her cheek as he continued to stroke her. Mel's eyes opened and locked with his for what seemed like an eternity. Mike lent forward and brushed a kiss on her cheek and then offered to help her sit up, as he adjusted her pillows and helped prop her up into the sitting position. Mel winced as she tried to get comfortable and Mike sat back down in his chair, worried he was making the situation worse. "Can I get you anything, Mel?" he questioned, wondering where to start and what to say. Normally, being in her company was so natural as they used to tell one another everything but now it felt awkward, vulnerable, and needed careful handling.

"Some water please," said Mel pointing over at the jug. Mike refreshed the glass and helped her guide it to her mouth and then replaced it back on the table.

He sat on the edge of the bed and took Mel's hand in his. "Mel, I'm so sorry for what happened to you, I don't really know what to say," he said fumbling to find a way to start the conversation.

"You don't have to say anything, Mike, being here is enough. You're the one person I wanted, thought of, when I woke earlier, the one person I trust," she added, as she tried once more to get into a comfortable position. "I don't really want to talk about what happened for the time being," she told him. "I'm not ready to face it but I do want you here. You make me feel safe," she told him.

"You're my bestie, Mel, and I'm going to take care of you," he said, taking her hand once more in his. "When you're well enough to leave here," he said, trying to phrase his words carefully. He was about to say well enough to go home but she didn't really have a home, not now, not after this. "When you are well enough to leave here," he repeated, "I want you to come home with me so that I can look after you. Now, I know you will probably argue that one," he said jovially, "but I won't take no for an answer," he said, standing up as if to give his argument some stature.

"I would like that," said Mel attempting a smile, knowing that she had nowhere else to go, but also knowing that she was comfortable around Mike and he would be her preferred choice.

They continued to chat for an hour or so. Idle, safe chat, anything that didn't involve her ordeal. Mike decided after struggling for conversation to focus on the Gordon case and bring her up to speed regarding the two sessions he had experienced. Mel was present during the first session with Doctor Leeson at the observation centre but now there was so much more to tell her, especially the progress witnessed at the long-term observation and rehabilitation centre run by Doctor Gyllensvan. Mike told her all about the reintroduction of the sisters and that they obviously understood what was being said to them. He filled her in on all the details, giving her a blow-by-blow account. Doing so not only helped with the awkwardness of Mel's situation but also gave her something to focus on, other than her own plight. Some might say it is escapism not facing the facts but there was plenty of time for that and, right now, Mel needed company, conversation and something else to concentrate on so that she didn't drive herself mad.

Mike yawned and rose to his feet, feeling selfish about leaving her yet again. "Mel, I'm gonna head home now but I will be back again tomorrow and will keep you posted on the case." He bent forward to kiss her forehead and smiled down at her.

Mel reached out for his hand and gripped it tightly. "Thanks, Mike," she said, holding on to his hand longer than normal. Mike understood completely, as he didn't want to let her go either and bent down and kissed her forehead again.

"Night, bestie," he said moving towards the door, "see you tomorrow."

Mike headed home, pleased that Mel was awake. This was a huge leap forward. She was coherent, showed no sign of amnesia and was comfortable about going home with him to recuperate. There was a long road ahead towards her recovery yet, which would include counselling sessions and much more but he felt relieved beyond belief that she didn't appear to have any physical signs of brain damage, which had been his worst fear. She was still Mel, his Mel. The journey home was no better than the inbound journey and was hindered by a crash just outside a children's home called The Sanctuary. It was an orphanage built in the seventies and was a haven for youngsters who were orphaned or had nowhere else to go. Police had sectioned off most of the road and a diversion had been put in place which had caused congestion the entire length of Holden's Hill. Mike waited patiently in the line of traffic just at the foot of the hill. He was sitting just outside the entrance gates to the home when the heavens opened. "Oh, for God's sake," he shouted, banging his fist on the steering wheel, before turning on his wipers. He could just make out the sign on the gates and then his attention was drawn to a smallish photograph of its founder. The light under the sign kept flickering in the darkness but every few seconds it lit up.

The traffic made a sudden surge forward and Mike then crawled the entire length of Holden's Hill until he eventually met the High Street. What a relief, thought Mike, as he moved into third gear and turned into Wood Lane, he was now on the straight and narrow and should reach home in the next ten minutes he thought. He wasn't going to need any assistance getting to sleep tonight he thought, desperately trying to stay awake behind the wheel. He was far too tired to drive and was thankful when he pulled up outside his flat. He made one last push to take the steps up to his front door and turned the key in the lock. Once in, he dropped his jacket to the floor, kicked off his shoes and headed to the bedroom. He sat on the edge of his bed and then laid backwards with his feet still touching the floor, almost paralysed through exhaustion, and closed his eyes.

He woke to the sound of church bells and then realised his phone was still in his jean pocket. He glanced across at the clock as he tried to retrieve his phone from its awkward position, wondering who was calling him at 8am on a Sunday morning. "For God's sake," he shouted out loud, when he saw Dhillon's name on the screen. "Morning, Sir," he said, almost screaming the words, as he sat up, adjusting his pillow so he could lean back.

"Morning, Mike, sorry to call so early but Niko's been spotted near his flat this morning. We received a tip off from one of his neighbours that he was seen at Mount Pleasant, the worse for wear," he told him. "He was seen climbing into a white Escort, after stumbling down the kerb and basically being retrieved from the gutter," said Dhillon.

"Best place for him," said Mike, sarcastically as he swung his legs over the edge of the bed and rose to his feet. "Did you get the plate?" he asked hopefully, thinking this could be the breakthrough and lead to a connection.

"Yeah, traced it to Miss Johnson from Loughborough," he told him.

"Ah, and let me see," said Mike, in an even more sarcastic tone, "was reported stolen this morning," he said, sitting back down on the bed.

"No, actually, we've spoken to Miss Johnson this morning, well, Paul has, by phone," he added. "He is on his way up there now to interview her."

"Do we know how she is connected to him?" asked Mike. Thankful for this lead, however small it might turn out to be.

"Aunt I think, but to be honest the fact that she knows him gives us something to go on," Dhillon said, trying to sound positive.

"What time was he seen?" asked Mike, thinking that she couldn't have been the driver if Paul was on his way to Loughborough straight after the tip off. "Around 5am this morning but the old dear didn't call us until after 7am – didn't think we were open," he said, smiling to himself at her logic.

"So, the aunt could be the one driving, picking him up then?" said Mike, making his way to the kitchen. He flicked the switch on the kettle and perched on the edge of a stool. "The old girl, what number is she?" he asked, suddenly wondering how much she got to see of his usual comings and goings.

"She's in the opposite block, Mrs Wilson, number 18, our guys have interviewed everyone in all three blocks in the hope that someone would know him. Her bedroom window is across the green, immediately opposite his," said Dhillon.

"OK, Sir, thanks for filling me in, think I will pay Mrs Wilson a visit this morning, see what else she knows," he said, as he reached up to retrieve a mug from the cupboard and ended the call. He made himself a coffee with three sugars and walked across to the sofa. He sat down and put his feet up on the coffee table, amused by the fact that he still had yesterday's socks on. He felt grotty and smelly, as he sniffed his armpits and knew he couldn't go anywhere until he had showered. He reached for his chin and stroked his stubble, surprised by its sudden growth. If I'm not careful I'll have a full-on beard, he thought, standing up to head to the bathroom. He showered quickly and attempted to prioritise his day into some sort of order, making Mrs Wilson his first stop and then to the hospital, he decided.

He arrived at Mount Pleasant around 9.45am, and headed for the block opposite Niko's. He was relieved that Mrs Wilson was situated on the ground floor when he spied the lift was also out of order in this block. Seems to be common practice round here, he thought, as he saw graffiti sprayed across the front of the lift doors and along the entire length of the corridor. It stopped just sort of

Mrs Wilson's front door and then continued thereafter, just as if the artist had decided to refrain from obscenities on the old-dears flat, as a mark of respect. Probably her grandson or some related yob, he thought cynically. He rapped on the door with his knuckle in the absence of a bell, which was hanging by its wire, and waited patiently for her to answer. After some shuffling noises and a door opening and closing, the front door opened by a petite woman in her mid-eighties wearing a blue bonnet, firmly tied under her chin.

"Good morning," she said brightly, stepping out into the hall, while pulling on a pair of matching gloves. "How can I help?" she said as she headed off down the corridor after closing her front door firmly. "You'll have to keep up, if you wish to speak or I will be late for church," she informed him. "I always like to make the 10am service," she added. "Are you one of those door-to-door salesmen?" she asked, before he had the chance to introduce himself. "Coz if you are, you're wasting your time knocking on my door," she told him, as she raced out of the front entrance and headed off across the green. He found himself racing along after her like a pet Labrador, trying to get a word in when she suddenly stopped in her tracks and turned to face him. "You're one of those nice policeman," she said, tilting her spectacles upwards to get a closer look. "Yes," she said, stepping back slightly as if to bring him into focus. "You're better looking than the two that were here the other day," she said with a wink. "Now come along, keep up or you'll make me late," she said, ushering him along.

"Mrs Wilson, if I could just have a moment of your time," he said, beginning to pant. He put his hand gently on her left shoulder in an attempt to halt her from her urgent pace. "Mrs Wilson," he said, turning her slightly to face him. "I am Detective Sergeant Brugge from Holden CID and I would like to talk to you about your neighbour in the opposite block, Melbourne Towers, Niko," he said, relieved that he was finally able to get a word in.

"Umm, I guessed as much," she said, glancing over at his flat window. "Horrid little man, rude, obnoxious and highly offensive," she said, shaking her head in disgust. "Spits, he does, spits all the time," she said. "Landed right by the side of my shoe once, when I was waiting at the bus stop," she told him. "Filthy animal he is. and as for his language, well, never heard anything like it."

"Fan of yours then?" he said smiling at her passionate account of his character.

"You may mock, but believe me, you stay well away from that one," she told him.

"What do you know about him, Mrs Wilson? apart from his delightful character, of course. Do you know any of his family members or friends? We need to trace him urgently. It's extremely important that we find him as soon as possible," he told her, stressing the importance.

"Never really see him with anyone, with the exception of an elderly lady who visits occasionally," she said, giving it some thought. "Know he runs a kebab shop and basically stalks the neighbourhood."

"Stalks the neighbourhood? tell me what you mean by that Mrs Wilson."

"Well, l he's always hanging about, lurking around in the dark."

"Do you know why he's hanging about, Mrs Wilson, lurking, as you describe?"

"Detective Brugge, I keep myself to myself and I try to stay out of his way but yesterday, as I reported to the station, I saw him climbing into a white van. I wouldn't have thought anything of it, except for the fact that I was advised that if I saw him to call the station. He was filthy drunk, falling all over the place," she added.

"Mrs Wilson, you mentioned he was at the bus stop. Does he drive? does he own a vehicle that you are aware of?"

"No, he never drives. I've never seen him drive, ever," she said. "Now I really need to get going," she told him, starting up her fast pace again. "Good day, Detective Brugge."

He watched her as she weaved her way across the green, stopping briefly to pat a small tabby cat, she then turned the corner and was gone from view. Mike stood motionless for a few moments longer staring at the tabby, when the thought suddenly occurred to him that Mel had a cat. A house cat that by now would be hungry, very hungry indeed. He would need to go back to Mel's flat to feed it. Actually, he thought, reconsidering, he had better retrieve it and take it back to his. He wondered if Mel had a cat box and then decided this was probably unlikely. Mel was broke and had been for a long time. She would have probably borrowed one should she have had the need to visit a vet. He walked back over to his van, thinking a pet shop should really be his next move and wondered if there was one en route to Mel's place. He typed 'pet shop' into his phone and switched on location. 'Grooming Lovelies' was the closest, on the corner of the High Street and would now be his next stop. Didn't think this would be on my agenda today, he considered, climbing into his van with a sigh. He made his way down into the High Street, pulling up in the slip road where there were parking meters that charged an extortionate rate. Relieved that the first fifteen minutes were free, he made his way into the pet shop, glancing quickly at his watch to keep note of time.

"Morning," said the shopkeeper, making her way back out from the rear of the shop with a small mongrel puppy on a pink lead.

Mike bent down to stroke the pup, as he greeted the young girl with a smile. "Morning," he said, as he rose back up from his crouched position. "Do you have any of those cardboard cat-carrier boxes please?" Mike asked, as he looked round the shelving for some tins of cat food. He selected two tins and then waited patiently as the young girl went to retrieve a box. She returned carrying two different types and presented them to Mike across the counter.

"The cheapest one," said Mike, placing the tins on the counter, "together with these," he said, pointing at his selection. The young girl scanned all three items and informed him that it would be £9.25. Mike retrieved a £10 note from his wallet and then placed a tin in each of his pockets, as he waited for his change.

"Thanks very much, love," he said, replacing his wallet in his inside pocket and grasping hold of the awkward shaped carrier, which was rather large in its flat-pack state. He left the shop deep in thought about his next move, which was to return to the rape scene.

He drove in a daze, hating the fact that he needed to go back inside Mel's flat. The place where it had happened, which was now a crime scene. He parked near the foot of the stairs and made his way up onto the upper terrace. He stared at Mel's front door, reliving the night that he had run up the stairs, two evenings prior, when Brian was crouched down calling her name through her letterbox. His heart started pounding as he pulled back the orange and white crime-scene tape and stepped through her unlocked front door. Two forensic officers were still analysing the scene and nodded at Mike as he entered. Mike knew them well and thought how different it felt when the shoe was on the other foot. He was usually sympathising with the victims and now a complete role reversal. He was the partner of the victim, he was involved, it affected him, it was personal. He stood at the top of the stairs staring at the speckles of blood that had splattered the walls.

"I've come to get her cat," he finally announced, giving himself a shake, as he descended the staircase.

"It's perched on the window ledge over there," said Elaine, pointing at the grey Persian-looking feline draped across the window ledge. Mike stared at it thinking she was the only witness to this tragic event. "You saw it all," he said, picking her up off the ledge and looking her straight in the eye. "If only you could talk," he said. He put her straight into the box, as she was starting to struggle in his grasp and he quickly closed the lid.

He looked at the blood that had gathered in a pool near the foot of the stairs and guessed that that was where the rape had taken place. There was a bloody handprint on the wall. Was it Mel's or was it that greasy, slimy, evil excuse for a human being. He had to get out of there, he couldn't spend another minute in a place that now represented evil. The stench was in the air and no matter how much they bleached the place at a later date, it would never be clean again. He started to make his way up the staircase and then stopped and turned.

"Elaine, Mel's clothes, can you bag up some of her stuff and drop it off at the station please? I've got to get out of here," he said, feeling nauseous. He stepped outside and leaned up against the wall, taking deep breaths. The cat, Lola, was starting to struggle and was meowing and clawing the inside of the box. Mike knew he needed to be quick and made his way down the terrace steps back to his van. Too late, he thought, as he climbed into his van. The smell of shit was now in the air and the fragrance was to linger the entire journey home.

"Cat litter, for fuck's sake," Mike shouted out loud to himself, he had forgotten about cat litter. He opened his window to get some breaths of air, feeling sick at the thought of Lola sitting in a pile of shit, which he would have to clean. He pulled in at a corner convenience store and bought a bag of litter and decided that he would have to put it into an old baking tin, as he wasn't going all the way back to the pet shop now. The day just gets worse, he said to himself, as he threw the litter in the back of his van. Forty-five minutes later he was standing in his kitchen watching Lola take her first pee in his roasting tin, where his Sunday dinner should be.

He opened his kitchen cupboard and then closed it again. Why did I do that? he thought to himself. The cupboards are bare. Did I honestly think the fairies had done my shopping and they were going to be laden with goodies? He watched as Lola made her way enthusiastically through a saucer of foul-smelling cat food and wondered what he would do for lunch. He decided to settle for hospital food. Yes, he would drive back to the hospital, use the restaurant facilities there and then visit Mel. Why not? he basically lived there now anyway.

Six

Monday morning arrived far too quickly and Mike was scheduled to sit in on a session with the Gordon girls at 10am. He felt nervous and apprehensive but was desperate to see what developments had been made, if any. He was meeting Nurse Somers and Doctor Gyllensvan at the nurse's station outside Isaac ward at 9.45 and was slightly ahead of schedule. He was pacing up and down, looking at all the pictures on the corridor walls of various doctors and nurses that made up the unit's team. Some looked quite scary and Mike thought that some looked like they should be committed themselves.

Nurse Somers arrived first, bustling in wearing a cape style jacket that made her look like a nurse from the Victorian times. "Morning, Mike," she said cheerily, as she unveiled herself.

Mike stood up as if to attention and shook her hand vigorously. "Morning, Julie," he said, wondering why she had just arrived, a little curious as to who was dealing with the girls at the moment. He then recalled the conversation during the previous session where he was advised that there was a night-shift team, obviously realising that Julie had to leave the hospital at some stage. She had a life of her own without doubt. Doctor Gyllensvan followed shortly afterwards and they made their way through into the observation suite.

"Good Morning, Mike," came Doctor Gyllensvan's greeting as he entered his fingerprints onto the recognition panel. "I trust you are well," he asked. Mike nodded as they made their way down the long corridor into a small room called the 'Think Tank'. This was the room where they made suggestions, decisions, plans for each patient. They discussed findings, made preparations and route paths for each individual. Patient's fates were decided in this room.

A consortium of doctors making final conclusions, verdicts This is where it happened, rehabilitation or committal.

"Mike, just to bring you up to speed," said Doctor Gyllensvan, taking his seat at the table. "We have decided to put Jane under hypnosis. This is Julie's speciality," he added, looking across at her as a form of acknowledgement and confirmation. "She has had a huge success rate using this method and we have found that it accelerates progress with a majority of our patients."

Julie shuffled her papers and looked across at Mike smiling. "Yes, I think that in light of the fact that we know nothing about the girls at all, their history, their plight, an insight into their world will not only help with their rehabilitation but could also help you with your investigation," she told him.

"It would be a window into their past," added Doctor Gyllensvan.

"My God, I had never even considered the possibility of hypnosis, taking them back, so to speak. I've always been really sceptical about that topic. I have reservations as to whether it's real," he said being honest with them. Julie smiled, shuffled her papers again and then assured him that however dubious he was, however doubtful, it was in fact 'real', as he put it.

"It's a very delicate, complicated process and needs skilful handling," she told him. It can be very painful emotionally for the patient and you need to know where to draw the line at each session. I usually only take them under for short sessions at the beginning, so that I can assess their progress," she informed him. "Sometimes it can be a downward spiral, and in some cases we have had to stop for the safety of the patient. However, in this case we know nothing, there is no history and we need something to work with, something to help them come to terms with, to come back from, to heal from," she added.

"We are going to start with Jane, as we have been monitoring her for longer and, being the eldest, she may remember more about how it began, assuming that this may have commenced from when they were very young," Doctor Gyllensvan advised. "The girls have been separated temporarily, during the session. Sally has been taken to a different room and will be monitored during the separation," he told him. "It's almost 10am and the room has been set." He got to his feet, "Julie, Mike, are you ready to go back?" Mike rose to his feet and followed them out of the 'Think Tank'. He suddenly felt really nervous, anxious. He had never witnessed anything like this before and wished Mel was with him. He would fill her in later, he decided.

They continued down the corridor until they came to the observation room connected to Jane's room, and Doctor Gyllensvan tapped in the relevant code and pressed his finger on the panel. The door slid to one side and they all stepped into the room. Inside, two doctors were already seated in the chairs with laptops and Mike was asked to take a seat. Doctor Gyllensvan sat down in the final seat and Julie switched on the viewing window.

"Mike, I would like to introduce you to Doctor Greenfield and Doctor Reynolds, who are specialists in this field," Julie informed him, nodding towards the two doctors present. Mike nodded an acknowledgement to them both and then turned to face the viewing window. "I'm conducting this morning's session with Jane so will now enter the room," said Julie. Nurse Julie Somers left the viewing room and reappeared inside Jane's room moments later.

Mike expected to see some kind of chaise longue for the patient to lie on, like in the movies but was surprised that the room was exactly as he had last seen it. Jane was lying on the bed looking up at the ceiling and Julie sat down at the table on a chair facing Jane. "Good morning, Jane," said Julie, giving her usual morning greeting.

"Jane rarely moves now to cower in the corner, she usually stays motionless," the doctor interjected, bringing him up to speed.

"Today we are going to try something different," she told her. She rose to her feet and slowly walked over to the projector window and realigned its projection so that the image was now on the ceiling. She changed the image to a night sky with thousands of twinkling stars. She then dimmed the lights. Julie stayed in the corner of the room, almost as though she was out of sight and then she spoke softly.

"Jane, we are going to count backwards from ten and when we reach one I'm going to click my fingers and you will be back in your childhood." Mike looked across at Jane, who was motionless, and then he turned to his right to look at Doctor Gyllensvan who was transfixed on the viewing window. He then focused his very being on what was about to happen.

Julie started to count backwards from ten. "Ten, nine, eight, seven…" she did this very slowly and calmly until she reached number one and then she clicked her fingers and spoke gently. "Jane, how old are you?" questioned Julie.

Suddenly from the darkness Jane sat up and slid her legs over the side of the bed. "Ten," she answered, "I'm ten, well almost," she added.

"What's your name?" questioned Julie.

"Roberta," she replied, jumping down from the bed. She started dancing round the room doing pirouettes. She stumbled and bumped into the table. "Oh, I can never do it properly," she muttered, "Anika's the dancer, I have to paint."

"What do you mean, you have to paint?," questioned Julie.

"Daddy likes Anika to dance ballet and he likes me to paint," she answered crossly, trying to perfect her dance moves.

"Can't you choose your own hobbies?" asked Julie. Roberta started dancing around the room in an awkward fashion, avoiding the question.

"Where are you at the moment?" asked Julie, "are you at home?"

"Yes," said Roberta, sitting down at the table.

"And where is home?" questioned Julie from the corner of the room. "Downstairs," she said angrily, "but I prefer it upstairs," she informed her. "Are you not allowed upstairs anymore, Roberta?" asked Julie.

"No," she said angrily.

"And why is that?" asked Julie.

"Because we're not real, we don't exist," she said, starting to cry.

"Please don't cry, Roberta, let's move on. Is your daddy a nice man, is he kind to you?" she asked.

"He's nice when we are performing," answered Roberta.

"What do you mean performing?" asked Julie.

"He likes it when Anika dances," said Roberta. "She's really good at it and it makes him happy, for a while anyway."

"What do you do while Anika dances?" asked Julie.

"I have to sit at my easel and paint. The scene has to be perfect or we have to do it again over and over until we get it right."

"What happens if you get it wrong?" asked Julie.

Roberta started to weep and sway back and forth until Julie interjected. "Roberta, I'm going to click my fingers and you are going to be eight years old." Julie immediately clicked her fingers and Roberta sat down on the floor cross legged. "What are you doing?" asked Julie, curious at this sudden change of position. "I'm waiting for Rachel."

"Who's Rachel?" asked Julie, curious as to whether there was another sister. "She's my sister," said Roberta.

"How many sisters do you have?" asked Julie.

"One," said Roberta, standing up as if she was looking up and down the street for her.

"I thought your sister's name was Anika," Julie asked, growing more and more curious.

"No, her name is Rachel," she confirmed.

"What is your name?" Julie suddenly asked.

"Linda, my name is Linda."

"Why are you waiting for Rachel and where are you going?" asked Julie. "Linda, Where are you going?" she repeated.

"I don't know," said Linda, starting to cry.

"Why are you crying?" Julie asked.

Linda started to howl like an animal and Julie knew it was time to end the first session. "Linda, I am going to count to three and then I am going to click my fingers. When you hear the click you will wake up and remember nothing of what has just happened." Julie counted to three and clicked her fingers and then she turned the dimmer switch to the lit position, brightening the room once more.

Jane lay motionless on the floor, curled up in a ball, totally unaware of what just happened. Julie slowly manoeuvred her back onto the bed and covered her over with the duvet. Julie made her way over to the door, dimmed the lights once more and quietly left the room.

Mike rose to his feet as Julie re-entered the room. He was trembling, unable to quite take in what he had witnessed. "I don't get it," said Mike, pacing back and forth. "I mean, is she more than one person, is she schizophrenic? What just happened in there?" he questioned, unable to absorb what he had just seen.

"Let's reconvene in the 'Think Tank," said Doctor Gyllensvan, "and order some coffee," he suggested. They made their way back up the corridor, stopping briefly while Julie requested three coffees from an auxiliary nurse, who seemed more than happy to oblige.

"There are several possibilities to consider," said Julie, as they re-entered the room. "Yes, there is the possibility that she is schizophrenic but there is also the possibility that she was stolen as a child, kidnapped and made to become someone else. Forced to replicate a scene that brought joy and happiness to someone," said Julie.

Doctor Gyllensvan nodded in agreement. "Yes, I have witnessed schizophrenia many times over the years and it does come in many forms. However, while we can't rule it out, this does point more to a kidnapping," he said. "My gut feeling tells me the girls were abducted as small children to fulfil someone's fantasy," he added.

Mike nodded in agreement. He too felt that this looked more like an abduction. "We have four names," said Mike, "four names," he repeated. Mike stood up and walked across the room. He stopped, turned and looked at them both. "Four girls," he said. "We therefore have to assume that something happened to the first two, for the replacement two to be abducted," Mike said. Mike had his detective head on now and the possibilities were endless. "Also," he said, "is this the first time he has replaced them. We could be looking at a series of abductions and possibly killings.

"This case was growing bigger by the second, and Mike knew he needed to get back to the station. Mike suggested that he would very much like to sit in on the next session and requested the date and time so that he could ensure he was present. There was no way he was going to miss the next instalment, as he tried to piece everything together like a giant jigsaw puzzle. He was typing the date and time into his mobile, when there was a light knock on the door.

"Enter," said Doctor Gyllensvan, looking up from his notes. "Your coffee, Doctor," said the young auxiliary nurse, entering the room with a small tray of coffees in polystyrene cups with a selection of milk and sugar sachets. Mike reached out to retrieve the tray from her outstretched arms and thanked her before placing it on the table. He then reached for a sachet, pleased that the nurse had been over generous with the sugar.

"What other option is there to consider," pondered Mike, recalling Julie's earlier comment about there being several possibilities.

"Well, that's what we will uncover session by session," said Julie. "I suggest the next session we move on a couple of years," she said. "Something changed to make the father move them from upstairs to below stairs."

"Yeah, what happened," said Mike. "She made the comment about not being real, not existing," he said.

Doctor Gyllensvan rose to his feet, confirming the date and time of the next session, shook Mike's hand and then said that he needed to move on to his next patient. Mike sat discussing possibilities with Julie for a further ten minutes and then decided he, too, needed to return to the station. He now had some names. He decided he needed to pursue missing persons again. Sisters missing for approximately ten years called Linda and Rachel and then we have Roberta and Anika missing possibly a decade before.

"Can you send me today's findings electronically, so that I can add them to my investigation report please, Julie?" Mike asked, as he rose to leave. "Also, anything that comes to light between now and our next session, please fill me in. This could now be far more than an abduction and anything you may find, however small, or insignificant you may think it is, please let me know," he added.

Julie escorted Mike from the observation suite, thanked him for his time and input and then returned to the girls.

Mike left the hospital in a daze, mulling things over and over in his head. It started with one girl on a blustery cold November night. Three weeks later there were two and now we have four names and lord knows how many others there may be, he thought to himself, as he drove out of the hospital car park. His mind was darting everywhere, he was hungry for answers. He was also hungry for food as his stomach let out a rumble. He'd missed breakfast completely and lunchtime was fast approaching and he needed something hot. He hadn't had anything decent to eat in days, just a series of pizzas and hotdogs and he was starting to feel deprived. Man can't work on hotdogs alone, he said to himself, with a half-hearted laugh. He felt a little better, his spirits were lifted slightly now that he had something to work on. He would go to the café for pie and mash.

He arrived back at the station at 12.20 armed with his hospital findings. He selected his coffee and made his way to his desk. Paul was typing enthusiastically into his laptop and obviously had something to report on, by the look on his face.

"How's things, Paul?" Mike asked, looking over his shoulder. "How did it go with Mrs Johnson in Loughborough?" he questioned.

Paul stopped and looked up. "Odd woman," he said. "Can't quite get my head around it all but she lives like Niko. Grubby, smelly, looks like she doesn't have two cents to rub together," he said. "Loyal though, says she's his aunt but the way she talks about him, you would think she had given birth to him."

"Aunt, you say, so is she the sister of his mother or father?" questioned Mike. "Well that's where it gets complicated," Paul said. "There is no reference to his birth parents at all. Get the impression he was adopted," he added. "She clammed up completely when I pushed for answers on this. Wasn't giving anything away. The woman is a bit of an outcast actually."

"Go on," said Mike.

"Well, can't find much about her either," he told him. "It's like both she and Niko were manufactured, as opposed to being born. No parental history, no sibling history. Somehow it's been lost or removed purposely along the way," said Paul.

"So that's their link then," said Mike. "We need to find out why their history has been removed and by who. Did she confirm she was the one who picked him up Sunday morning?" Mike questioned.

"Yes, she was but she has no idea where he is now," he said.

"Well, he doesn't drive, so I suspect he's in Loughborough somewhere, probably under her floorboards," said Mike sarcastically. "Keep digging, Paul, someone knows something." Mike walked back over to his desk, then stopped and turned. "What's her first name, Paul?"

"Doreen," said Paul. "Doreen Johnson with no social security number, no birth record, exactly the same as Niko," he told him.

"And Niko's last name?" questioned Mike.

"Well, according to his rent book it's Niko Demetriou, but I assure you it's fictitious, the man doesn't exist."

"Paul, one last thing, how did she react when you told her that her pride and joy had raped someone?"

"She wouldn't say a bad word about him," he said. "Said he was a troubled boy when younger but didn't have it in him to do something so terrible."

"He's pulled the wool over her eyes over the years then," Mike said, sitting back down at his desk.

"Have Ben and Billy got any further with their house tours in Gordon Square yet?" Mike questioned further. "Yeah, they have managed to search some of the houses where residents were willing to oblige without search warrants. Obviously the ones that are wholly owned, where they occupy all four floors and basement," he added. "Nothing suspicious uncovered only some wealthy wine collections that are worth dying for," he said with a smirk, "but there are two homes that refused entry and we are trying to obtain search warrants, which is difficult without a justifiable reason, and one guy that lives in the States, the majority of the time but we have been unable to reach him."

"OK, good work. Well, I have some findings of my own to do with the Gordon girls, so will be calling a briefing where I want everyone present at 2pm," he advised. Mike set to work preparing his briefing notes and catalogue his findings electronically for all to share. He made two silhouette photos representing Roberta and Anika, changed the names from Jane and Sally to Linda and Rachael on their photo ID pictures, and added all the new information to the photo chart in the briefing room. Back at his desk, he then started to prepare his speech for the briefing. At 2pm sharp he walked into the briefing room with Inspector Dhillon and brought everyone up to date.

"Good afternoon, everyone," said Inspector Dhillon, thanking everyone for being in attendance. "We have some new developments we need to share to ensure that everyone is up-to-speed. Firstly, I am going to bring everyone up to date with regard to the Niko Demetriou case, and then I am going to hand you over to Mike for an update on this morning's session with the Gordon girls." Inspector Dhillon filled everyone in about how Niko, together with his aunt, having no record of existence anywhere. He went to great lengths, covering everything from the interview with Doreen Johnson to the interview with Niko's neighbour, Mrs Wilson. "Well, they couldn't have appeared out of fresh air," said Inspector Dhillon, trying to make sense of it all and bringing his briefing to a close. "I want everywhere checked, adoption records, children's homes, rehabilitation units, young offender institutions, everything, leave no stone unturned. Someone knows something," he told them, "and I want answers," he said, handing over to Mike in an almost aggressive tone, to continue with the Gordan case.

Mike stepped forward to begin. He stood in front of the briefing wall pointing out the new developments and then described in great detail the morning's hypnosis session to the group. "So, you see," he concluded, "while we can't rule out schizophrenia, everything points to abduction. The information we have to date means that we are looking for two siblings called Roberta and Anika. What happened to them, what was their fate? We are also trying to find the birth parents of siblings Linda and Rachel, who their relations are, who reported them missing and when. From the short hypnosis session carried out, everything points to Linda and Rachel being the replacements for Roberta and Anika," said Mike. "We also have to bear in mind we have no idea of the time scale between the two missing sets of sisters," he added. "If this was a fantasy replacement, have any other children/sisters had to play out this fantasy and, if so, where they are now. Yes," he said, taking note of Karen's gasp. "We cannot rule out that there could be more and there could be bodies to uncover. Children grow up and, in this case, would become surplus to requirements. We have researched everything over the last ten years to date and drawn a blank. I now want you to go back twenty, even thirty-plus years, whatever it takes. Two children called Roberta and Anika went missing or died many years ago and someone knows something. I want to know when and how. Please find out their fate," he said, willing everyone to pull together. Mike felt he gave the briefing justice, he had given it his all. He had given over all the facts, everything he had garnered so far. He now wanted answers.

It was almost 4.30 when Mike decided to throw in the towel for the evening. He felt exhausted, the day had been filled with so many developments and Mike wanted to tell Mel what he had uncovered so far. Mike stood by the window, staring out into the car park, wondering how she was doing. He missed her. "Night," he shouted, grabbing his jacket off the back of his chair. "I'm going to head off to see Mel," he told Paul and Karen, who were still working tirelessly.

"Night," said Karen, acknowledging his departure. "Please give Mel my love. Mike, I would like to visit her, please let me know when she's up to having visitors."

"Will do, Hun," he said, smiling over at her.

Paul stood up and nudged his arm. "Hang in there mate," he said. "Send her my love." He sat back down and returned his attention to his notes. Mike nodded at Tina as he passed the vending machine and he stepped out into the cold night air.

He decided to head back to the hospital via The Old Bakery, which was Mel's favourite tea shop. It sold the most delicious sandwiches and scones and he and Mel often used to go there when they were mulling over cases. Mike nodded at Fred as he entered the bakery and then greeted his wife, Sheila, with a kiss on both cheeks. They were a lovely couple and had been running the shop for as long as he could remember. Fred, an oversized, short man, who's physique emphasised his desire to enjoy his own pastries and cakes, slipped out from behind the counter to give Mike a welcoming handshake and thump on the back.

"Mike, where have you been? I was just saying to Sheila that we haven't seen you and Mel for weeks."

Mike wondered how much detail he should give with regard to Mel, after all he didn't want to discuss Mel's private life with all and sundry. He decided to remain tight lipped about her ordeal and to breeze over the details. He wanted it to be Mel's decision as to who should know. "Fred, how are you, old buddy," he said, returning the welcome gesture with enthusiasm. Mike glanced down at his apron which was covered in jam with crumbs stuck at various points. "You been enjoying the jam Danish again," he said pointing at the evidence with a smirk.

"Ah, you know me, Mike, can't get enough," he said chuckling.

"Yeah, I think he eats more than we sell," said Sheila, winking at Mike.

"Come and sit down," said Sheila pointing at a vacant table. "Where's Mel?" she questioned, as she pulled out a chair for him.

"Sheila, I can't stop today, love, as much as I would like to," he told her. "Mel's in hospital and I am on my way up there but I wanted to take her some of her favourites," he said.

"Oh, what's happened?" she said, "I hope it's nothing serious," she added, perching on the chair she had just retrieved.

Mike struggled to think on his feet and decided to say she was having some tests. "She should be out in a few days, but in the meantime can you put one of your cream teas together for us, so that I can take it up there?" he asked.

"My pleasure," said Sheila, standing back up. She popped behind the counter and selected some of Mike and Mel's favourite sandwiches. She then selected two scones, complete with jam and clotted cream and then made her way over to the window display. Without evening pausing for consideration, she selected a coconut slice, together with an iced bun with a cherry and popped them all into two cake boxes. "On the house," she announced, placing both boxes carefully on the glass countertop.

Mike gave her a hug and shook Fred's hand again. "Thanks, guys," he said, feeling a little emotional at their kind gesture.

"Now, you give Mel our love," Sheila instructed, "and please come back again soon, with Mel," she added.

"Will do," said Mike, retrieving the boxes from the counter. He waved at them both, blowing Sheila a kiss and stepped back out into the cold. Such caring friends, thought Mike, as he climbed back into his van.

He arrived at the hospital just as the evening meals were being served and was just in time to offer Mel an alternative. He walked through her door, holding both boxes up high, offering to trade her macaroni cheese for two cream teas. It was no contest. Mel shoved her tray to one side and Mike laid both boxes on the table, right under her nose. He kissed her on the cheek and opened both boxes at once.

"So, you've been to Fred and Sheila's without me," she said smiling.

"Not quite," he said sitting down on the edge of her bed. "I went to Fred and Sheila's for you," he said. "Got your favourite," he added pointing at the coconut slice.

"So I see," she said, picking it up. Mel never did anything in the right order, she often chose her sweet before her savoury, yet another little quirk Mike loved about her. She ate it enthusiastically, as did Mike, deciding to eat his cherry iced bun first, following by example. For a few moments they took refuge from Mel's ordeal and enjoyed the sweet taste of their favourite cakes.

"I've got loads to tell you," he said, wondering if he should include the Niko, findings. He decided to work up to that and started with the session with Jane. Mike described how he met Doctor Gyllensvan that morning at Isaac ward and sat in on a hypnotic session conducted by Nurse Julie Somers. "I've never witnessed anything like it," said Mike, giving her a blow by blow account. "Shook me up a bit, to tell you the truth," he said, pulling at his hair. He stood up and walked over to the window. "Mel, there is the possibility that this is just the tip of the iceberg. I mean how long has this been going on for and how many victims are there?" he questioned.

"Well, I guess you need to start with Roberta and Anika," said Mel, pleased that she had something else to concentrate on. She loved the fact that Mike had come straight in with her favourite coconut slice and then went straight into the Gordon case. He knew her so well, he knew how she ticked and that it would be her choice to talk about things when she was ready. She felt safe with him, he was the only person in the world she trusted.

"Yeah, I've got everyone checking missing persons, sisters over the last thirty-plus years," he told her. "My worry, Mel, is that children grow up and if they have been abducted to replace two children, what happens when they get too old to play the part." He shivered, considering the possibility that they could have been replaced numerous times. "And what does the perpetrator do with them afterwards?" he questioned. "The Gordon girls are in their late teens. Where have they been all this time and are there two other children out there now, as we speak, around eight and nine years of age playing out this guy's fantasy?"

Mel reached out for his hand. "You'll get him," she said, as he snuggled up

close to her.

"We'll get him," he corrected her. "Mel, we always work together and I value your opinion and any input, however small," he said, trying to make her feel part of the case still.

"Any news as to when you can get out of here?" he questioned, pleased to move on as the case was driving him insane.

"By the weekend, I've been told," she informed him. "I've told them that I'm coming home with you and they have agreed to this, subject to a set of guidelines, rules, you know the usual shit," she said. Her leg was no longer in a hoist but was heavily plastered from the groin to her ankle, so she would probably require crutches. He then looked at her bandaged wrist and arm in a sling and wondered if she would manage without the aid of a wheelchair. Mel could see him pondering over her injuries and told him not to fuss. She told him that they were going to do a detailed assessment and she would be sent home with all the necessary equipment needed to aid her recovery.

"Mike, they have told me that I have been booked into some counselling sessions and I have asked if they can be conducted at your flat, is that OK?" she questioned. "I really don't want to have to come back here," she told him.

"Of course, that's fine," he told her. "Whatever's best for you."

"Hey, I collected Lola and took her back to my flat," he told her, changing the subject.

"Oh my God, Lola, how could I forget her?" she said sitting up straight, as if suddenly in shock. "Oh, Mike, how could I have forgotten about her?" she repeated, tears running down her cheeks.

"Hey, stop that," he said, pulling a tissue from the box on the side cupboard and passing it to her. "What you've been through, I'm surprised you remember your own name," he said, giving her a cuddle. "Look, she's come to no harm and has settled into my place quite well," he told her. "She's become acquainted with my baking tin," he said with a smile.

"Baking tin?" quizzed Mel, thinking he had lost the plot. Mike told her about forgetting about a litter tray and how he had to improvise, which made Mel giggled a little.

"What are you like?" she said, giving him a nudge. "So, you went back to my flat then?" she quizzed, suddenly turning pale.

"Yes, I needed to retrieve Lola, Mel, and I have organised for some of your clothes and personal stuff to be dropped to me at the station, so that you will have what you need at mine," he told her. "Mel, while we are touching on that subject, Niko's been sighted near his home address and we have traced him to an aunt in Loughborough. We have interviewed her but she claims to know nothing about his current whereabouts but it would appear he is now in Loughborough," he said. "Both their identities are in question as they appear to have been erased from existence," he told her. "They have no birth records or NI numbers, a real mystery but we've got people on it and we will find him, Mel, we will," he repeated.

He moved quickly off the Niko subject, reaching into the box for a scone and took a giant bite. Cream oozed out of the sides and jam dropped into his lap, distracting Mel immediately. She fussed over him, passing him a tissue, mothering him in her usual manner. His distraction plan had worked and she too decided to have her scone as her next course. Mike left the hospital around 7.15 and made his way back to his flat. He had so much to think about, so much to do. He pulled into his parking space and switched off the ignition and sat there in thought for a round ten minutes. He needed a beer. He didn't want to sit by himself at home mulling over everything, feeling guilty about Mel. He climbed out of his van, crossed the road and headed to his usual bar, Bernie's.

Seven

The days passed quickly filled with visits to the hospital, preparing for Mel's release and forthcoming counselling sessions. It was also a week of non-stop enquiries, interviewing witnesses, links to Niko's past and updates on the Gordon girls' progress. Mike worked flat out and had never been so tired in his entire life. His nose was feeling exceptionally sore, as he had had it manipulated back into position two days prior. He had had to go under general anaesthesia and had spent the day in Holden General, as a day patient. What a day – that was followed by a sleepless night. Yesterday he had spent the entire day at his flat as he wasn't allowed to drive and by the evening was suffering from cabin fever. His only company was Lola and two mobile calls to Mel.

It was now Friday morning and he was heading back to the hospital but this time to see Doctor Gyllensvan again. Julie Somers had informed him that they were going to put Jane under hypnosis again at 10am. This was a session he had been mulling over all week, wondering how it was going to pan out. What would they uncover? What agonising nightmare had been afflicted upon the girls and for how long had they had to endure it? He had set his alarm for 6.30 that morning as he needed to catch up on some paperwork at the station before leaving for the hospital. He was behind, due to his nose surgery and was now playing catch up. The sound of a horn brought him back to reality, as he had drifted off into his own thoughts again.

"Come on, mate, I ain't got all day," came the sound of an aggravated driver from behind. "That's the second set of lights you've missed," he shouted, banging on Mike's side window, after climbing out of his car. Mike put his hands up to gesticulate an apology, mouthing the words 'sorry' through the closed window.

The driver shrugged and made his way back to his car. Mike selected first gear to move off and the lights changed again, just as he headed off over the line. Mike could see in his rear mirror that the driver had been caught by a third set of red lights and was waving furiously at him through his windscreen.

"God, I must get myself together," he said to himself out loud, as he pulled into the hospital car park, shaking his head. He had really drifted off back there and was wondering if it was the after effects of the anaesthetic. He climbed out of his van after doing three laps of the car park trying to find a vacant space and then headed over to the pay and display machine. He wondered momentarily how many hours parking he would require. There was no telling how long the session would last and then there would be the after-session in the Think Tank. He opted for three hours and then headed back to his van to display his ticket.

He made his way down to the observation suite, inside the psychiatric centre, housed in the basement area of the hospital. He descended five levels in the lift, followed by a further flight of stairs and made his way along a short corridor which led to the nurse's station. "Morning," he said in an over the top cheery voice, in an attempt to mask how tired he actually felt. The guard looked up, turning his attention away from the small handset he was holding and nodded towards the guest register. He then gestured towards the row of seats along the back wall.

"Lost ya voice?" Mike said jovially, feeling slightly agitated by the guard's lack of professionalism.

The guard placed the handset down on the counter and rose to his feet. "Sorry, I have been on duty all night and missed last night's match. My nephew sent me some of the highlights and I was just watching the winning goal as you walked in," he told him, defending his lack of acknowledgement.

Mike had lost touch with reality and didn't even know who was playing. "No worries, mate, but I'm here to see Nurse Julie Somers and Doctor Gyllensvan, when you've got a moment," he said in a half sarcastic tone. Football wasn't his thing, so he couldn't empathise on this but was anxious to get inside the centre as quickly as possible. It was 9.49 and he didn't want to miss this opportunity. This could be the breakthrough they were waiting for.

"You're the first to arrive," said the guard, switching his handset off and placing it inside the desk drawer, "but I expect they will be here any second as punctuality is vital here," he told him. He rose to his feet again, as the swing doors opened and Doctor Gyllensvan walked in alongside Julie Somers. They nodded at the guard and then walked towards Mike, welcoming him with a generous handshake.

"Morning, Mike," said Doctor Gyllensvan, releasing Mike's hand and turning towards Julie. "Shall we go in," he gestured, making his way over to the security reader. He punched in the code and placed his finger over the recognition panel and the door was released. "After you," he gestured with a sweeping movement holding the door to one side for Mike to enter.

"Thanks," said Mike now leading the way along the corridor, towards the Think Tank. Mike could hear screams coming from one of the rooms, at the far end which was harrowing to say the least and he found himself feeling quite disturbed. His imagination was running riot, as was his curiosity. What was happening inside that room? Was that one of the Gordan girls he could hear?" he pondered to himself. Julie could see Mike's reaction to this and quickly reassured him that some of the patients were extremely disturbed and very vocal and that it was not unusual to hear screaming.

She held the door open to the Think Tank, and Mike chose the chair closest to the door as he sat down at the table. Julie was armed with several folders, as was the doctor, which they spread out on the table in front of him.

"It has been quite a week," Julie announced, starting off the conversation, as she took her chair.

Doctor Gyllensvan stood over by the window, poised, waiting to interject. "Indeed it has," said the doctor, as he perched on the windowsill. "We will go into it in more detail with you after this morning's session, as today's findings may resolve some of our questions," he told him. "In the meantime, we have decided to move on with our session to when the girls were taken to what they describe as 'downstairs', as we need to establish what happened down there.

"Yes," said Julie, "I am hoping that I may, depending on how Jane copes with the first part of the session, move her on several years. This, of course, can only be determined as we go along, as I can't compromise her safety, but we will stretch it as far as possible," she told him.

Doctor Gyllensvan glanced at his watch and announced that it was time to proceed and made his way over to the door. He stopped, looked over his shoulder and directed his next statement at Mike. "Mike, the next hour or so could be extremely disturbing for you and I need to forewarn you that if at any time you are unable to continue, please leave the room. The last thing we need is to start counselling you," he said with a half-smile. Mike gestured that he was sure to be fine and followed him and Julie out of the room. Mike knew that he was actually nervous, let alone anxious and the screaming from earlier had highlighted the fact that this was likely to be a triple X production.

Mike and Doctor Gyllensvan took their seats in the viewing room, next to a doctor/clerk who was typing furiously into his laptop and Julie made her way round to the door leading to Jane's room. Doctor Gyllensvan advised Mike that, once more, Sally had been moved to a separate room during the session and would be brought back to her sister later in the day. He also told him that they were still calling her 'Jane' for the time being so as not to confuse the hypnosis sessions with real time, until Julie gave the all clear to do so. Mike looked through the viewing window and was surprised to see that Jane was in the exact position she was in the last time they did a hypnosis session and was lying on her bed facing the ceiling as Julie entered the room.

"Good Morning, Jane," said Julie, in a cheerful voice, as she pulled over a chair and placed it by the side of the bed. She sat down and placed her hands in a grasp. She always did this as a reminder not to reach out to her, as any contact could cause a violent reaction, as they had witnessed on previous occasions. "How are you today?" asked Julie in a very quiet tone. There was, as expected, no response but undeterred Julie continued to speak softly, explaining step by step what she was about to do. She rose to her feet and walked over to the window projector and aligned it up towards the ceiling. She switched it to a night-sky projection, just like before, and then she dimmed the lights. Millions of twinkling stars lit up the ceiling which you couldn't help but focus on. She stood as before in the corner of the room out of sight and gently spoke to Jane.

"Jane, I am going to count back from ten to one very slowly and then I am going to click my fingers. When you hear the click you will be thirteen years old," she told her.

Mike felt so tense, he had almost stopped breathing, as he waited for Jane to be thirteen years old. "Ten, nine, eight, seven…" Julie continued to count, until she reached number one and then she clicked her fingers sharply. Jane sat up on her bed and raised her hand to her ear, as if he was trying to listen out for something.

"Hello," said Julie from the corner of the room. "What is your name?"

"Roberta," said Jane, jumping off the bed and moving over to the door.

"And how old are you Roberta?" asked Julie, ensuring they were carrying on along the same timeline.

"I'm thirteen," she responded, crouching down by the door.

"What are you doing?" Julie quizzed, wondering why she was crouched with her ear to the door.

"I'm waiting for Father," she told her, in a sad voice.

"He's coming," she shouted out loudly, running away from the door. "Anika, quickly get your ballet shoes on and get into position," she instructed, as she quickly lifted the needle on the record player across onto the vinyl. It started to crackle and the sound of operatic tones filled the room. Roberta immediately pulled out a chair from the table and sat down with her arms poised, as if she was holding an artist brush and started making sweeping brush strokes into thin air. Roberta rose to her feet, shouting Daddy, Daddy you're home, we've missed you terribly, she shouted, throwing herself at him. Her father sat down in the cosy wingback chair by the fireside and Roberta jumped on his lap and snuggled up.

Anika started pirouetting around the room for their amusement. "Look, Daddy, I'm Cinderella," she said gracefully as she pirouetted past them. Their father smiled and clapped cheerfully until Anika stumbled knocking over Roberts's artists easel, making the painting flutter down onto the floor. Their father rose to his feet, throwing Roberta off his lap until she spun across the floor crashing into the Welsh dresser which housed their best china tea set. The dresser wobbled back and forth, knocking several of the dainty china cups off the top shelf, smashing down onto some delicate ornamental figures, causing them to crash down onto the floor. Roberta gasped as she tried to pick herself up, trembling. Blood was pouring from her left brow and was dripping down her face onto the broken china pieces.

"I'm sorry, Daddy," said Anika weeping as she tried to gather up some of the broken pieces. Anika watched as Roberta stumbled, trying to stand up straight. She couldn't stand without holding on, she felt dizzy from the blow to her head and then she vomited everywhere.

"You've ruined it," shouted their father. "I've come all the way back to see you, you ungrateful, worthless, good-for-nothing pair of idiots, and you can't do one thing for me, one bloody thing, that's all I ask of you." He turned on his heel and left the room, slamming the door.

"Noooooo," screamed Anika, rushing over to the door. "Roberta, don't let him go. Daddy, please don't go, please feed us," sobbed Roberta and Anika in unison.

"Please, Daddy, please," sobbed Roberta, "our food ran out days ago," she screamed through the keyhole. "We've got nothing left," she sobbed, curling up into a ball, "we've got nothing left," she repeatedly sobbed. Anika started thumping on the door, screaming over and over until her knuckles became so sore, blood started to drip onto the floor. Then she let out a piercing scream. The door suddenly opened, knocking them backwards. They both stared at him covered in blood, desperate.

"You disgust me," he shouted, "you are not my children. You smell, you're disobedient and stupid and it's time you went," he screamed. He threw a carrier bag of food across the room, the contents spilling out across the floor.

"We are trying," said Roberta, sobbing, "but I'm not nine anymore, Daddy, and Anika's getting too old to pirouette around in such a small space," she pleaded, "and we're tired, hungry and lonely and we want someone to take care of us, feed us, love us," she said between sobs.

"I've told you before, you don't exist, you're not worthy of love and you're lucky I took you in," he screamed. He slammed the door, turned the lock and was gone.

Roberta stumbled over to a pack of buns that had landed close to her and ripped open the plastic. She handed one to Anika, who started shovelling in large pieces and swallowing without chewing, choking, splattering and crying in between mouthfuls. The operatic tones were still playing in the background and echoed around the room playing triumphantly amongst their sobs of despair. They sat cuddled up for what seemed ages until the light showing through the small narrow window turned to dusk. This narrow window, high up the wall, almost touching the ceiling was their only way of knowing if it was night or day. They had two rooms and a bathroom. One room was their bedroom and the other was their sitting room. This room had to be kept clean and tidy at all times, not a thing out of place. It was painted a soft pastel green and large oil paintings hung on the walls. There was a mock fireplace to the left, complete with mantle clock, with a wingback chair placed either side. Adjacent was a Welsh dresser, which housed an extremely expensive antique dinner service. A four-seater table and chairs stood in its centre and in the far corner, as if set to stage, was an easel with a half-finished painting carefully placed on it. In the opposite corner was a portable ballet rail. On the back wall was a book cabinet filled with educational books and a sprinkling of novels, which had been Roberta *and Anika's only window into the real world. This room could not be personalised by them. This room had been carefully prepared and duplicated a life that went before and was now a shrine to happier times.*

Roberta wiped away Anika's tears with her sleeve and attempted to stand up. Her head ached so much but she needed to keep going. She needed to look after Anika who was fading fast. She held onto Anika's hand and led her to the bathroom, where she carefully bathed her sore knuckles and the cut on her own forehead. There was hardly anything left in their medical box, with the exception of a few plasters and an out-of-date antiseptic cream. She put some cream on Anika's knuckles and her own brow and then placed a plaster on her brow to stop the blood running down her face. It was quite a deep cut and probably needed stitches, but that was never likely to happen. Then she led Anika back out to the sitting room and sat her down at the table while she picked up the rest of the food items. They had no means of cooking and had to wash up in the bathroom. All of the food provided had to be eaten cold and was usually tinned. Their father's visits had become fewer and fewer with several weeks in between and the stocks had often depleted long before his return. She swept up the broken china and wiped the blood from the floor. She then turned and stared at the door. The door that they had been led through over four years ago, a door that they were never allowed to go out through, a door that could lead to their freedom, that was now stained with blood.

"We're going to die, aren't we?" questioned Anika, sobbing at the table. "Why don't we exist Roberta*? I mean quite clearly we do. Why does he say we don't?" she said whimpering as she stroked her knuckles.*

Roberta chose not to answer but busied herself picking up their food items, working out how she was going to make them last. How long was it going to be until his next visit? and what did he mean by 'it was time they went'? She marked another line on her home-made calendar and sat and waited.

Mike was completely transfixed, absorbed so intensely that by the time he heard Julie moving her on to another period of time, he realised that he had risen out of his chair and was standing with his face almost pressed against the viewing gallery window. He hadn't even realised he had changed position, until he found himself rubbing the window with his sleeve, to clear the glass that was misting from the deep breaths he was taking. He had been totally fascinated and intrigued by the adaptation that had taken place. While they could quite clearly hear her interacting with her sibling and so-called father figure, they had to interpret the responses in line with her answers and suspect that they may not all have had the same experience by definition or interpretation.

Mike could see Julie was now kneeling down on the floor in the corner of the room, in the darkness of the shadows. She was probably exhausted, totally drained from guiding Jane as safely as she could through this harrowing session. Jane was now sixteen years old.

The door opened and their father entered the room followed by a meek looking woman. She looked scared to death and was trembling from head to foot. Roberta and Anika were no longer required to perform their fantasy ritual and were now required to cower in the corner and were not allowed to look, speak or interact in any way. Usually food items were delivered silently with no interjection whatsoever. Just as if they didn't exist and that it was some kind of store cupboard their father occasionally opened. This had been their existence for several years and they had come to realise that they were never going to leave. This time, however, their father fully entered the room, pushing the woman to the forefront. He spoke gruffly, introducing the woman as their new carer and that his visits were now going to get fewer and fewer. He placed a number of bags along the wall by the side of the door and then turned and left without so much as giving any other instruction or understanding of what he was now planning.

Roberta and Anika slowly rose to their feet. They didn't know how to react or interject with another human being. They had been imprisoned for so many years they had forgotten what it's like to see another person.

"Hello," said Roberta, walking nervously over to where the woman was standing.

The woman was coughing relentlessly and was staring down at the floor, shaking violently. She was petite, frail and looked like a parlour maid, complete with grey dress and white apron. Her hair was blonde and tied firmly in a bun and she didn't look that much older than Roberta. Roberta suddenly felt sorry for this woman. She knew how horrible their father was and wondered what had happened to her that was so terrible that her fate was to be the same as theirs.

Roberta reached out to touch her hand. "Hello," she repeated. "My name is Roberta and this is my sister, Anika," she said pointing over to her sister.

"Hello," spluttered the woman, with a slight accent, in between coughs. Tears started to stream down her face, she couldn't stop shaking and Roberta could see that this poor woman looked frightened to death and probably didn't even know why she was there.

"I'm Helena," she finally spluttered.

"How do you know our father?" Anika asked curiously, moving in closer to take a good look at her.

"I work in his kitchen," she finally answered, after considerable pauses between coughs. "He said I was to look after you," she told them.

"But why did you agree to it?" asked Roberta, wondering how this was sold to her.

"I didn't," she said, starting to wail and rock back and forward. "He called me into his office and said he had a new role for me and then he gave me a

drink. The next thing I knew he was pushing me through this door. He must have drugged me," she said, walking over to the door. She turned the handle and pulled at the door, over and over. "It won't open," she screamed, shaking the handle.

Anika took her hand in hers, leading her away from the door. "It's locked, we've been prisoners here for years," she told her.

Helena started to rock back and forth and let out a piercing scream, it settled into sobs, followed by whimpers and then she went silent. Her fate had become interlocked with theirs.

Julie watched Roberta sitting in the middle of the room rocking back and forth whimpering. She glanced at her watch and decided to call an end to today's session. The session had lasted over an hour and it was seldom that she would allow a session to go beyond an hour. "Roberta, I am going to count to three and then I am going to click my fingers. When you hear the click you will wake up and remember nothing of what has just happened." Julie counted to three and clicked her fingers and then she turned the dimmer switch to the lit position, brightening the room once more. Roberta sat motionless in the middle of the room. She had stopped swaying and was totally still, staring into space. Julie carefully guided her back over to the bed and helped her climb up and lay down. She covered her over with the duvet and made her way over to the light switch. She spoke very softly, as she dimmed the light and then she quietly left the room.

Mike was still standing in the same position, face pressed against the glass, when Julie re-entered the observation room.

"Mike," said Julie, in an attempt to bring him out of his transfixed status. "Mike," she repeated, placing her hand on his left shoulder.

Mike spun round as if he had totally lost track of where he was. "Sorry," he muttered, shaking his head and sitting back down in one of the observation chairs. "There's a third person," he muttered, pulling at his hair. "A third person," he repeated, as if he couldn't quite get his head around this new development unless he kept repeating it. "Who is she and more to the point where is she now?" he questioned. "My God, where is that poor woman now?" he said out loud.

Doctor Gyllensvan suggested that they should now reconvene for further discussion and led them all out of the observation room and down the corridor towards the Think Tank. It was as if all hell had broken loose as they made their way along the noisy corridor. Screams could be heard coming from several of the rooms and the sound of bangs and crashes could be heard, as if the items were being thrown against walls. A door suddenly opened and two burly security guards were trying to restrain a patient with the help of a doctor and a porter. The patient looked like a giant gorilla, as if he had been on steroids and was exceptionally strong. He looked ungroomed with a wild bushy beard and long spirally hair. His only item of clothing was a pair of white y-fronts, which he had clearly soiled. Despite his restraints, he was giving it all he had and was giving his assailants a real run for their money, as they spilled out into the corridor. He obviously saw them as the enemy and was doing all he could in a bid for freedom. The patient was now foaming at the mouth and was spitting at the porter, as they wrestled him to the floor. He was grunting like an animal, as they secured their hold on him, until eventually he succumbed to the injection that was finally administered.

Mike couldn't believe the morning he was having and what he had witnessed both in the observation suite and the hospital corridor. His mind was darting everywhere as he was led into the discussion room. He sat down, nervously, feeling his limbs trembling, trying to keep a hold on his emotions. Christ, to work amongst this everyday would be enough to drive you insane, he thought to himself. He then thought, momentarily, how the doctor and Julie coped with this on a day-to-day basis. He suspected that it must have warped their judgement in some way or other.

"Right," said Doctor Gyllensvan. "I'm going to keep this brief this morning, as I have a hectic schedule ahead of me." The doctor looked agitated and distracted and his concentration span had obviously been shifted in some way or other, to the extent of him advising that he was going to leave him in the capable hands of Julie. Mike wondered what it could possibly be that could be more pressing than the session that had all just experienced. Mike had never witnessed anything like it in his entire career but guessed that this was just another day for the doctor who had seen it all before. Doctor Gyllensvan instructed Julie to send him the electronic notes of this morning's session and told her that he would meet with her again that afternoon around 3pm. He then shook Mike's hand and bowed out of the meeting.

Julie could see that Mike found the doctor's sudden departure unnerving and attempted to lead the meeting herself. "Unfortunately, Mike, in our line of work, it is sometimes necessary to bail out of one patient's quandary and into another, she told him. "The patient in the corridor is one of Doctor Gyllensvan's long-standing case studies and has just been committed indefinitely. Doctor Gyllensvan's drive for rehabilitation is always at the forefront and the time invested in that patient has almost brought him to his knees. Now shall we move on?" she said, opening one of her folders in front of her and removing her pen from her top pocket. Mike nodded, thinking how stressful all this must be and what it must do to a person's emotions. It was hard enough in his line of work with everything that went with being a copper and everything he witnessed. He often sat staring at the wall in the evening, his stomach churning, feelings of grief overwhelming him but this, this was an entirely different level of emotion, this had taken him out of his comfort zone entirely.

"I think we can say, without a doubt, that this is an abduction," Julie stated, bringing the meeting back on track. From what we have learned from our previous session, the girls were already 'downstairs' as it is referred to, by the age of ten. We have to assume that they spent some time upstairs as this is where they appear to have some happier memories. The blood results have placed the girls biological age at around sixteen and eighteen, so they were captive for around ten years before escaping. Assuming they did escape and were not just abandoned."

"Abandoned?" Mike questioned. Mike hadn't even considered that possibility. "What makes you think they may have been abandoned?" queried Mike. "Surely the abductor wouldn't just turf them out into the night for fear of being caught, traced!" said Mike.

"What if he was dying, or merely had simply had enough of the whole thing, or was too old to care anymore and was getting careless?" suggested Julie.

Mike's attention was suddenly drawn to the father's age. How old was this guy? he wondered, and had he become careless, as suggested?

Mike found it hard to concentrate, let alone process any of the information that had come to light and now there was another missing person in the equation, Helena. His head was spinning and his mind was in total chaos and he felt he needed to dissect it piece by piece and then place each piece carefully back until he had the full picture. The only problem was, he didn't have all of the pieces, not yet, but he would and he wasn't going to rest until he had every single segment.

Mike rose to his feet as a signal that he was drawing a close to today's session. He had been overloaded with new findings and Julie was going to reconvene with the doctor at 3pm for further medical assessment, so it seemed like a good place to leave things for today. He needed a coffee and time to think, and then he needed to deliver these new findings to his colleagues. Mike shook Julie's hand, thanking her for including him once more in the hypnosis session and requested to sit in again on the next one, to gather more pieces to this overwhelming investigation. Julie promised to keep him informed as to the date and time of the next session and then she led him back down the corridor and out into the reception lobby. The guard from earlier had long since left his post and had been replaced by a young male student, who looked frightened to death to have been placed there. Mike signed out in the visitor's book and nodded at the student nurse, who stuttered a form of goodbye and then he made his way back upstairs, away from all the madness and out into the fresh air. He fumbled in his jacket pocket for his cigarettes and finally retrieved them from his inside pocket. He was trembling slightly, the after effects of being witness to such an awful ordeal, and he could feel his hands shaking as he attempted to light one in the cold wind. He leant back against the wall just outside reception and tried desperately to make sense of all that he had just witnessed.

His stomach let out a loud rumble, bringing him back into reality. It was almost noon and he had been on the go since before sunrise. His body was telling him it was time for some nourishment but his stomach was still churning from his experience. He definitely needed something, especially a coffee, so decided to stop off at the pie and mash café. They did all sorts of savouries and the thought of a pasty suddenly felt appealing. He headed back over to his van and climbed in behind the wheel. "Right," he said to himself out loud, prioritising the rest of his day. "Let's grab a coffee and a pasty to go, and then head back to the station." He had so much to do, he wanted to make time to visit Mel and organise her transfer to his place, which was scheduled for tomorrow afternoon. He was going to see her doctor shortly before her release to discuss her care package and counselling sessions that were now to take place at his flat. And then there was the Niko case running alongside. Fuck, how the hell was he going to fit it all in.

Eight

He arrived back at the station just as Elaine was leaving. "Hey, Mike, how's it going?" she asked. Mike could see she had done as requested and had bagged up some of Mel's clothes and personal belongings and had left the items in some carriers next to his desk. "Thanks for doing that," he said, nodding towards Mel's belongings. "You know what a lady needs." he said with a smile. "I probably would have selected all the wrong stuff," he said in a grateful tone. There was no way he could have stayed longer at Mel's flat that day, the crime scene, as it had been tainted, ruined, but he knew he needed to make plans to remove the rest of her belongings and would have to go back at some stage.

"How's Mel doing?" questioned Elaine, as she perched on the edge of Mel's desk.

"She's on the right track but it's going to take time, Elaine," said Mike, sitting down at his desk.

"Give her my best, Mike," said Elaine.

"I will, she's being discharged tomorrow but I expect it will be a while before she's up to having visitors," he told her.

"Of course," said Elaine, as she rose to leave, "but send her my best, Hun, and tell her I will look in on her soon." Mike's attention was then drawn to the orange flashing light on his answer phone. It wasn't there earlier, as he had checked all his messages before leaving for the hypnosis session. He nodded goodbye towards Elaine and then pressed to retrieve his message.

Mike paced up and down while listening to his message and then he played it again. It was from Mrs Wilson, she had suddenly remembered something about Niko. The message was brief and Mike played it three times before finally realising where he recognised the name 'Sanctuary' from. Mrs Wilson had seen Niko coming out of the children's home called The Sanctuary a while back but thought nothing of it but she had seen him again that morning and thought perhaps he should know, in case there was anything in it. Fuck, that means he's back in town, thought Mike, worrying again about Mel's safety and the proximity of the home to the hospital, and what was Niko's connection with that home. Mike looked across the empty office. There was no one available to assign this to. He would have to go himself. He wasn't going to hold back on a lead like this, he needed to go and go now.

He headed back out of the station doors as Paul was coming up the steps.

"Hey," said Paul, pausing on the third step. "How did it go in the hypnosis session this morning, Mike?"

Mike stopped, pleased that Paul had shown up when he did. Police visits were usually conducted in twos and he needed him to accompany him to the children's home. "Paul it would take me all afternoon to tell you about what was unearthed in this morning's session but something has come up," he told him. "Niko has been seen coming out of The Sanctuary children's home on Holden's Hill – and not for the first time. Mrs Wilson left me an answer-phone message this morning, while I was at the hospital and I'm on my way there now," he told him. "If you've got nothing more pressing on for the next hour or so, do you want to accompany me down there?" he asked. "I can fill you in on the hypnosis session en route," he told him, as he continued down the steps.

"Sure," said Paul, turning back round and following him down the steps towards his van.

Mike knew Paul wouldn't say no. He loved being out on a case and took every opportunity to be in the thick of it. He was also good at what he did, he was thorough and Mike knew he would pick up on anything he missed.

"So, how did it go then this morning?" questioned Paul again, as he climbed into the passenger seat of Mike's van.

"Quite harrowing actually, Paul." Don't know if you've ever witnessed hypnosis, other than the daft stuff we see on TV, but by God it's totally gripping and makes you feel like you're there witnessing their ordeal first hand." Mike pulled out of his parking space as Paul was buckling his seat and then headed for the exit.

"No, not first hand," said Paul, "but I've seen some recordings of a few cases but nothing along these lines."

Mike decided to lead the conversation as to what he experienced that morning, as he knew that if he gave Paul half a chance to lead on a topic, he would cover every minute detail with such scrutiny that his mind would be blown before they reached the home. Mike described how Jane had been placed under hypnosis back into her childhood and had re-enacted a very poignant scene endured at the age of thirteen, which was violent and disturbing. He then went on to describe how the session moved onto a scene played out at the age of sixteen. "When I say 'played out', Paul, what I mean to say is that Jane was actually reliving it as if it was in real time. We actually watched her relive that day bit by bit and it was really disturbing. When Helena was tossed into the room it really took my breath away, as you can imagine. I mean, we now have another missing person in the equation and we have no idea what her destiny was or indeed her fate." Mike gave Paul a fairly brief but accurate account of what he had witnessed that morning and then moved on to Mrs Wilson's answer-phone message.

"What the fuck is Niko doing going in and out of that children's home, Paul, and what is his connection there?" he questioned.

"Lord knows," said Paul, "but hopefully we are about to find out." They pulled up outside the ornate gates that stood proudly at the entrance to the grounds and pressed on the intercom, which was housed inside a post, in easy reach of the driver's side window.

"Good afternoon," said Mike, responding to a faint voice intermittently sounding between a lot of radio interference. "My name is Detective Sergeant Mike Brugge and I'm here with my colleague Detective Constable Paul Osman from Holden Police CID," he began. Before Mike had the chance to say anything else as to why they were there, the gates started to shudder and then swung open. Mike looked across at Paul, shrugged, and then selected first gear. Mike drove slowly up the gravel driveway, marvelling at the stunning grounds and prestigious mansion house that spread before them. It really was a grand affair and had surely been some wealthy person's family home at one time or another. Mike approached the end of the drive, which led up to a small roundabout with a lawn and flower bed, leading on to the grand entrance. This house had stood here for centuries and Mike could imagine horse and carriages pulling up with butlers and footmen assisting the gentry, the aristocracy and members of the upper-ruling classes. He could see a small car park area to the left of the entrance but instead he decided to park right outside the grand front doors. There were no footmen or butlers helping them out of his rusty old van but there was a stern looking woman dressed in grey standing on the steps to welcome them.

"Good Afternoon," said Mike reaching out to shake her hand as he climbed the front steps. He introduced himself and stepped back for Paul to do the same.

"Come on inside," she ushered. "It's far too cold to stand on parade out here," she told them. She closed both doors firmly behind them and led them into an office. "So, what can I do for you today, gentleman?" she asked. She sat down behind a bureau-style desk and clasped her hands together on the desk. "Sit down," she instructed.

There was a real sense of headmistress about this woman and it made Mike feel like he was ten years old, as he took one of the seats immediately in front of her desk. "Thank you for seeing us without an appointment," he said. "I realise that you are extremely busy running a home but we need to ask you a few questions that, hopefully, won't take up too much of your time."

"Continue," she instructed again with a piercing stare.

"Do you know a man called Niko Dimitriou?" Mike asked. "He's been seen coming and going from this home and we would like to know what his connection is here."

"That name means nothing to me at all," she told them sternly. Mike felt as though she was looking right through him as if he wasn't there and then realised that she hadn't actually even had the courtesy of introducing herself.

Mike reached into his top pocket and pulled out a picture of Niko and placed it on the desk immediately in front of her. "This may help," he suggested tapping at the photo. "He may be known to you by another name. Incidentally, Miss…" he then paused waiting for this stern headmistress-type woman to fill in the gap. "Miss?" he offered again.

"Sorry, gentleman, how rude of me, I'm Miss Rosenburg, and unfortunately I have no idea who this man is," she told them, rising to her feet.

"Miss Rosenburg, may we take a look around please, and I would like to question some of your staff, if that's possible," Mike requested.

Miss Rosenburg's expression gave way to a crooked smile and then she gestured over towards the door. "Follow me, gentleman," she said as she moved towards the door. "I will give you a brief tour and then I will send some of our full-time staff members into the drawing room afterwards," she offered. "Some of our staff members are temps and haven't been here long, they come and go, you understand."

Mike and Paul followed the stern Miss Rosenburg out of the office and along a short corridor leading to the lounge area. It was quite a pleasant room and some teenage children were sitting around a table playing cards. It was a large lounge, as one would expect in a mansion of this era, it was grand but somehow didn't look fitting for children. While it was adorned with spender, it lacked colour, and this area of the house had definitely not been adapted for children.

Miss Rosenburg led them through whistle-stop style, pausing momentarily in each room. The far end of the house looked more cheerful. It was colourful and bright with a series of rooms configured for various activities. As they turned the corner Mike could see some youngsters taking part in a music lesson, which made Mike wince from the screeching sound of the recorders. This was followed by some percussion sounds that ended with a little nipper clapping together some symbols enthusiastically. Next to the music room was the art studio where the walls were adorned with children's paintings. A teacher was kneeling on the floor next to washing up bowls containing red and blue paint and children were dipping their hands in and doing finger painting on large sheets of white paper spread across the floor. The room was full of cheer as laughter and giggling echoed around the studio. Through the large sash windows, Mike could see some kids playing football. Looked like five a side and Mike smiled as he watched a small bald-headed man with a whistle, attempt to settle an argument that had unfolded on the pitch. Miss Rosenburg was doing her best to convey the homes best assets to their full potential as she bustled from room to room, bringing the tour to a close in the dinning room where the tables were being laid for lunch service. The next wing is the school area where we have five classrooms and a small science lab, and the upper level is mainly dormitories, she informed them. She then glanced at her watch and suggested that they should reconvene in the drawing room so they could address her staff. "Please keep it brief, gentleman," she once more instructed, "as it's almost one thirty and the bell will go shortly for lunch service," she told them sternly.

She led them into an impressive drawing room with a cosy inglenook fireplace which had just been lit, the flames were just taking hold. Above the fireplace was an oil painting of a distinguished gentleman with a grey beard and green velvet jacket, wearing a maroon cravat. Mike guessed he was probably the owner.

"Wait here, gentleman, I will be back shortly," she said pointing over to the sofa."

Mike and Paul once more sat down to order and waited for her return.

"Blimey," said Paul, making himself comfortable, "she's not giving much away. That tour must have taken less than ten minutes," he said, looking at his watch for confirmation. "A house of two halves," he said. "One half crafted for the purposes of providing a home/schooling facility for orphans but the other half gave me the creeps," said Paul, studying the impressive but dark drawing room they were now seated in.

"Yeah, but back in the day, I expect it was someone's family home and was probably quite splendid," said Mike, staring once more at the portrait over the fireplace. "Can't quite work out how Niko would fit in here, though, and why is she denying all knowledge of him?" questioned Mike.

"Well, maybe she doesn't know him," suggested Paul. "He might have something to do with the grounds," he added.

"What, like a caretaker or gardener?" he quizzed. "Nah can't see that somehow, she would have to vet all employees, especially where kids are involved. He would have had to have a DBS check anyway," said Mike.

"Yeah, but that would be quite difficult with no identity records, Mike. Think, the guy has no record, there's nothing to check. Cash in hand number, perhaps."

"Well, I would like to look round the grounds before we call it a day anyway," said Mike.

Miss Rosenburg re-entered the room with four members of her team, which she lined up in front of them as if she was organising an identity parade. These are four of my longest serving members of staff who have been with me for many years, she offered. They have all exceeded fifteen years of service and know every single member of the team, including kitchen and groundsmen.

Mike rose to his feet and walked over to the window. He had suddenly felt hemmed in and suppressed. He also felt he had lost control of the session, which was quite clearly now being led by Miss Rosenburg. He cleared his throat and then addressed his audience with a new found vigour.

"Good afternoon, ladies," he said, moving in to shake their hands. "I am Detective Sergeant Brugge and this is Detective Constable Osman," he said, acknowledging Paul's presence from the sofa. "We are currently investigating a case involving a Mr Niko Dimitriou and we are urgently trying to track his whereabouts," he told them. He reached into his inside pocket and retrieved the photo. He hated looking at the photo, it made him feel sick to the pit of his stomach. It really was a face that only a mother could love, he thought to himself, as he passed the photo to the woman nearest to him.

Mike watched with interest as they passed the photo between them, noting that they all barely looked at it and all stood staring at the floor. He looked across at Paul, wondering what his take was on it, as for him, he thought they had all been prepped. He was just about to ask if any of them thought he might be connected by a third party, such as a tradesman or delivery agent when the sound of the dinner bell made him jump, causing him to drop Niko's photo on the floor.

"Now that's what you call being saved by the bell," he said, trying to retrieve the photo from underneath the coffee table.

"Sorry, Gentleman, that's all we have time for today," she said, as she gestured to her team to return to their duties. Mike watched as the women were led out of the room like soldiers and then followed to order. What a farce, completely choreographed thought Mike, as he looked across at Paul.

"Thank you for your time today," said Paul, deciding to take over from Mike, as he could see he was really agitated. Mike nodded a form of goodbye and followed Paul towards the front entrance. Miss Rosenburg closed the front door while they were still standing on the top step, ending the session forthwith.

"What the fuck was that all about?" said Mike, as they walked over to the van. "What a bitch," he added.

"What about the grounds, Mike?" said Paul, pausing, as he looked across the vast lawns.

"There's about two acres I recon," said Mike, trying to estimate, as he stared as far as the eye could see. "At the back of the estate is woodlands," he said, "I know that because there is a small gate leading from the wooded area into Marshalswick Lane. I've parked there numerous times when I've used the café but never thought too much of it. There is a small sign on it saying 'Private Property', but to be honest, there's nothing secure about it," he told him. "Think we should drive around and enter through the back and see what's what?" he suggested.

Paul shrugged, agreeing with his suggestion and they climbed back into the van.

They drove back down the gravel driveway towards the gates, which opened without any intervention by them. "Must be watching us out the window," said Mike sarcastically.

"Yeah, unless they are censored," suggested Paul. They made their way down Holden's Hill and turned onto Marshalswick Lane and parked a short distance from the gate Mike had referred to. Mike glanced at his watch, pleased that it was still quite early. He didn't fancy poking around in the woods in the dark. Paul opened the small narrow gate, which surprisingly was unlocked, and held it open for Mike to enter. Mike noticed there was a padlock but it was rusty and was lying on the floor amongst the autumn leaves, discarded. They both stood on the other side of the gate motionless, wondering which way to go.

"Not really sure what we are hoping to find," said Paul, wondering what it was Mike was trying to achieve.

"I just want to see if there are any sheds or greenhouses or maybe a lockup, you know, what the groundsmen would use," said Mike, heading into the thicket. "There must be something, a house of this standing. Or one of those summer house things," suggested Mike, remembering the last film he watched with Mel where there was one down by the lakeside. They rustled their way through the trees which led into a clearing where there was in fact a small pond. To the left was a shack-style cabin, which looked like it was inhabited.

"What do we have here then?" said Mike, pleased that he had decided to explore the grounds after all. Outside the shack was a small campfire with a kettle suspended over it, like in an old western movie, alongside a long log, obviously used as a seating area.

"It's probably a den built by some of the older kids from the home," offered Paul, as he moved in closer. There was a washing line suspended between two trees where a tartan blanket had been pegged. It looked dirty and damp and looked like it had been there for sometime. Around the campfire were numerous cigarette butts scattered all over the floor.

"Looks like those kids enjoy a good puff," said Mike, picking up a discarded cigarette box from the fireside floor.

Not convinced, he picked up the tin mug that was resting on the end of the log and sniffed at the discarded contents and then replaced it back on the log. "Enjoy whisky, as well, those kids," said Mike, sarcastically, wondering if they had hit the jackpot. He walked over to the shack door and dragged it open, as it was hanging by one hinge. The cabin was bigger than expected and extended further back than assumed from the outside. "This looks like it used to be someone's favourite place," said Mike, as he looked around. There was a small wooden table, two chairs and a single bed and it was full of someone's personal possessions. Everything looked old and worn with a musty damp aroma. There was a shelf on the wall over the bed stacked with books and papers and Mike could see there was a photograph leaning against one of the books. He reached out for the old photograph of a young boy of around sixteen playing footie with a man, possibly his father. He replaced the photo and turned to look at a small basket filled with old whisky bottles, two of which were half full. He pulled his phone out of his pocket and took two photos of the cabin so that he could analyse them later in detail, when Paul called from outside.

"Mike, come out here a minute?" Mike popped his head out the door.

"What is it?"

"These ashes are warm," said Paul poking around in the campfire ashes. "Someone's been here within the last twenty-four hours," he said.

"Paul, I don't think this is used by the kids from the home. I think we need to keep this place under surveillance. Yeah, I will get the lads back at the station on it," deciding to assign this new development to Jim and Dave. Mike took two more photo's outside the cabin and then followed Paul back to his van.

Mike's thoughts then drifted back to Mel. She was coming home tomorrow and he really needed to get organised. "Paul, I'm gonna drop you back at the station and then I need to get my place prepped and stocked for Mel's release tomorrow," he told him.

"Yep, drop me off, I want to brief the team and get today's notes on the system so everyone is up to speed with everything," he told him.

Mike knew he could rely on Paul and was pleased that he had joined him at the home. They pulled out of Marshalswick Lane and headed back to the station and then Mike headed towards town. Again, Mike was held up in traffic trying to get into town. Not surprising really, he thought to himself, we are in December now and the shops and roads leading into town were jam packed with Christmas enthusiasts. Mike decided going into town was a foolish move, he could get what he needed from Harvey's the little store at the end of his street. He turned into a side street and attempted a three-point-turn in the smallest of spaces and just about achieved it within a hair's breadth of someone's van. Phew, that was a close one, he thought to himself, as he pulled back out onto the main drag. He switched on the radio and adjusted the channel, as usual, and settled on some jazz.

There were five parking bays outside Harvey's and Mike was pleased that the last one was free. Mike jumped out of the van with renewed vigour, deciding that this was a good choice, rather than go up against the Christmas masses in town.

"Afternoon, Harvey," he shouted, grabbing a hand basket from the stack outside the front door. Harvey was rearranging some Christmas trees, which he was trying to support with the aid of a chain against the wall. "Can I help you with that Harv," he offered, watching his friend struggle.

"Nope, think I've got it, Mike," he said, stepping back to check he had them all secured. "Mrs Robson wanted the one at the very back," he said chuckling.

Mike laughed. He knew Mrs Robson, as she was his neighbour and he also knew how indecisive she was.

"She's had me at it for the last half hour," he told him. "How you doing, Mike?" he asked, thumping him on the back.

"Yeah, fine thanks, Harv. Mel's coming to stay with me for a while, as she's recovering from a broken leg from a fall, so I need to stock up my cupboards," he told him. He really didn't want the neighbourhood knowing Mel's plight and he knew Mel would hate it.

"Ah really, poor girl, give her my best, mate. Right, what can I get ya," he asked, stepping back inside and behind the counter.

Mike glanced at the deli counter and selected some cold cuts of roast beef and some honey roast ham. He wasn't the best of cooks and needed some quick fixes but he also wanted stuff that Mel could easily manage when he was at work. While Harvey was busy weighing and wrapping the cold meats, Mike made his way up and down the two isles, selecting some salad bits and a crusty loaf. He was debating what he could give her for her welcome meal and decided to run with his signature dish, spaghetti and meatballs. He placed all his groceries on the counter at the checkout and Harvey rang them all through the till.

"Anything else I can get you, Mike," he said glancing over at his favourite dumpy beers in the fridge.

"Yep, add a pack of my usual, Harv, and some milk," he said. "There is one further thing, Harv," he said, starting to chuckle. "One of those trees," he said smiling. "The one at the back," he added.

Harvey smiled as he reached for the key to unlock the padlock on the chain. "You sure you want the one at the back," he said, as he raised his fists into the boxing position, pretending to offer him out.

"Na, the small one at the front will be fine, Harv, only pulling your leg." Mike had made the split decision to put up a tree to make the place feel more welcoming, more Christmassy in the hope that he could bring a little cheer into Mel's world.

"Got anything to hang on it, Mike?" he asked thinking this was the first time Mike had brought a tree from him.

"Got a point there, Harv, what ya got?"

"Well, I've got some lights," he said, making his way back inside. He reached up onto the top shelf and handed the box to Mike. "Should be enough for a tree that size," he told him, "and here's some multi-coloured baubles, on the house," he said, slipping them into his carrier bag.

Mike thanked him, settled his bill and then made his way back to his van, waiving a cheery goodbye to Harvey. He was a good bloke and had run that store for the last two decades. Mike opened the door to the rear of his van and shoved the tree in as far as he could, followed by two carrier bags and then he drove the two-minute journey to the end of his street.

He dumped his shopping on the kitchen floor and then made his way back down to the van for the tree. He was just wondering where to put it when he stopped by the side of his Morgan and stared. Bloody insurance company, still dragging their heels with regard to where the responsibility lay. Something else for him to have to sort, he thought, as he dragged the tree up the short flight of steps.

He unpacked the shopping and washed up the dishes that he had left lying around the place and then he went off to change the sheets on the bed. He was going to give the bedroom over to Mel and he was going to use the sofa for the time being. He then ran a vacuum around quickly and wiped the coffee table over with a cloth. The place looked OK, a little dishevelled but no worse than usual. A typical man-clean, he said to himself with a smirk. He stood for a while at the foot of the bed, wondering if he should unpack Mel's things or whether he should leave that to her. He decided to clear out the bottom drawer of his chest and then placed some of her clothes within. He hung two jackets, three blouses and a dress up in his wardrobe and then he placed her toiletries and make-up items in the bathroom. He stood staring at her perfume bottle momentarily and then sprayed some onto his wrist subconsciously. God he missed her, the smell of her suddenly overwhelming him. He stood transfixed for a few moments longer and then his thoughts turned to the tree. "Now, where am I going to put this tree?" he said out loud to himself.

He settled on the right-hand corner of the room, as it could be viewed from the sofa and was probably the only place it would fit. He unpacked the lights and strung them around the tree as best as his artistic eye could manage and then he randomly placed the baubles. He flicked the switch and stood back to admire his handiwork. Looks OK, he thought proudly. Brings a bit of Christmas cheer, he decided, and in any case he knew Mel would love it and that was the main thing. He looked at his watch and then grabbed his jacket, which he had left lying over the back of the sofa, and made his way back down to his van. Visiting time had started half an hour ago and Mel would be wondering where he was. He climbed into his van thinking about the sleeping arrangements. "What a plonker," he said out loud to himself as he turned on the ignition. He changed the sheets a day too early and would now have to sleep on the sofa tonight. Oh well, he thought, I'm gonna be on the sofa from now on anyway.

He arrived at the hospital just before 7pm, stopping briefly at the hospital shop for two coffees. He then made his way to Mel's ward and waited as usual for someone to release the doors. "For God's sake," he said out loud, pressing the buzzer again and banging on the window to attract someone's attention. Once again a visitor released the doors by pressing the button on the wall from within. "Thanks," Mike shouted to the old chap who was making his way back towards the nurse's station. This system really sucks, he thought, as he turned immediately right into Mel's room.

"Hey, Mel," he said, swooping in with a kiss for both cheeks. He handed her a coffee and perched on the edge of her bed. "How you doing?"

Mel put her coffee down on the bedside cabinet and then put both arms around his neck. "I've missed you," she said, almost in a whisper. "You're late tonight," she questioned, still holding onto him tightly. She released her grip and looked right into his eyes.

Mike suddenly felt really exposed, vulnerable, as he looked back into her eyes. "I'm sorry Mel," he said, avoiding her gaze. What was happening here, he thought? He suddenly felt so drawn to her, like he didn't want to ever let her go. He stood up and walked around the bed and sat down in the wingback chair. "I've been preparing the flat," he said, "for your release tomorrow. Wanted everything to be ready for you," he said with a smile. "Have you been given a discharge time yet?" he asked, wondering if it would be morning or afternoon.

"Yeah, eleven o'clock, after the doctor has seen me," she told him.

"OK, well I'll come up around ten thirty as I need to see what the doctor has to say, recommends, so to speak," he told her.

Mel reached out for his hand which she held onto tightly. "Thanks Mike, thanks for everything," she said, her eyes boring into his very soul, "I don't know what I would have done if I didn't have you," she told him.

"Hey, you will always have me, Hun," he said, stroking her cheek softly.

"Not if you go to South Wales," she said with a tear rolling down her cheek. South Wales, was the furthest thing from his mind.

He had actually forgotten Dhillon's proposal, as he had been so caught up with everything that was going on. "Look, let's not worry about that for the time being, Mel," he said, wiping her tears with a tissue from the box on her table tray. "We've got enough to get on with at the moment and I certainly don't have time to swan off to South Wales," he told her, trying to make her smile.

"Not now maybe," she said, "not for the time being but what about Dhillon's offer?" she questioned.

"Well, you're my top priority," he told her, "so stop worrying."

"Hey do you want to hear about the Gordon case?" he asked, in an attempt to steer the conversation away from South Wales.

"Yeah, of course," she said, adjusting her pillows and sitting up straight ready to receive the latest instalment.

"Well, I sat in on another hypnosis session, Mel. Has to be one of the most harrowing things I've ever witnessed," he told her. "This time, Mel, Nurse Somers took Jane through from the age of thirteen to sixteen, it was absolutely horrendous." Mike spent the next half hour explaining blow by blow what he had experienced, leaving nothing unsaid. "So, now we have another missing person, Helena," he told her, "and what was her fate, Mel, is she dead? What happened to her? It's really haunting me, to the extent that I think we are going to be digging up her remains, if, of course we could locate the house. There is one other thing," he said, taking her hand in his again. "Niko has been seen going in and out of The Sanctuary children's home. You know, the big mansion house at the top of Holden's Hill," he said, hoping that this wouldn't make her panic.

"What!," said Mel, letting go of his hand. "What's his connection there?" she questioned, her mind darting from one sinister thing to another.

"Well, we don't know yet," said Mike. "Paul and I went there this afternoon," he continued, "but drew a blank. The matron, or whatever you want to call her, Miss Rosenburg, claims to have never seen or heard of him and neither have her staff."

"Did you look around the home?" Mel questioned.

"Yes, including the grounds, Mel. We found round the back of the mansion house, about an acre away from the house, some woodland. It's accessible from Marshalswick Lane via a small gate. Anyway, we found an old cabin, well more of a shack really," he told her. "I expect it was quite nice at one time or another but is quite dilapidated now. Anyway, it looks like someone's hideaway, it's got some personal possessions, books, papers, etc. Outside was a small campfire with log seating and a kettle was suspended above the fire pit. The ashes were still warm, so we now have the place under surveillance."

"Surely is just a den that the kids from the home use?" queried Mel.

"Don't think so, Mel, there's fag butts everywhere."

"What? you're telling me that you never had a secret ciggie behind the bicycle shed at school," she said, giggling.

"Course, but this place had a basket of whisky, mainly empty bottles but whoever uses the place is a heavy whisky drinker and that's an odd choice for kids, Mel."

"Yeah, you're right, if it was beer, perhaps, but whisky that's too heavy duty," she said remembering how she hated the taste of whisky as a child and even the smell used to make her feel sick. "You think Niko's hiding out there don't you?" questioned Mel.

"We have to rule it out, Mel. He's been coming in and out of the home grounds and yet none of the staff recognise him. We've got to check it out, Hun."

"Yeah, course," said Mel, feeling a little vulnerable, as the mansion house was a stone throw from the hospital.

"Hey you're coming home with me in the morning and I'm not going to let anything happen to you, you hear?" he said, reading her mind.

"Sure," said Mel, pulling the blanket up under her chin.

"Right," said Mike, standing up, "is there anything I need to bring in the morning?" he asked.

"Yeah, there is actually," said Mel, "some boots or trainers for my feet, some underwear, jeans and a top," she requested, "and my coat."

Mike thought momentarily about whether he had unpacked any trainers. He hadn't actually unpacked any footwear at all. "What size are you, Mel?" he suddenly questioned.

"Six, why did you forget about my feet?" she asked, smiling.

"'Fraid so," he said, "but I'll pick some up in the morning." He kissed her on the cheek and told her that he would be back at 10.30 sharp with all her stuff and not to go anywhere without him.

He walked out of the hospital in a daze. How fucking stupid, he hadn't even considered her feet or the fact that it was the middle of winter and Elaine hadn't included a coat. He made his way back to his flat, parked the van and headed to his usual bar.

He woke to the sound of church bells at 8am prompt, draped across the sofa. He had set his alarm so that he would have time to nip into town for some trainers for Mel before collecting her from the hospital but somehow the thought of a shopping trip seemed really unappealing after sinking too many beers last night. He sat on the edge of the sofa with his head in his lap. Why did he do that? He was going to stop at two, but two turned into six, followed by a whisky chaser, as he sat wallowing by himself in one of the booths. He rose to his feet and made his way to the kitchen, flicked on the kettle and then headed towards the bathroom. He brushed his teeth for a full five minutes while he organised his day in his head and then he stepped into the shower. He was dressed and back in the kitchen within fifteen minutes with a small carrier containing Mel's clothes. He then fed Lola, made himself a coffee to go, as he didn't want to hang around. He wanted to get a move on as he had to choose a pair of women's trainers and a coat, and it had felt bad enough selecting a pair of panties and a bra from his bottom drawer. It made him feel so uncomfortable that he just wanted to get to the hospital and hand the stuff over.

Where was he going to get trainers on a Saturday morning without having to travel into town, he pondered. I know, he said to himself as he pulled away, the market along Pilgrims' Way. It was a small market, mainly fruit and veg sellers but it did have a number of clothes stalls and definitely had one that sold trainers, as he had eyed up a pair last year for himself when he went down there for some new work boots. It was also not too far from the hospital so would work well with his timetable. The market was right at the bottom of Pilgrims' Way, housed in the car park area of the community hall. The only problem was parking, as the market utilised the car park area, it made it necessary to park in neighbouring streets. It had been under discussion to move the market onto Pilgrims' Way itself but as yet was still in the place it had been for decades. Mike parked at the foot of Pilgrims' Way and walked the entire length of the road which was uphill. By the time he reached the top he was panting and stopped to draw breath, perching on someone's garden wall. He really was unfit and seriously needed to include some cardiovascular activities into his lifestyle. He gave himself five minutes and then headed into the market.

Although it was only 9.15, the market was already bustling with early shoppers eager to secure the bargain of the day. Mike wandered along the isles rather enjoying the banter and comradery that was exchanged between stall owners and punters and stopped at the coffee and breakfast wagon. He paused wondering if it would be too criminal to take a few minutes out for a bacon butty and then decided he couldn't pass up the opportunity. He watched mouth wateringly, struggling with the difficult decision of choosing between ketchup or brown sauce, which also seemed to be the conundrum for the chap in front of him in the queue. He found himself ordering a bacon bap with extra onions, together with a strong coffee, and took refuge at one of the spare tables under the awning. Mel would back him all the way, he thought as he took another bite from the steaming hot bap. He sat watching the hustle and bustle of the market, smiling at the effort the stall holders made with the tinsel and Christmas decorations, when he suddenly realised he was perched opposite the boot, trainer and shoe stall. Perfect, he thought, relieved that the stall still existed.

He finished his coffee and lit a cigarette, a pastime that was now becoming more and more habitual. Mel would be so cross if she knew. He really was going to have to reign himself in. He walked across to the shoe seller and perused the contents of his stall. He picked up a plain white pair, mimicking a well-known brand. Mike knew the market was full of fakes but who cared, they would serve a purpose. "Got these in a six, mate?" Mike asked, holding up the right foot of the display trainer.

"Sure, let me check my stock," the guy told him, as he rummaged through the shoe boxes stacked in the back of his van. Within a minute or so he was back with a box containing the trainers in a size six. "Fifteen quid please, mate," the guy offered, holding out his hand.

"Cheers," said Mike, passing him a twenty pound note. The guy rustled in his money belt and handed him back a fiver and Mike moved on in search of a jacket.

What the hell did he know about choosing a lady's jacket, he thought, as he wandered around aimlessly. He stopped at the last stall along the aisle where a woman was selling padded bomber-style jackets and was modelling one as an example. Mike glanced at all the different colours and settled on a navy one.

"What size do you need, Hun?" questioned the young girl running the stall. Mike didn't have a clue and hadn't even considered this obvious requirement.

He looked at the girl serving and said, "What size are you wearing? you look around the same size as my friend?"

"Twelve," she answered, "you need a twelve," she confirmed. She rustled amongst her stock and handed it across to him for his approval.

"How much, love?" he questioned, hoping he had enough cash on him.

"A tenner to you," she said as if she was doing him a favour.

"Right," said Mike smiling as he pulled his last ten pound note from his wallet, "Guess it was meant to be."

He walked back down the hill, rather pleased with himself that he had managed to achieve his objective and he felt certain Mel would approve of his choice. How was he doing for time? he suddenly wondered, hoping he wouldn't miss Mel's discharge appraisal. Nope, he was fine, still had twenty minutes.

Mel was perched at the end of the bed when he arrived and Daisy was helping her brush her hair. "Good morning, my two beauties," said Mike, smiling, as he entered the room with all his bags. He popped everything onto the bed and gave Mel a kiss on both cheeks. "How's the patient today, Daisy?" he asked, sitting down next to Mel.

"Yes, she's co-operating this morning," she said, giggling as she replaced the hairbrush on the bedside cabinet.

"Did you bring everything I asked for, Mike?" questioned Mel, pulling out the contents of the bags.

"Yep, but I didn't bring your jeans, Mel, you would never get them over the cast. Only thought of that shortly before I left the flat but thankfully there were some tracksuit bottoms amongst your stuff."

Mel pulled out her favourite tracksuit bottoms and smiled. "Ah, you brought my happy pants," she told him smiling, "my loungewear," she said looking across at Daisy. "Well, everyone has their comfy pants for lounging," she said pulling out her sweatshirt and holding it up for approval.

"Right, Mel, got you these," said Mike, opening the lid of the shoe box, "but don't get too excited, they're fakes," he said, handing them over to her.

"Ooh, there nice, Mike, great choice," she added, as she turned one over to check they were a six.

"And I got you a jacket, Mel, as Elaine sorted your stuff for me and she didn't pack one."

Mel pulled the jacket out from the bag with one hand and smiled. "It's perfect and you got the right size," she said, kissing him on the cheek.

"OK, young lady, let's get you dressed before Doctor Richard arrives," Daisy suggested, ushering Mike out of the room. Mike waited outside, pacing up and down, eager to get going. He really hated hospitals and he had spent far too much time in them recently. Daisy opened the door around five minutes later and invited him back in, just as Doctor Richards and his team arrived.

Mike extended his hand out to Doctor Richards, in a more humble fashion than the previous week. He remembered with embarrassment his unconstrained conduct and felt his cheeks flush as he shook the doctor's hand.

Doctor Richards shook it firmly and moved straight into his assessment of Mel. "So, how are we doing today, young lady?" he said, holding Mel's chin up, while he checked her pupil dilation.

"Ready to go home," said Mel, hoping that nothing would stop this from happening. She was feeling rather shaky and had experienced a night terror around 3am. She had woken in a hot sweat, heart racing, and had experienced a panic attack, probably from the thought of Niko being so close to the hospital. She wanted to keep this totally secret as she didn't want anything to interfere with her discharge. She knew that her emotional state was in a delayed status, like suspended animation, and that bit by bit it was going to come back to haunt her. But she also knew she would rather deal with her rehabilitation with Mike than in hospital, so was desperately determined that nothing was going to stand in the way today.

The doctor checked the notes hanging on the clipboard at the foot of the bed, to verify that her temperature and blood pressure were within an acceptable range and then checked her sprained wrist. Her neck brace had been removed the evening before but the doctor went to great lengths, examining her neck, together with the top of her spine. "How are your headaches, Mel, are they easing in their intensity?" he questioned again while taking another look at her pupils, together with the bruising around her eyes, temple and chin. Mel shook her head and told him that she was fine but the truth of the matter was she had experienced a severe headache yesterday, that had lasted all day. "Right Mel," said Doctor Richards, returning the clipboard to its original position, I see no reason why you can't go home today. We have allocated you some crutches but you will need some aided support with their use, while your wrist is gaining strength and we will obviously need to see you in around five weeks with regard to the cast removal and some physio sessions. I understand from my colleague that you would prefer to undertake some counselling sessions at home, as opposed to sessions within the hospital environment?" Mel nodded in agreement, she just wanted to go home with Mike. She looked over at Mike with a look that Mike recognised instantly. It was time to go.

Mike assisted Mel into her new bomber jacket and helped her into a wheelchair to aid her departure down to the hospital front doors. They both thanked Daisy for all her help and then Mike took one last look around the room to ensure they left nothing behind. There was nothing, Mel didn't have anything. She had been brought into reception in a torn dress and a hospital blanket from the ambulance driver. She had worn hospital gowns all week, as it had not been feasible to collect her belongings from her apartment, and now she was leaving in fake trainers and a market jacket. He looked down at her broken body as she sat in the wheelchair and felt real sadness. He wasn't going to let her down again, he was going to look after her, whatever it took. Damn South Wales, why did that offer have to come up now!

They were escorted by a nurse called Flo down to the front entrance, who waited with Mel while Mike brought the van round to the front porch. Flo assisted Mike with Mel's transfer into his van, so that they were considered safely off the premises and the liability ceased. Mike turned on the ignition and Mel fumbled with the radio channel choosing a suitable station and somehow, for that split second, things felt normal.

"Mike, it's kind of en route anyway, but do you think you could drive past The Sanctuary, just want to see its splendour. Never really paid too much attention to it before but you made it come alive when you were describing it?"

Mike looked at her and smiled. He had really missed her ways. The way she needed to see everything in minute detail and have every single detail etched on her mind. "Yeah sure," said Mike, "I'll pull up outside the gates, you'll get the best view from there."

"Have you met the owner?" questioned Mel, as they approached the gates a few minutes later.

"No, but there is a portrait hanging over the fireplace in the drawing room of a distinguished looking chap in a maroon cravat and green velvet jacket, which I suspect is him, and," he said, stopping outside the gates, "look at that sign, there is a small photo of its founder, I think it is the same person, just younger."

Mel strained to see and could just about make out a guy with a beard. "Do you know if he lives in the home or somewhere else?" questioned Mel, her attention now drawn to the house up on the hill.

"No, I didn't ask but that will be a question for later, now that you've raised it. What are you thinking, Mel?" asked Mike, knowing how her mind operated.

"Just think we need to check it out," she said. "It's quite something isn't it," said Mel, taking in the sweeping driveway and sculptured lawns.

"Mike, drive round the back to Marshalswick Lane please," she suddenly asked.

"No, Mel, we have that under surveillance and I don't want to draw attention to it. And in any case, that's kind of a weird request, seeing as we think Niko might hang out there. Actually, I'm not sure if it's brave or crazy but the answers still no, Mel. I took some photos of the cabin in any case, I'll show you them later, now let's head home."

"I didn't want to go in, Mike, just a drive-by," she said, reassuring him that she wasn't crazy.

"The answers still no, Mel."

They pulled up outside Mike's flat ten minutes later and Mike raced round to her side and opened the door. "Allow me, my lady," he said grinning, assisting her out of the van.

"Morgan's not been sorted yet then?" questioned Mel, staring at it in its sorry state, as she leant on Mike's arm for support.

"Nope, poxy insurance company is dragging its heels but don't get me started on that," he told her. "Now, young lady, how are we gonna get you up those stairs?" he questioned. "It may have to be a fireman's carry," he suggested, laughing. "Yeah, this is going to take some working out," he said, gesticulating various carrying positions and making her laugh. They settled on a hoist and hobble ascent until they reached the top, laughing. "I've really missed you, Mel," he said, blushing with sudden embarrassment.

"I've missed you too, Flossy," she said laughing.

"Now don't start that nonsense," he said, turning the key in the lock with a smile. He assisted her through the front door and said, "for you my princess," gesturing towards the tree.

"Oh, Mike, it's beautiful," she said, turning toward him smiling. "Interesting colour scheme but beautiful all the same," she told him.

"Well, it was from Harvey's up the road, as opposed to Knightsbridge," he said, jangling one of the baubles.

"Hey, Lola, mummy's back," said Mel, catching sight of her stretching out and then curling back up into a ball. Lola was draped across the arm of the sofa, completely oblivious to Mel's need to be reunited with her, as Mike assisted her over.

"Right, let's get you settled on the sofa and then you can watch me prepare my signature dish," he said, picking up his apron, as he watched Mel get reacquainted with her beloved cat. "You taking anything that could interfere with a beer?" asked Mike, opening the fridge door.

"If I was, I wouldn't care," she said, making herself comfortable, "I'm so overdue a beer, Mike."

Mike opened two beers and joined her on the sofa. "Do you want to see the photos I took of the cabin, or is that a bit too creepy?" he asked.

"No, you know I want to see them, Mike, show me," she said, trying to pull his phone out of his grasp.

"Hang on, Miss Impatience, let me pull them up," he said, passing her the phone.

"This is the part of the cabin I keep thinking about, Mel. You see, to me that looks like a place someone has spent a lot of time in, over a long period of time," he said.

"Yeah, it does look lived in," said Mel, widening the image on the screen. "Actually, if you ask me, it looks like somewhere that was lived in but not any more," said Mel. "To me it looks neglected," she said looking up at Mike. "You can almost imagine the smell of damp, its history, whatever went before."

"Somewhere that someone visits you mean?" said Mike, watching Mel swipe onto the next picture.

"Yeah, perhaps somewhere that meant a lot to someone once or somewhere that someone doesn't want to let go of or can't part with," she suggested. "Simply can't let go of," she added. Mike sat staring into space, his mind darting from one possible explanation to another, when Mel suddenly touched him on the arm. "Hey, you OK?" she said, wondering what was going through his mind.

"Yeah, I was thinking, what if Niko was a resident at The Sanctuary when he was a youngster and the cabin was somewhere he used to hang out, Mel?" he said, swigging at his beer. "He's got no papers, Mel," he said standing up and walking over towards the kitchen. He opened a cupboard, retrieved a pack of spaghetti and placed it on the counter. "No birth records, no national insurance number, nothing. Perhaps he was an orphan, Mel?" he suggested, as he gathered his ingredients from the fridge.

"Orphans have papers, Mike, they were still born to someone," she said, looking across at him.

"Yeah, but it seems weird to me that both him and Doreen basically don't exist on paper anywhere."

"What are you getting at, Mike? Do you think Doreen's from the home as well?" she questioned.

"Not just her, Mel, what about the Gordon girls," he said. "They've been missing for years and no one has reported them missing, like they don't exist either."

"What? do you think the Gordan case is linked to the home, Mike?" she said, as she watched Mike mix mince meat with breadcrumbs and an egg.

"I don't know, but I'm going back, something didn't feel right," he told her. He put two saucepans on the hob and started to prepare the sauce.

"Can I help you, Mike," she said giggling from the sofa.

Mike burst out laughing. "Help me?" questioned Mike, laughing and crying at the same time while chopping up an onion. "You can't cook, Mel, and right now you can't walk either, so I think it's best you stay where you are," he told her, reaching for a garlic clove. He placed the onion and garlic into the pan with a tin of tomatoes and added some herbs. Give me a minute to fry off these meatballs and add them to the sauce and then I can set them to simmer and I will be right back with you, young lady," he said, finalising his signature dish.

He grabbed two more beers from the fridge and returned to the sofa, retrieving his phone from Mel's hands. "Come on, let me have it," he said, coaxing it away from her. He swiped to the next picture showing the campfire and log seating and then looked across at

Mel. "Told you the campfire ashes were warm didn't I?" he questioned, picturing the fire alight and the kettle above it boiling to make tea.

"Yes, you did," she said, with a frown. "Who've you got on it, Mike? surveillance I mean," she questioned.

"I've assigned Jim and Dave to do tonight's watch and then Billy and Ben are taking over at six in the morning," he told her. "Right let me get this pasta on," he said, returning to the kitchen, "and give my speciality sauce a loving stir."

"You OK to eat it on the sofa, Hun?" thinking it would be a bit of a challenge at the breakfast bar on a bar stool.

"Yeah, I think that's the safest option, Mike."

Mike continued stirring his sauce, his mind now awash with all sorts of possibilities, wondering if Niko, in some way, had something to do with the Gordan girls. Or even if he had nothing to do with the girls it didn't mean to say that the girls didn't reside there at some stage. Mike decided that he would take the girl's photos back there, when he next visited. Wouldn't do any harm and it now needed to be ruled out.

"You been in contact with Pete, Mel?" he asked, as he tested a pasta strand. "Wow that's hot," he said, spitting it into the sink and regretting his actions. Deciding it was too al dente, he left it on the boil for a few more minutes and turned to face Mel. She was staring into space, totally oblivious to his question, making Mike question whether she was blanking the question out or merely just caught up in her own nightmare. He decided to ask the question again, as he retrieved two bowls from the cupboard. "You been in contact with Pete, Mel?" he questioned a second time, wondering if he should have saved this question till later. He really didn't want to ruin Mel's appetite, as he knew she wasn't ready to face reality and needed to escape from the truth for the time being.

Mel continued to stare at the wall and then stated that she had no intention of telling him, ever. "I don't want people knowing, Mike," she said, turning to face him. "I can't help the fact that our work colleagues know, we are police officers after all, but I don't want anyone outside that ring knowing," she told him sternly. "It's my business and my decision," she said, bringing an immediate close to the conversation.

"OK," said Mike, retrieving the pasta from the colander and transferring it to the bowls. "It's totally your call and I will support any decision you make," he told her, reconfirming her faith in him.

He tested the sauce and ladled the meat balls over the pasta, and grated some parmesan over the top. "Here you go," he said, passing one of the bowls to her, together with a fork. "You want some pepper on that, Hun?" he asked, grabbing the pepper grinder from the counter, as he retrieved his own bowl.

Mel nodded, accepting the grinder, as she smiled at Mike's efforts laid out before them. "This is delicious, Mike," she told him, sucking up a spaghetti strand without any finesse.

Mike laughed at her as he watched her wipe her face with her sleeve. "Yeah, you missed a bit," he said chuckling, pointing to her chin. He was so comfortable in her company and had really missed her being around and was so grateful that she was back. They spent the rest of the afternoon and early evening listening to music until they both fell asleep on the sofa. Mike stirred around 10.45, deciding it was time to throw in the towel. He had to be back at the psychiatric unit first thing, as it had been decided to put Jane under again, one last time.

"Hey, Mel," he said, giving her a gentle nudge, "time for bed, Hun, he said, stroking her cheek. He helped her across to the bedroom and over to the bed.

"Mike, just cover me over please, I'm too exhausted to get undressed," she said to him laying her head on the pillow. Mike dimmed the light and stepped back out into the front room. "Mike, don't leave me," she called, sitting up rubbing her eyes. She pointed to the other side of the bed, indicating that she wanted him to lie down next to her. "Please stay," she asked, "you make me feel safe."

Mike smiled and walked back towards her. He lay down next to her and put his arm protectively around her. "I will always keep you safe, Mel, I promise."

Nine

Mike sat waiting outside Isaac ward for Doctor Gyllensvan and Julie to make an appearance. He was a little ahead of schedule and was working out his timetable for the day ahead. He was nervous about leaving Mel at home, without his support, but he didn't want to miss the final hypnosis session with Jane. Doctor Gyllensvan's evaluation of the situation had concluded that one more session would be sufficient to undertake a good evaluation of the girl's plight to enable him to rehabilitate them, with the best possible outcome. Julie had indicated that she felt it would serve no purpose to risk any additional sessions due to their intensity and felt that they had sufficient knowledge to work towards a successful restoration of function and, hopefully, future happiness. She had also stated that she felt that it could be detrimental to undertake hypnosis sessions with Sally, who seems the more vulnerable of the two. Jane's sessions had provided adequate knowledge of their ordeal and would serve towards both outcomes.

He rose to his feet as he heard footsteps coming up the corridor, hoping that it would be them. The doors swung open and Doctor Gyllensvan and Julie breezed in carrying stacks of folders. "Good Morning Mike," he said cheerily, reaching out for his hand, as he attempted to juggle his folders. His temperament seemed somewhat improved from the last time he had been in his company, where he had seemed distracted and disturbed.

"Morning, Julie," said Mike, acknowledging her presence, as she reached out to enter the security code.

"Morning," she said pressing her finger onto the recognition panel. "How are you getting on with your investigation?" she asked him curiously, stepping back as the doors opened.

"Slowly," he answered, suddenly feeling frustrated at the lack of leads he had, "but I have some stuff to check out later, which may throw up some answers," he told her. He followed them down the corridor and into their usual room, where he chose the seat by the window. "How are the girls doing, Julie?" he asked wondering if there had been any change since he last saw them.

"There have been some significant changes since we reintroduced the girls," she told him, opening one of her folders and retrieving one of the loose papers. "Bringing them back together seems to have exhilarated their progress with regard to communication," she told him, smiling.

"Yes, we have observed conversations between the siblings which have proved invaluable," said the doctor, glancing down at his notes. "One of the more interesting developments we have witnessed is Jane, or should we refer to her as Linda, she has been questioning their true identity," he said rising to his feet. "Yes, we have observed her telling Sally that she remembers, or thinks she remembers, that their names were Linda and Rachel and not Roberta and Anika. They have spent so many years suppressed, locked away, made to be someone else that they have been brainwashed to the extent that the younger of the two appears to have no memory of what went before," he told him, as he walked over to the window. He stopped, turned and looked directly at Mike. "Today's session is primarily to continue with the chain of events that we have learned so far but I don't think this will lead us to the girl's origin but may lead us to the perpetrator," he told him. "Now let's go in," he said walking over to the door.

Mike wondered how much of his childhood he could remember before the age of seven and concluded it was very little and that was without having undergone trauma.

He followed the doctor out of the room and Julie closed and locked the door, leaving the folders available for their return later. Thankfully, today there were no screams or tormented sounds coming from any of the rooms, making their journey down the corridor less agonising. Mike waited while the doctor tapped in his code, leaving Julie to make her way round to Jane's room. Once more, Mike sat in the front row of what was to be the most harrowing production to date. He watched as Julie went through her usual routine of setting the projection stars on the ceiling and dimming the lights, wondering if they would learn today the fate of Helena. Mike jumped nervously as he heard Julie click her fingers and then they were transported back below stairs into the horrific world that had become their nightmare.

"Anika, bring me another damp flannel," Roberta instructed from the bedroom, as she bathed Helena's forehead. "We need to keep her temperature down as much as we can," she told her. Roberta had just finished reading a novel from their collection about a nurse who catered for a small hamlet called Carleton St Peter in South Norfolk and was using her new-found knowledge to help Helena who was seriously ill. This was hindered by their lack of any medical knowledge, as the first aid box lay open on the bed devoid of anything useful. Helena was seriously hot and sweating profusely and was now completely delirious. She was screaming out in pain and there was nothing the girls could do to help her.

"What's wrong with her?" questioned Anika, a tear rolling down her cheek. "Why is she screaming like that?" she added.

"I don't know, Anika, I'm not a doctor but I think it's to do with her terrible cough." The book she had been reading covered a section about a man who had bronchitis that led to pneumonia and he had died. She didn't want to tell Anika this but was seriously worried that Helena faced the same fate. "I'm scared," said Anika, starting to cry. "What if she dies, Roberta, what will we do then?" she questioned between sobs.

"Anika, I really don't know," she said feeling helpless and frightened all at the same time. "We need something to fan her with, to keep her cool," suggested Roberta. Anika selected a pamphlet-style book from the shelving and flapped it back and forth over Helena's face. She watched as Roberta tried to tip some water into her mouth but this made her gag and then she threw up over

everything. Anika burst into tears again and then started to gag from the smell, rushing from the room. Helena was gagging and gasping all at the same time and then a terrible rasping and rattling noise came from her mouth.

"What's happening," said Anika from the doorway. Roberta, stood up and stepped back, shaking uncontrollably, as she watched her friend scream out in agony. Helena started to shake violently, lifting up from the bed, thrashing back and forth, she gave one final, rattling gasp and dropped back on the bed, her head hanging to one side.

"No," screamed Roberta, "no, don't die, Helena, don't die," she screamed. She placed her hand on her chest but there was nothing, no movement, no life, totally still. "She's dead," said Roberta looking down at her, the woman who had become their true friend, who was now laying on her bed with her mouth wide open staring up at the ceiling, was dead.

"She can't be," said Anika, starting to panic. Anika raced out of the bedroom, across the living room and started banging on the door. "Help us someone, help us," she screamed over and over. "Please help us," she shouted. She dropped to her knees and started sobbing uncontrollably and then she curled up into a ball. Roberta sat on the bed opposite staring at her dear friend, tears running down both cheeks. They had both grown to love Helena deeply during the year she had been confined with them and she had enriched their lives with tales and stories of her previous life and what the outside world was like. While she was only a few years older than Roberta, she had led a full life before coming to England, which turned out to be the worst decision of her short life. Roberta stood up and pulled a sheet over her, so that she didn't have to see the look of torment on her friend's face, and then she laid down on the other bed and waited.

And wait they did, as another two weeks went passed and their food supplies depleted. Roberta looked across at Anika who was rocking back and forth and now seemed totally unreachable. They hadn't eaten in four days and the smell of rotting flesh was overwhelming. They were both too frightened to go into the bedroom and had confined themselves to the living room entirely. 'I'm so hungry," said Anika, rocking back and forth, willing her father to return with their food supplies. They faced yet another night sharing their accommodation with a corpse when suddenly the lights started to flicker over and over until finally they went out, leaving them in total darkness.

"What's happening?" screamed Anika, clinging onto Roberta for dear life.

"I don't know," said Roberta, "must be a power cut or maybe the bulb's blown," she told her.

"I can't do this," screamed Anika, "I can't do this," she repeated, running towards the bedroom. "I want Helena," she sobbed opening the bedroom door.

"Wait," screamed Roberta, "don't go in there," she said, trying to prevent her from entering. It was too late, she had pulled the sheet off Helena, revealing the most horrific sight. Helena had turned green with patches of red, her face was completely bloated and her eyes looked like they were popping out of their sockets. Liquid was oozing out of her open mouth which had frothed all over her cheeks and pillow. The smell of gas was overwhelming and Anika vomited involuntarily all over her. She then dropped to the floor and wailed. Roberta sat down on the floor next to her sister and held her in her arms. They rocked back and forth until Roberta let out the most horrific scream.

Mike watched completely transfixed as he watched Julie bring an end to the session, which had become too harrowing for Jane to continue. You could see the look of panic on Julie's face as she counted down explaining that as soon as she clicked her fingers she would remember nothing of the session undertaken. Roberta was rocking so violently back and forth, she kept hitting her head on the floor over and over. Julie was trying desperately to prevent her from further injury as she continued to count down, until she finally reached the point where she could click her fingers. Julie was sitting in the middle of the floor cradling Jane in her arms, gently swaying back and forth, stroking her face.

Mike could feel himself trembling as he watched Julie go through the motions of guiding Jane back over to the bed and covering her over. He turned and looked across at the doctor who was still facing the viewing window and showing no signs of moving. Mike felt that he had lost the use of all his limbs, they felt heavy and as though all the blood had been drained from his very being. He honestly thought that he must have stopped breathing at some point, as he slowly felt his circulation return. This session had pulled him in far too far and was becoming dangerous. It was one thing watching a movie where you knew it was total fiction but another thing entirely when you knew this was genuine suffering. God, how long did they have to endure sharing their space with a corpse? Mike wondered and how long did they go without food and lighting? It was unimaginable.

Doctor Gyllensvan was still staring through the viewing window when Julie re-entered the room. "OK," she said, observing the doctor's transfixed expression. "That definitely re-confirms that that will be the final session, for the time being," said Julie. "I think it would be detrimental to continue and could seriously hinder their progress," she told them, reiterating her earlier comments.

Doctor Gyllensvan nodded in agreement, as he rose to his feet. "Yes, for a while, I did seriously wonder if we had gone a step too far in there but you pulled it back just in time, Julie, well done," he said, ushering them all out of the viewing room. They had all taken something different with them, as they made their way back to the Think Tank. During each session they could only hear Jane's side of the conversation so had had to interpret the flow of the conversation by her answers and responses. Therefore, they had all a different interpretation of the events that had taken place. They now needed to put this information together, so that they could unravel, comprehend and decipher the code, the missing dialogue to complete the script for analysis.

Mike could feel his mobile vibrating in his pocket as they made their way back down towards the Think Tank. He retrieved it from his pocket and saw it was Mel. She had received a non-scheduled visit from a counsellor who she had refused to allow access and had now worked herself up into a panic. Damn, thought Mike, knowing this would really unnerve Mel. He sat down at the table, knowing he would need to make a hasty return to his flat and that he needed to bring his dealings with the doctor to a premature close.

"Doctor Gyllensvan, I have received an urgent call from my partner and need to get back to the station ASAP," he said, slightly altering the facts. "Very horrifying session today and highlights without doubt that they were mentally abused, imprisoned and starved for over a decade." Mike could feel his hatred for this abuser running through his veins and knew that he wasn't going to rest until he had him behind bars. "I would also like to thank you for allowing me to sit in on the sessions, which will, without a doubt, help us build a picture of the perpetrator and hopefully lead to his arrest."

Doctor Gyllensvan shook Mike's hand and asked to be kept up to date with his investigation and then Julie held the door open to aid his departure.

"Thank you Julie," I appreciate all of your input. Please continue to keep in touch regarding the girl's progress," he asked, as he shook her hand.

"Indeed, likewise," she said, as she watched him walk back up the corridor. Julie nodded at the security guard, who was standing just inside the double door, to release them, allowing him to step back out into civilisation.

Fucking hell, that was chilling, he thought to himself, as he signed out of the visitor book and made his way back up the staircase. How long had the corpse rotted before being removed and where was it now? he wondered, as he weaved his way through the car park. That was by far the worst session and he suddenly felt so grateful that he wouldn't have to witness any more.

His attention turned to Mel. Who had come knocking on his door? No sessions had been booked yet, which made Mike feel really uncomfortable about this unscheduled visitor. He had wanted to go back to The Sanctuary first, before returning to his flat but now he would have to turn things around. Mel came first. He drove down Holden's Hill, stopping at the lights and stared at the mansion set back in the distance. What had gone on there? What unimaginable horrors had emerged from that house? The lights changed and Mike's thoughts turned back to Mel. He wondered if the visitor had been male or female. Mel hadn't indicated in her short text and now Mike's mind had gone into overdrive. He could feel his anxiety rising and the short ten-minute drive felt like hours.

"For fuck's sake," he shouted out loud, stopping at yet another set of lights. "How many lights can there be on one road?" he screamed again, thumping his fists on the steering wheel. He pulled up outside his flat seven minutes later and took the stairs two at a time. "Mel, it's me," he shouted as he turned the key in the lock. The door opened slightly, stopping sharply from the security chain. "Hey, Mel," he said wiggling the chain, "let me in ."

Mel slowly made her way over to the front door with the use of one crutch. Her wrist was still far too weak to operate two. "I'm coming," she yelled as she hobbled towards the door. She released the chain and stepped back from the door.

"You OK?" said Mike, pulling her towards him for a hug.

"Yeah, guess so, but I'm worried, Mike, as I haven't booked any sessions yet and I really doubt they would send someone unscheduled, especially a male. "They sent a guy? Mel, I don't think that was the hospital, surely they wouldn't be so thoughtless. What did he say?"

"He knocked on the door and stupidly I called out, asking who it was, that immediately gave the game away that I was in and alone," she told him, "and when I heard a man's voice saying he was the counsellor, I just knew he was lying."

"Have you called the hospital?" said Mike, pacing up and down.

"Yes, they know nothing about it," said Mel, hobbling over to the sofa. She sat down with a sigh. "He's back for more, Mike, isn't he?" she said, a tear rolling down her cheek.

Mike paced up and down, articulating with his fists. "I'm going to kill that bastard when I get him, Mel. I'm gonna crush him. He thinks he doesn't exist now, well I'm going to wipe him off the planet." Mike pulled his phone out of his pocket and dialled Paul. "Paul, get me someone over to my place now," he instructed. "I think Niko just paid Mel a visit. In fact, send me two guys. I want one inside the flat and one outside surveilling," he instructed. He threw his phone onto the sofa and continued to pace.

"Hey, Mike, calm down," you're making me even more nervous," she said, trembling from the thought of Mike taking on Niko.

"Did you see him through the window or anything?" questioned Mike, sitting down on the sofa next to her. He took her hand and kissed it. "Did you see anything, Mel?" he questioned again.

"No," said Mel, "I was hiding. Stupid really, as he already knew I was in here, after I called out."

"Hey, it's not stupid, you must have been petrified," he said, letting go of her hand and standing up. "I'm not leaving you here alone, Mel, not any more," he added. "I want someone with you at all times, until we catch that bastard," he told her firmly.

"Mel, I'm going to stake out the cabin area tonight with the lads," he told her, walking over to the window. He pulled the blind to one side, looking out for his colleagues and then returned back over to the sofa.

"But I want you here with me," said Mel, taking hold of his hand.

"I know, Hun, but the lads have been at it around the clock and I just can't sit here doing nothing," he told her. "You're perfectly safe, Mel, you're being looked after, I promise."

Mel knew she wouldn't be able to persuade him otherwise, she'd worked with him far too long to know you couldn't change his mind if he was set on something. "OK, Mike, but be careful, he's a ruthless bastard," she said, knowing how vicious he was.

"So am I," said Mike, walking over to answer his front door.

Tina came through the door like a tornado, blown in from the west. "Is she OK, Mike, what happened?" she asked, walking straight past him to get to Mel.

"We think Niko tried to pay her a visit," he said, stepping back as she raced passed. She sat down next to Mel and reached out for her hand, giving it a squeeze. Mel smiled as she dried her tears on a crumpled-up tissue, discarded on the coffee table.

"I don't want to leave her here on her own," he told her, "I want someone with her at all times," he instructed, grabbing his jacket from the back of the sofa.

Tina nodded in agreement, "I'll sit with Mel, to keep her company and Ed's outside surveilling the place," she confirmed.

Mike kissed Mel on the forehead and promised to call her later, thanked Tina and then headed back down to his van. He just couldn't stand around doing nothing. He felt helpless and just couldn't settle, not now he knew Niko was on the prowl. His place was a mere ten minutes from the cabin and he now felt certain that this was Niko's hang out. It was only 1pm but he felt like he had put in a full day already. It was a miserable day, overcast and smoggy and the thought of sitting about watching a woodland area didn't exactly fill him with joy. He drove to the station to switch cars. He was worried Niko might recognise his van so decided this was his best option. He called Ben and told him that he would take over and then gracefully pulled into position between two parked cars, a few yards from where Ben and Billy were parked. Ben pulled away slowly after seeing Mike pull up and then he sat and waited.

He hadn't done any surveillance stuff for years, as he usually gave it over to the rookies but he had his best men on this. There was no pulling rank on this one, everyone was taking a turn. He bit into a sausage roll he had bought en route and then opened a can of coke. It was going to be a long afternoon.

His head was reeling with possible scenarios as his thoughts drifted from one case to the other. To him the two cases seemed to be merging and he seriously wondered if the Gordon girls originated from The Sanctuary. He fished his mobile from his jacket pocket and selected Paul's number. Paul answered on the third ring and seemed a little out of breath. "You OK, mate?"

said Mike, wondering what he was up to.

"Yeah, just climbed a flight of stairs," he said, drawing breath. "What's up?"

"Paul, I've been running things over, trying to tie everything together and I keep merging The Sanctuary with both the Niko and Gordon case. I am now beginning to wonder if the Gordon girls originated from The Sanctuary as well," he told him.

"Go on," said Paul.

"Well, we already suspect that Niko has a strong connection with the home and I think that also applies to Doreen, who possibly worked there but now I'm wondering about the girls. Mainly due to the fact that there is no record of two sisters going missing," he told him.

Paul sighed, "Yeah, I see where you're coming from," he said, slowly piecing it together. "My thoughts keep taking me to the fact that Niko and Doreen have no records and it seems the girls are the same. All four don't seem to exist anywhere. Where are you now?" questioned Paul, thinking he would like to revisit the home.

"I'm on watch at the cabin," he said, "but I was hoping you could go back to The Sanctuary!"

"Yep, I'm on it, Mike," he said, "I'll leave now."

"Paul, take the girls' photos with you. I know they are probably a decade out of date but show them using the name Linda and Rachel and see what reaction you get. Oh, and take one of Doreen as well, as I think she may have worked there, possibly in the kitchen," he told him. "Cheers, mate." He ended the call and took another bite of his sausage roll. Everything points to that home, he thought.

He made numerous calls, checked on Mel a couple of times and then started to fidget. God, this is so boring, so laborious, he thought, trying to get comfortable. It was almost 4pm, dark and absolutely freezing and he really needed to stretch his legs. He kept checking his phone hoping that Paul had pulled something out the hat, when it suddenly rang making him jump. "Hey, Paul, how did it go?" he asked, regaining his composure.

"Yeah, I get the feeling they are hiding something, Mike. Not too sure about the girls, as too much time has gone by and the staff have changed numerous times over the years, but Doreen's photo seemed to provoke a reaction with some of the kitchen staff, although they all denied knowing her, of course. But I could tell that some of them did, as their expressions changed, almost froze and then, you know when someone babbles too much, denying all knowledge but over-does it, well that's how it appeared," he told him.

"OK, well thanks, Paul, I'm still at the cabin and will be for a few more hours but nothing to report yet," he said, suddenly sitting up. Mike hung up quickly and reached for his binoculars, aiming them at the gate leading to the cabin. "What the fuck was that?" he questioned out loud, thinking he had just witnessed someone going into the gate. He sat motionless, momentarily, thinking about his next move. He began to question whether he actually saw something, trying to replay it in his mind. It was definitely someone but whether it was Niko, he couldn't tell. Time to find out, he decided. They could be completely wasting their time staking this place if it belonged to someone totally unrelated to the case.

He gave it a few more minutes to allow whoever it was to make their way into the thick of the woods, before climbing out of the car. He could feel himself shaking a bit, as this could be a real big moment, coming face to face with Niko. What he had done to Mel outraged him, sickened him and tormented him daily. How was he going to remain professional when he wanted to rip his fucking throat out? He opened the gate quietly and slipped into the woodland, treading carefully so as not to make a sound. God, this is impossible, he thought as leaves rustled under foot and then a twig snapped and then another. He crept as best as he could, sheltering behind each tree, until he reached a good viewing point and stopped. He stayed hidden by the thicket, watching and wondering, willing it to be him. Please let it be him, he prayed. He could see a light shining inside the cabin and the silhouette of a large figure with his back to the window frame. Another oil lamp was swinging outside the front door, lighting up the log-seating area. Whoever it was had already lit the campfire, which was beginning to take hold and the whole scene looked like something out of an old western. Mike waited patiently pondering his next move. He decided to wait awhile. After all, if he had lit the fire then he had every intention of sitting by it, he decided. He needed to see his face, make absolutely certain before he pounced. The fire was really beginning to build, which in turn emphasised the bitter cold from where Mike was hiding and he could feel the damp seeping into his bones. All he had on was his leather jacket and he was absolutely frozen to the core.

The door of the cabin slowly opened, dragging along the floor, and the silhouette made his way over to the log seating and sat down. Was it him? he questioned, watching the man rub his hands together over the fire and then swig from one of the whisky bottles. He strained to see, kicking himself for leaving his binoculars in the car, as he tried to capture his features in the light of the flickering flames. Fuck, it's him, it's definitely him, he said to himself over and over. He would never forget that ugly face, full of hatred and evil. He froze, wondering about his next move and how he would approach this piece of shit. He had to get this right, he couldn't afford for him to get away, he needed to call it in. He struggled with his conscience, battling between right and wrong, knowing what he should do but how could he, how could he be professional, not after what he had done to Mel. He watched as he took another swig from the bottle and then watched as he spat into the fire, making it hiss and spit. A total fucking animal thought Mike as he leaped from the bushes.

Mike ambushed him head on, forcing him backwards off the log, crashing into the front of the cabin. He then grabbed him by the throat and dragged him over to the fireside, before Niko had time to defend himself.

"Who the fuck are you?" Niko shouted, trying to fend Mike off.

Mike stopped and stared, rage running through him like never before. "Who the fuck am I, you question? I'll tell you who the fuck I am, you sick, twisted bastard. I'm the partner of Mel, you know the beautiful young woman you raped and tortured and left for dead," he said, spitting in his face. "You've ruined her life, you sick, evil bastard. How could you do that to someone? How could you take something that's not yours from someone so helpless, so defenceless?" he screamed. "What kind of a man are you that could take something so innocent and destroy it, turn someone's world to shit?"

"She's no innocent, she's pulled the wool right over your eyes," he said rising up off the floor. She's always got men coming and going from that apartment but you're too stupid to see it. Her tops are always far too low, if you ask me she was gagging for it," he told him, almost spitting the words at him.

Mike flew at him with such force, the final hinge on the door snapped forcing it down on top of them both. They struggled underneath the door, trying to break free until the rage in Mike superseded and he forced it off towering up over Niko. Mike reached for a rock and held it up high over his head. "Answer me you fuck. How could you take someone's world and turn it to shit?" Mike was trembling as he held the rock over Niko's head. He knew if he did this he could never take it back but he wanted to kill him and he could taste the hate.

"Because it was done to me," screamed Niko, forcing Mike backwards, while he was off guard. "Because it was done to me," he said, trying to stand up and then dropping to his knees, "because it was done to me," he repeated a third time…

Mike stopped, tried to regain some order to his thought process, feeling sickened at the thought of almost killing someone. He too was on his knees as Niko cracked, whimpering.

"What do you mean?" questioned Mike, wiping the blood from his mouth with his sleeve. "Doesn't give you the right to do it to someone else," he said, trying to get up off the floor.

"I loved him," said Niko in a childlike voice, not really making sense. "He was everything to me, I lost everything, including my life, the life I knew as a boy," he said, looking up towards the sky. Niko's voice sounded different. like he was a young boy, a teenage boy, frightened and vulnerable. He was almost whispering as though he was a child again and it made Mike feel like he was about to relive a very powerful moment in his life. Something he had kept hidden, buried, but was about to spill.

"I was fifteen at the time, innocent as you put it, when my world came crashing down," he said trembling. "My life was mostly good, with the exception of my mother," he said, his voice growing shaky. "She was a whore, having affairs left right and centre, which eventually drove my father to drink, when she left. My father was a great man and I loved him but she wore him down, which resulted in him taking solace in the whisky bottle."

"What the fuck has this got to do with Mel," said Mike growing angry. "This is not a psychiatric session and I'm not the local priest. You want to repent, well you can pray all you like in prison," said Mike, dragging him up by the collar.

"I killed them," said Niko, "I killed them," he shouted. Mike released his grip, making Niko stumble backwards onto the floor again.

"Killed who?" screamed Mike. "Who did you kill?" he repeated. "Two little girls," he said whimpering, "two little girls," he said in a whisper.

Mike grabbed him by the collar, staring straight into his face. "What two little girls?" screamed Mike, shaking him violently.

"Roberta and Anika," he said, choking on the words, as he repeated them.

"Mike, stop," shouted Paul, verbally forcing him to release his grip on Niko, "let me take it from here," he said, rushing forwards in an attempt to separate them.

"It was him, Paul," said Mike, staggering backwards, totally blown away by Niko's confession. "He did it. He killed Roberta and Anika," he said, rage taking hold of him again. "Take him in, take that sick bastard in," he instructed, unable to believe what he had just heard.

Paul grabbed hold of Niko by the collar and arm and led him through the woodlands towards the car, reading him his rights as they went. He had felt uncomfortable about Mike doing a stakeout by himself and had decided to join him. Thank God he had, he thought, as he encouraged Niko into the back of his car, after handcuffing him.

Mike sat down on the log, unable to believe what Niko had just confessed to. "Jesus, I didn't see that coming," he said out loud.

Paul drove Niko back to the station in silence and Mike followed on behind. Mike's head was now spinning, wondering how long ago these murders took place and why these girls were not reported missing. Were they from The Sanctuary, too, he wondered? Mike arrived back at the station, as Paul was booking Niko in, so he made his way to the gents to clean up. He looked in the mirror and sighed. Least his nose wasn't broken, just a fat lip to contend with, he thought. He washed his face and dried it on some toilet roll and then reached for his comb in his pocket. He was about to go into the arena and he wasn't coming out until he knew everything. He made his way back out to the check-in desk to clarify what room Niko had been taken to and then he headed down the corridor. He stopped outside the door, took a deep breath and then turned the handle.

Paul was sitting in the interview room opposite Niko and the tape recorder was set ready to record. Mike sat down next to Paul and pressed the record button. "This interview is being conducted at Holden Central Crime Investigation Department on Monday the 16th December 2019, at 5.20pm. Present in the room is Mr Niko Dimitriou, Detective Constable Paul Osman and Detective Sergeant Mike Brugge," said Mike, following protocol.

"Today at approximately 4.20pm Niko Dimitriou was apprehended in the grounds of The Sanctuary Children's Home, where he confessed to the murder of two young girls, Roberta and Anika, surname, as yet, unknown," said Mike, going straight in for the jugular.

"No," screamed Niko. "I didn't murder them, I didn't say I murdered them. It was an accident," he shouted. "An accident," he repeated, his voice now almost whispering. "My father had driven us into Ramchester, something he often did on a Saturday," he said, his eyes darting between Mike and Paul. "There was a bar there, his favourite, all his mates went there," he added. "He was once again drowning his sorrows and had one too many for the road, so to speak," he said looking up at the ceiling as if recalling it bit by bit. "This was a regular occurrence, only this time he was way over the limit and could barely stand. He drove an articulated lorry for a living and as we didn't have a family car, he used to use that on weekends. He was teaching me to drive and sometimes he used to let me drive back from the pub." Paul went to interject but Mike raised his hand, preventing him from speaking, as he didn't want Niko to change his mind about confessing all. He wanted him to spill it all out now, while he was vulnerable, before he regained any strength.

"He was really bad so I had to help him outside, as he was stumbling all over the place. It was getting late and the locals in the pub had mentioned a storm was heading in our direction and I really wanted to get on our way. I knew I would have to drive, as he could barely stand up. I had done it loads of times before but I was nervous, as I wanted to get it over with before the rain came in. I really struggled getting him into the cabin as he was so heavy but eventually I managed to buckle him in. It was just starting to spit when I climbed up into the cabin and I was praying we would make it home before it got too bad. We were about halfway when the storm hit hard and I could barely see a foot in front of us. By then my father had fallen asleep and kept falling towards me as we went round the bends in the mountain. The wind was howling and the rain just kept falling and the windscreen wipers just couldn't take it away quick enough. I couldn't see and I was so scared, so scared," he repeated, "I was only fifteen for fuck's sake. I turned the bend and then I saw a light, someone waving furiously in the road." Niko placed his head in his hands, tears rolling down his cheeks, he wiped them away, viciously with the sleeve of his leather coat and then tried to regain some strength. He gulped and then continued. "It was too late, they were in front of me before I could stop and I ploughed them off the side of the mountain. I froze, unable to move and my father was reaching over to me. He had blood streaming down his face, as somehow he had managed to unbuckle himself en route and had hit the windscreen full on. There was an explosion and I knew I had killed them but I just couldn't move. My dad's last words to me was to save myself and to transfer him into the driver's seat and then he died. I didn't know what to do, I was in shock. But then there was a second explosion, which somehow encouraged me to drag my father into the driver's seat. I shouldn't have done it. I basically let my father carry the can for wiping out a family. I killed four people that day, two little girls, their mother, Mary, and my father."

He stopped and looked up, he had spoken totally uninterrupted for twenty minutes. "But I never murdered them," he repeated. "I was fifteen, fifteen," he repeated, trembling from his confession. Mike was trying to do some mental arithmetic in his head, to establish how long ago this tragedy had taken place, if Niko was around fifteen at the time.

"What year was this?" Mike asked, finally interjecting after letting Niko spill all.

"December 1976," he said, staring at the floor, "1976."

Mike looked over at Paul, totally bewildered. No wonder there was nothing in the news about these girls. They had been focusing their search over the last ten to twenty years, in relation to the ages and established captivity of the Gordon girls. This scene of events spanned over forty-three years. The Gordon girls had been in captivity for round ten. If these girls were the replacements for Roberta and Anika, then the likelihood was, thought Mike, the true horror unfolding, the likelihood was there would be further victims.

Mike rose to his feet and started to pace up and down. He stopped, turned and stared directly at Niko. "What is your relationship with

The Sanctuary Children's home?" he questioned, wondering if Niko had resided there after the accident.

"Well, after the accident I went to stay with foster parents but I just couldn't settle. The guilt of letting my father take the blame, ruining his reputation and letting everyone think he was drunk behind the wheel was too much to handle and I started getting into trouble. My foster parents soon realised I was broken and decided I couldn't be fixed. They placed me there."

"What happened to your mother?" questioned Paul, wondering why she didn't come forward.

"I have no idea, she left long before and I never heard from her again. She was a slag, if she hadn't of tortured him with all those men, this would never have happened. She drove my father to drink," he said, starting to get angry again.

Mike could see that Niko hated his mother and that this extended to all women. He looked upon them as nothing but whores, all tarred with the same brush.

"She ruined his life and mine," he said, a look of hatred unfolding across his face. "This is all her fault," he said, starting to get agitated. Mike could see that Niko's normal demeaner was starting to reappear and he knew he needed to press on if he was going to get any more information from him.

"Were you happy there?" asked Paul, deciding too that they needed to extract as much from Niko as possible before he shut down.

"I was at first but that soon changed," he said, a look of despair overshadowing him.

"What happened?" asked Mike, wondering what changed.

"The home changed hands. Originally, it was a short-stay foster home but a guy called Joseph Treville bought it outright and turned it into a full-time home for children to live permanently, where they could be educated and live as one big family."

"Didn't you fit in? What changed?" asked Paul curiously.

Niko stood up from his chair and placed his hands on each corner of the table, a look of rage unfolding on his face. "He was the father of Roberta and Anika. Yes, I had wiped out his entire family. I couldn't believe that fate had brought us together again." Niko looked as though he was about to pick the table up and throw it across the room but instead he sat back down and buried his head in his hands. "Joseph Treville had been paid out thousands in insurance compensation from the crash and had bought The Sanctuary outright. I think his original aim was to try to replace his family with a new, larger one and be a father figure for every needy child that entered the establishment but one day he snapped and a monster unfolded."

"Go on," said Paul, looking over at Mike. "Did he know that you were in the vehicle that ploughed his entire family off the mountain side?"

"Yes, he had read everyone's case notes. He was very thorough and wanted to help everyone and seemed like a really nice guy at first. I spent a lot of time in his company and he was very sympathetic that I had been involved in the tragedy and treated me like a victim of circumstance. He actually treated me like a son and we grew very close. We used to sit in the wingback chairs placed either side of the inglenook fireplace in the evenings and talk for hours.

"However, the guilt wore me down and late one evening after a long heart to heart, I spilled out the truth that it wasn't my father and that I was the one driving the lorry. This horrendous look of torture unfolded on his face and then he flew out the chair and grabbed me around the throat. I thought I was going to die as he kept pressing and pressing but then he lifted me up off the floor and threw me against the wall cabinet. Everything came crashing down on top of me and then he leaped on me, beating and beating me. When he finally stopped he looked up to the ceiling and howled like an animal. I could see the veins popping in his neck and he was a fierce red colour and he was spitting rage. He was frothing at the mouth when he finally stood up and then he left the room.

"Doreen, the housekeeper found me and nursed my wounds and tried to keep me safe from the horrendous beatings. She became my only friend."

"How long did the beatings go on for?" Mike asked, picturing the whole harrowing scene.

"Years," said Niko. "I used to hide out in the woods in the log cabin and Doreen used to bring me food when she could. Can I have some water?" he asked, staring at the floor. He looked beaten, he had been carrying this series of events his entire life.

Mike spoke into the tape recorder, advising that they were going to reconvene in half an hour and brought the first part of the session to a close. Mike walked out of the room, instructing the guard standing outside to bring Niko some water and then he headed to the coffee machine with Paul in tow.

"Fucking hell," said Mike, reaching for his glasses. He selected his usual and leaned against the wall. "What did you make of that?" he said, pondering whether to go outside for a cigarette.

"I think something snapped inside Joseph Treville that night, something so terrible that he metamorphosed into a schizophrenic monster," said Paul. "I've read books, some fiction, some theory where a perfectly normal person gets pushed to the limit and snaps. It triggers something inside their subconscious where two personalities battle it out. In most cases one dominates the other, takes control, and in some cases the lesser personality doesn't know the sinister side exists."

"Do you think Joseph Treville abducted the Gordon girls?" asked Mike, adding another sugar sachet to his coffee.

"Time to find out," said Paul, heading back down the corridor.

Mike called out to Karen, who was typing furiously into her keyboard. "Karen, please call Mel and let her know we have Niko in custody. I don't want her freaking out, thinking he's still at large," he told her, "and let the guys on the case know our current position."

Karen nodded in acknowledgement and proceeded to put Mel's mind at rest.

Mike and Paul re-entered the interview room and Mike pressed record on the tape. "Interview reconvened at 6.45pm on 16th December, 2019, at Holden Central CID. Present in the room are Niko Dimitriou, Detective Constable Paul Osman and Detective Sergeant Mike Brugge.

"Niko, we have a series of questions that we need to ask you but the one most pressing on our mind is, do you know two girls by the name of Linda and Rachel, we don't have a surname? They are now around sixteen to eighteen years of age but you may have known them ten years or so ago when they were young children?"

"What are you trying to pin on me?" he suddenly said, standing up again from behind the table and holding on to each corner, like before. I'm not a murderer and I have no interest in kids," he said in an almost spitting fashion.

"We are not suggesting you had anything to do with their abduction but it's looking extremely likely that Joseph Trievelle may have had something to do with it. Please, try to think if those names mean anything to you," asked Mike, trying to restore some order to the session.

"Loads of kids pass through that home," said Niko. "Some, they find new homes and some stay for years," he told them.

"Why did you stay so long after your revelation?" asked Paul.

"Because I had nowhere else to go," he said. "I was so young, naïve, and I had no one. Eventually, when the beatings got so bad, I stayed full time in the cabin and Joseph thought I had run away. Doreen used to sneak food to me but then she got caught. We basically stood trial together in front of him. We were on our knees begging for forgiveness as he thrashed us both. Then he dropped a bomb shell. He said we would never work again and that we would have no life at all. He produced from his inside pocket two death certificates. Joseph Treville was so wealthy he had his finger in every pie possible. He had dealings with corrupt priests, police officers and several figures of high standing. We both have a gravestone, you know," he said holding his head in his hands again. "In Holden's Hill Cemetery," he added. "Yeah, says we both died in 1981."

"But we can't find any listings of you anywhere in the public records," questioned Mike.

"Well, that's because my real name is Nicolas James," he said, tears rolling down his face. "That monster basically killed us, ruined our lives completely. We haven't been able to work properly since, because we don't exist."

"How come you run the kebab shop?" said Mike, trying desperately to make sense of things.

"I do and I don't," he said, sniffing and wiping his nose on his sleeve.

Mike looked across at Paul. "Go on," said Paul, trying to make himself comfortable in his chair.

"I managed to get in with a new crew. Prostitute ring, sleazy stuff really but it paid and I was able to send money to Doreen, after all, I owed her. Her life was ruined trying to help me," he added. "But once again Joseph stepped in and paid them off and once more I was tossed out onto the streets. I then met a bloke who owned the block on Kingsbury Rise who gave me some work here and there, and again, Joseph intercepted, only this time, he made it so that I got all the shit jobs. Yeah, I'm basically the rent collector and I have to keep an eye on the kebab shop. Not much of a résumé is it?" he said, in a voice that was now almost squealing like he couldn't believe his life had come to this. He snarled and then stood up. "Yeah, they call me the rent boy," he said snot dripping from his nose. He sat back down, his chair wobbling beneath him.

"Does Joseph Treville live at The Sanctuary?" asked Mike, suddenly wondering if he might live off-site.

"No, Gordon Square," said Niko placing his head down on the table. "Number 55," he added. "Spends most of his time in the States now though," he told them, looking back up. "Remarried years ago and had another family. From what I hear, spends very little time in England."

"OK," said Mike, standing up and looking over at Paul. They now had an address on Gordon Square and Mike knew, he just knew that this would be where their prison cell had been. Mike went through the process of charging Niko with the rape and assault of Mel and then he brought the interview session to a close at 7pm.

Ten

Mike raced down the corridor, yelling at everyone that they now had an address on Gordon Square and that he wanted a team round there now. Mike's heart was racing, he knew by being witness to the hypnosis sessions what horrors were about to unfold. He looked over at Paul who was grabbing his jacket and then they both took the front steps two at a time.

They pulled into Gordon Square at 7.15pm, blue sirens flashing. Several police cars swerved to a halt around them, stopping at number 55. Curtains were twitching as neighbours desperately tried discreetly to view the evening's entertainment, some bolder stepping out onto the street to get a better view. Mike rapped on the door knocker and then repeated his action a few seconds later. He called through the letterbox ensuring that there was no doubt about who they were. Mike stepped back repulsed by the smell that was seeping through the letterbox and then he gave the order to kick in the door.

He stepped back to allow an officer to force the door, shouting across to Paul that something or someone was dead in there, as he heaved from the pungent smell of death. Mike pulled his jumper up over his nose as he stepped into the grand hallway with a sweeping staircase. The smell was overwhelming and the walls were awash with bluebottles, floor to ceiling. The floor was moving, alive with maggots, blue bottles and other insects, as Mike weaved his way through to the front room. The door was slightly ajar and Mike hesitated momentarily before entering and then stood rooted to the spot. There, sitting by the fireside, was Joseph Treville, clutching at his chest. His head was resting to one side, with his body slouched, as if he had attempted to stand and then staggered backwards falling in his final moments. His eyes were bulging from their sockets and maggots were feeding off the mucus contents. A small part of him was green but the majority of his skin was dark red and his organs had started to liquify, producing the worst pungent gas imaginable. Some of his finger nails had dropped down onto the carpet, along with a tooth and he was covered in blisters. He had obviously been here for some time and Mike quickly calculated that it would have been around five to six weeks. A post-mortem would confirm this, of course. Perhaps it had been longer he considered, as he was unable to determine at this stage how long he had been dead and whether it correlated to when they found Jane.

He stepped back to let the coroners analyse the scene, and avoid contaminating any evidence and then stared at a photo album lying open on the table. He retrieved a pair of surgical gloves from the coroner taking samples from the surrounding area of the corpse and gasped as he saw what was presumably the real Roberta and Anika, staring back at him. He pulled on the gloves and turned the page and let out another gasp. There was Anika in a pink tutu and ballerina slippers pirouetting around a front room. She was blonde and pretty and looked extremely happy. In the corner of the room was Roberta, sitting at her easel, painting, looking totally absorbed and at peace with the world. It was a charming scene and represented what was probably a typical scene that their father came home to night after night. One he quite clearly couldn't let go of. He turned the pages again, over and over until he stopped at one of Mary, his beautiful wife. Her auburn locks framed her face and Anika and Roberta sat poised either side of her. He closed the album and placed it in a plastic evidence bag and then turned to look at the room.

There was a wingback chair either side of the inglenook fireplace, which seemed to be the theme he created over and over.

"Mike come down here," shouted Paul from below the stairs. Mike stepped out into the hall and headed towards the basement door. "Mike," came Paul's voice again, a little more urgent.

"Coming," said Mike, making his way down the staircase. There was another door at the bottom of the staircase which had a bolt top, middle and bottom. No one was getting out of there, thought Mike. He stepped into the room and gasped again. The room was identical to that in the photo album. It had been painstakingly staged, piece by piece with precision accuracy but now resembled something out of a horror movie. Mike looked around inch by inch, allowing the hypnosis sessions he had witnessed with Jane transport him into their world. He pictured the second session where Jane gave a detailed account of Anika falling during a visit and her being beaten when the re-enactment had been ruined. He also imagined what it must have been like being locked up with a corpse. The corpse of a person that had become their best friend. Joseph had obviously gone mad, psychotically disengaged to what was real and had created a living hell for these girls for the sake of fulfilling his own psychotic requirements.

Mike walked into the bathroom and picked up the medical box that had been described in one of the sessions. It contained some out of date ointment and an empty plaster wrapper. Mike placed it carefully back down on the bathroom cabinet and then stepped through to their bedroom. He stared at their beds, wondering which one Helena had met her fate, and then later decomposed in.

This was truly the worst scene in all the years he had worked in the force to witness and he felt sick to the pit of his stomach. He walked back into what would have been their main living area and stared at the empty cans piled up in the corner. These girls had been starved, surviving on cans of beans and macaroni cheese. This was a living hell and now the bastard won't even face his punishment. He stood staring as the crime scene investigators gathered evidence and placed it in plastic bags, labelling them accordingly. This was hell on earth and he wondered if the girls would ever recover to an acceptable degree, he suspected this would be unlikely.

"Paul, we need a team out the back, these houses have small yards and I suspect there will be bodies. We have a thirty-year gap to fill between Roberta and Anika dying and the Gordon girls being abducted. There is likely to be at least two more sets of girls if not three," he said sadly.

Mike made his way back upstairs and into the blue bottle, maggot filled reception hall. He stepped out onto the front steps and took a deep breath. He needed some fresh, untainted air. He sat on the bottom step and lit a cigarette and pondered his next move. So much had been uncovered today. One minute they were going nowhere and the next, they were almost at the end. Fuck this had been a heart wrenching case, he thought sadly.

Paul emerged sometime later, looking harrowed and somewhat disturbed. He was a gentle guy and Mike knew this case had troubled him deeply. It had affected them all.

"OK, Paul, let's call it a night, the crime scene investigators will be bagging up evidence for hours yet."

Paul nodded, he had a wife and son to get home to and he needed to hug his son before he went to bed.

They drove back to the station in silence, both deeply disturbed by the evening's findings.

"Night Paul," said Mike, as he stopped directly outside the station doors. "Night," said Paul, fishing for his car keys from his inside pocket. He climbed out of the van, pressed the button on his fob and headed over to his car. Mike sat for a further five minutes, running over the evening's events and then he headed home to Mel.

It was 9.45 but he knew Mel would be OK. She had been informed via Karen that Niko was in custody and Tina may still be with her for all he knew. He pulled up outside his flat, took a deep breath, and then made his way upstairs to give a blow by blow account to his partner, his best friend, the woman who suddenly meant everything to him.

"Hello," he yelled coming through the front door with sudden renewed vigour. At least he was able to report that Niko was in a cell and couldn't possibly cause her any more harm and that's reason enough to celebrate, he decided. He had so much to tell her. Mel was lying peacefully on the sofa with Lola in her arms. She had obviously stirred when he had called out but she looked relaxed, a sight he hadn't witnessed in ages. The look of relief shone out like a shiny trophy. They had won, he was behind bars. Mike sat down beside her and pulled her into his arms. "We've got him, Hun, we've got him," he repeated.

A tear rolled down Mel's face and then she pulled Mike to her. "Looks like someone got you too," she said, gently touching his swollen lip.

"Right, let me get us a beer," said Mike, feeling a little embarrassed at the sudden level of emotion felt by both of them.

Mel smiled, "Yeah, that would be great," she said adjusting herself on the sofa.

Mike handed her a beer and sat down. "Have you eaten anything today?" he asked suddenly, "cos I'm starving," he said, standing up and walking back over to the kitchen area. "Tell you what, I'll boil some pasta and just tip a sauce over it," he said, smiling.

"Perfect," said Mel, swigging a mouthful of beer. Mike stood washing his hands over and over, attempting to rid himself of the foulness. He felt contaminated and desperately needed a shower.

He set some pasta on to boil and headed to the bathroom. "Be back in a minute," he told Mel, as he pulled off his jumper and sat on the edge of the bed. God, that was so harrowing, he thought, as he pulled off both socks. He stood back up and unbuttoned his flies and headed to the bathroom. He reached out to the shower control, turned it on full throttle and then dropped his jeans and pants to the floor. Never before had he witnessed such a shocking scene and he knew that it would haunt him for a long time to come. He showered swiftly and returned to the kitchen just in time to save the pasta from boiling dry.

"You OK?" questioned Mel, knowing from all her years of partnering him that he needed time to digest his findings.

"Yeah, think so," he said sadly, as he opened the lid of a tomato-based sauce and placed it in the microwave. "Just can't believe the suffering they must have gone through, Mel, it's gut wrenching," he said. He plated up the pasta, grated some cheese and then wrestled the scalding sauce from the microwave. "Damn that's hot," he said flicking the lid off into the sink. He assembled both plates and headed over to the sofa handing a fork to Mel.

"Wow that looks great," said Mel, grateful for something hot and filling, as she took her plate from him.

Mike placed his down on the table and leaned back against the sofa, raising his arms up over his head into a clasp. "What a night," he said, reaching for his beer. He took a swig and turned to Mel. "Mel, I don't know where to start," he said reaching for his pasta. "Guess the cabin is probably the best point," he said, his stomach suddenly churning from the realisation that he had nearly killed Niko with a rock. He took a deep breath and began the gruelling story of how he saw someone going through the gate in Marshalswick Lane. "Wasn't sure it was him of course," said Mike, taking another swig from his beer, "but there was only one way to find out," he told her. "I hid out of sight, until I saw the silhouette of a man coming out of the cabin to sit by the campfire. I waited until I got a clear view of his face, so I could be absolutely certain it was him," he told her.

Mel sat poised, pasta sauce all over her chin. "It was him, wasn't it," she asked, interrupting him at this crucial point in his storey.

"Yes, it was him," he said, recalling his smug look as he swigged from a whisky bottle.

"I could feel the rage in me, Mel," he said, placing his pasta plate down on the table. "What he did to you," he said, tears rolling down his face. "I just couldn't stand what he did to you," he repeated.

Mel reached out to him and touched his hand. "I know," she said, tears welling up in her eyes. "But you got him," she said, "you got him."

Mike looked up and stared directly into her eyes. "I nearly killed him. I leaped from the bushes, obviously taking him by surprise and knocked him to the floor. We wrestled until I got the upper hand and then I held a rock above his head."

Mel could feel Mike's hands trembling, as she took a tighter grasp. "But you didn't Mike, you remained professional," she said, turning his face towards her.

"No, I wasn't professional, Mel, I stopped because he suddenly reverted into a child-like mode. His voice was different, subdued, frightened and he started to talk about his childhood, what had been done to him. It was really weird and then he suddenly confessed to killing two little girls. Anyway," he said, pulling at his hair, Paul turned up, separated us and we headed off to the station."

Mike rose to his feet and headed over to the fridge. "Another beer?" he offered, pulling two from the shelf.

"Yes," said Mel, placing her pasta plate onto the coffee table.

"We've been interviewing him all evening," said Mike, flipping both lids across the kitchen floor. "Mel this is going to blow you away but you know how we have established that the Gordon girls are the replacements for two little girls called Roberta and Anika, who until tonight we had no idea who they were?"

"Yes," said Mel, feeling herself start to tremble.

"Well, they are the daughters of the founder of The Sanctuary children's home, Joseph Treville." said Mike, returning to the sofa.

Mel shook her head. "How on earth did you find that out tonight?" questioned Mel, wondering how this had come about, after Niko's arrest. "Oh no," said Mel, "that's the two little girls that Niko murdered, isn't it, the ones he confessed to," she questioned.

"He didn't murder them, Mel, he was the driver of a lorry that ploughed them off the side of a mountain, over forty years ago, when he was a teenager."

Mel could barely take it all in. "But I don't understand," said Mel, trying to place the pieces together. "Oh God, Mike, Treville abducted the Gordon girls to replace his daughters," she suddenly said, the realisation overwhelming her.

"Yes," said Mike, "the harrowing account of events has been horrendous. We got an address, Mel, Joseph Treville's address, where he held the girls all these years and it was truly a chamber of horrors."

Mike's phone started ringing the sound of church bells from the kitchen counter top and Mike rose to retrieve it from its place. "Hi," he said, seeing Paul's name on the screen. "What's up?" he questioned, turning to face Mel. "Oh no," said Mike, his face turning grey. "I'll be right there. Fuck," said Mike. "They've found another room. I'm going to have to go back down there, Hun. Will you be OK?" he questioned, feeling guilty about leaving her again.

"Yeah sure," said Mel, wondering what other room and wishing he didn't have to go. "I'll be fine," she reassured him.

Mike pulled on his shoes and kissed Mel on the cheek. "I will try not to be long," he told her, as he grabbed his jacket from the side.

Thank God he had only just opened his second beer, he suddenly thought, as he climbed back into his van. He glanced at the passenger seat which was filled with sweet wrappers and sausage roll pastry flakes, remnants from his earlier mission, he thought, as he turned the key in the ignition. Another room, he considered, now what on earth would he want with another secret room and what was he about to uncover. He pulled outside number 55 where Paul was already standing on the front steps and nodded across to him. "What did they find, Paul?" he questioned, as he climbed out of the van.

Paul looked at Mike, with a harrowed expression. "Inside the master bedroom," said Paul, signalling for Mike to follow him in. "Inside the wardrobe actually, there was a secret door leading to another room," said Paul, heading towards the stairs. Mike followed Paul up the bluebottle-infested staircase and into the master bedroom, where both wardrobe doors were wide open.

"What the fuck," said Mike, as he headed inside the wardrobe doors and then stood rooted to the spot. "Oh no," said Mike, almost dropping to his knees, as he steadied himself by the side of the bed. It was a shrine to his dead wife and probably replicated his marital bedroom, before the accident. There on the bedhead was an auburn wig and hanging on a coat stand in the corner of the bedroom was a fur coat, the one he had seen his wife Mary in, in one of the photographs from the family album.

The room had most definitely been habited as it was full of personal possessions. "My God, it wasn't just the girls he had abducted, he had also abducted a replacement wife," said Mike, the realisation dawning on him. The forensic team were busy bagging up evidence and taking samples of the bedding and carpet and were emptying the bathroom cabinet as they studied the scene.

"How many women did he abduct over the years and where were they now," Paul questioned.

Mike nodded, wondering the same thing, as he turned to go back outside. He stopped as he approached the doorway, pausing momentarily at the sight of piles of empty cans of beans. Whoever had been imprisoned here had experienced a similar plight and had been neglected and starved. This was a house of horrors and he needed to get outside. He made his way down the staircase and headed towards the back garden. The garden was awash with yet another forensic team who had floodlit the entire lawned area, presumably digging for remains. The suffering that had gone on in this house, thought Mike, and where were they all now? he questioned. He sat down on the wall and lit a cigarette, as he watched the team dig. The replacement Mary… or Marys he thought, were probably raped over and over for his own satisfaction. He was a monster but had managed to escape justice. He looked up as Paul came out to join him.

"Doesn't bear thinking about, does it?" stated Paul, as he lit a cigarette and joined him on the wall.

"Nope," said Mike standing up.

"Do you think the women came from The Sanctuary, like Helena?" asked Paul.

"Almost certainly," said Mike, watching the remains of a dog, presumably a family pet, be exhumed from the flower bed in the far right-hand corner. "The Sanctuary will be our first port of call in the morning, Paul. Meet you there at 9am sharp."

Eleven

As Mike approached the grounds of The Sanctuary, he was surprised to find the gates were already open. Most unlike the grand headmistress, he thought, as he drove around the flower-adorned roundabout stopping directly in front of the steps, as before.

Paul was already there but had parked a courtesy distance from the house, unlike Mike. "Morning, Mike," said Paul as he walked towards him.

"Were the gates open when you got here?" he questioned, staring down the drive.

"Yes," he said, "surprisingly so."

Mike began to wonder if word had reached the home about Joseph Treville's house being raided last night. There were lots of witnesses, so he suspected someone had tipped off Miss Rosenburg.

Mike rang the doorbell twice before a petite woman in an apron, presumably kitchen staff, opened the vast front doors. "Good Morning," she greeted, stepping out onto the step. "How can I help?"

"Good Morning," said Mike, reaching for his ID. My name is Detective Sergeant Mike Brugge and this is Detective Constable Paul Osman from Holden CID. We would like to see Miss Rosenburg, if possible. but if not we have a warrant to search the premises and interview all staff," he told her.

"Miss Rosenburg is not feeling herself this morning, Detective, and has taken to her room," she informed them.

"Can we please come inside so that we can commence?" he asked, looking over his shoulder as three more police cars pulled onto the drive. The petite woman stepped to the side and pushed the door so that they could enter. "Can I take your name?" said Mike, "and your role here please?" he said, reaching for his notebook from his inside pocket.

"I'm Molly Green and I work in the kitchens but I also do some cleaning around the home," she said quite proudly.

"Have you been here long?" asked Mike, trying to guess her age. She looked around thirty and had shoulder-length auburn hair.

"Around six months," she answered shyly, "perhaps seven. Mr Treville gave me the role," she said triumphantly. "Said I resembled his first wife."

Mike felt suddenly sick, he was having a conversation with what was presumably Treville's next victim. My God, what a lucky escape she had had, he thought. If he hadn't had that heart attack, she could have been the next Mary.

"How did you meet Mr Treville?" he asked, thinking she had an American accent.

"I met him in the States," she said coyly. "He was my saviour, offering me this role and bringing me over here," she said. "He was so kind to me, when I had nothing," she told them, "but I haven't seen him for a while and he's not answering my calls."

Mike looked at Paul who was thinking exactly the same. He was bringing his victims over from the States, lost souls, people that had no family, so no one would be looking for them.

"Molly, can you take us to someone who has worked in the kitchen for the longest period of time please?" said Paul, thinking this was a good place to start.

"Mrs Jones has worked here for over forty years," said Molly, "as she keeps showing everyone her long-service certificate that Mr Treville awarded her a few years ago. She's very proud of it," she added. "It's her day off today and she usually goes into town but she hasn't left yet," Molly told them. "She's in the kitchen pantry having breakfast at the moment."

"Can you take us to her please, Molly?" asked Mike, thinking that they needed to act fast before she slipped into town.

Molly suddenly looked a little nervous. "Oh, she won't like being interrupted," said Molly, hesitating slightly.

"Too bad," said Mike. "Which way is the kitchen pantry, Molly?"

Molly pointed in the direction of the pantry and Mike ushered her along to lead the way.

"Mrs Jones, I presume?" questioned Mike, as they entered the kitchen pantry.

"Yes," said Mrs Jones, rising to her feet and replacing her napkin on the table. She looked totally shocked at having her breakfast disturbed, as she reached to take the ID badge being waived in front of her.

"I am Detective Sergeant Mike Brugge and this is Detective Constable Paul Osman from Holden Central CID, and we would like to ask you a few questions."

Mrs Jones gave Molly a look of disapproval, which made Molly disappear forthwith.

"What can I do for you, gentleman?" she asked pointing to the two chairs either side of the table. She reached for two cups and placed them in front of them and then raised the teapot. "Tea anyone?" she asked, looking at them both in turn.

"Yes please," Paul said, thinking why not? they could be here all morning.

"Coffee please," said Mike looking at the filter-coffee pot on the side. Mrs Jones rose to her feet, lifted the pot and returned to the table, agitated at his front.

"Mrs Jones," said Mike, reaching for the sugar bowl, "we would like to ask you some questions about Mr Treville."

Mrs Jones stiffened, coughed, cleared her throat and sat back down. "What is it you would like to know exactly?" she questioned.

"Mrs Jones, Mr Treville was found dead yesterday evening in his house on Gordon Square."

Mrs Jones released her grip on her cup and rose to her feet, knocking her chair backwards as she stood. "Dead?" she questioned, dabbing her spillage with her napkin. She sat back down in the chair shaking and then placed her head in her hands. "How did it happen?" she questioned between sobs.

"We suspect a heart attack but the coroner's report will confirm that," said Paul, thinking she obviously had a good relationship with him and perhaps didn't know he was a monster.

"Now I know this is obviously a shock," said Mike, deciding to take over, "but we need to ask you some questions. How long have you known Mr Treville?" Mike asked, as he studied her demeanour.

"Over forty years," she said, a tear rolling down her cheek. "I was here when he turned this place into a home for children who had nothing," she said proudly.

"Did you have a good relationship with Mr Treville?" asked Paul, as he took a mouthful of tea.

"Yes," said Mrs Jones, trying to catch her breath. "He was like a son to me," she told them.

"Do you know someone called Doreen who used to work here in the kitchen?" asked Mike. He watched carefully as she paused before replying. "Presumably you must have known her if you have been here so long," he added, trying to ensure that she didn't deny all knowledge of her.

"Yes," she replied, "I knew her."

"And Niko or should I say Nicholas who had a close relationship with Doreen? What do you know about him?" he added.

Mrs Jones coughed again and reached for her napkin to dry her eyes. "Yes, Nicholas was a difficult boy, hard to control," she added. "Doreen was too soft with him and mothered him, overly so. Sadly, they both died," she told them. "They are buried in Holden Hill Cemetery," she informed them both.

"How did they die, Mrs Jones?" questioned Paul.

"Swimming accident," she said, rising to her feet, as if she was bringing the questions to a close.

"Mrs Jones, please sit down or we will have to do this down at the station," said Mike, growing really fed up with everyone's lack of co-operation.

Mrs Jones sat down and called out to Molly. "Molly, please fetch Miss Rosenburg from her room," she instructed, before Mike had the chance to intervene.

"What do you know about the beatings Nicholas used to endure at the hands of Mr Treville, Mrs Jones?"

"I don't know what you mean," said Mrs Jones, starting to tremble.

"Mrs Jones, Nicolas used to endure the most horrific assaults at the hands of Joseph Treville and Doreen used to try to protect him. Now isn't that the truth?" he asked in a loud agitated voice.

"I don't know anything about that," said Mrs Jones standing up and walking over to the window, as if needing to distance herself from her attacker.

"Mrs Jones, correct me if I am wrong, but surely a woman as closely connected as you say you are to Mr Treville, a woman who is in charge of the kitchen and has been here for over forty years, knows something about the suffering of a young teenage boy."

"No, I don't," she repeated.

"What do you know about two young girls around eight and ten brought here around ten years ago called Linda and Rachel?"

Mrs Jones started to tremble uncontrollably and then started to stutter. "I remember, I remember," she repeated, "two young girls being brought here in the middle of the night. They were orphans to a prostitute who had died due to a heroin overdose and had no family. Mr Treville took them in but by the next morning they were gone," she said.

"Gone where, Mrs Jones, where did they go?"

"Mr Treville said they had gone to a family in Switzerland and were just passing through and had caught the early-morning flight."

"Didn't you think that was a bit odd, Mrs Jones?" questioned Paul, "that two little girls came in the middle of the night and were gone by morning? Was that a regular occurrence here?" he questioned.

"It had happened a couple of times before," said Mrs Jones. "Mr Treville used to try to find suitable homes for children, that was his mission and these things had been arranged prior, so they just passed through."

"Did you know their surname, Mrs Jones?" questioned Mike, growing more and more impatient.

"Blossom, I remember specifically because they arrived in the spring so it kind of stuck in my head," she told them, talking into her hanky.

"That's enough, Mrs Jones, thank you," said Miss Rosenburg. "Detective Brugge, why are you questioning my staff again?" said Miss Rosenburg standing sternly in the doorway.

"Miss Rosenburg, as you are aware we are dealing with an abduction and possibly a multiple murder enquiry. Now we do have a warrant to search these premises but, as it is a children's, home, we are fully aware of the implications of causing disruption to the children here, so we plan to minimise this as much as possible. I have decided that due to the gravity of the situation, I would like to question you further at the station, together with Mrs Jones," he said, determinedly.

"Are we under arrest Detective Brugge?" questioned Miss Rosenburg, as she stared mercilessly at Mrs Jones.

"At present, Miss Rosenburg, you're merely helping us with our enquiries, which I am sure a woman of your standing would wish to cooperate with," he said sarcastically.

Miss Rosenburg hesitated briefly, then half-heartedly agreed to accompany them down to the station, along with a sniffling Mrs Jones.

"Paul, take them with you and I'll catch up with you later," Mike told him while out of earshot. "I want to take a look around Joseph Treville's study before returning to the station."

Paul nodded, he was thinking the same and wondered what might be uncovered in the depths of the archives here at The Sanctuary. Paul ushered both Mrs Jones and Miss Rosenburg out of the home, after a series of delays provoked by two very awkward, troublesome, laborious old ladies.

Mike spent most of the afternoon, searching through Joseph Treville's office, filing cabinets and the The Sanctuary archives, while his team sympathetically searched the rest of the home, which sadly unearthed the possible plight of two further sets of girls and three 'Mary' substitutes. Mike looked at the pile of papers on the floor that he had painstakingly scrutinised until he felt certain that he had covered everything since the night of the accident forty-three years ago, leading up to the present day. He bagged everything up, along with some photographs and passed them across to Jim. Jim and Dave had been working their way through the kitchen-staff records that had uncovered Helena's true identity.

"Jim, she was only twenty-seven, had her whole life ahead of her," said Mike, passing the document back to Jim.

"Yeah, does make you wonder whether he had intended for her to be Mary originally but possibly changed direction with his requirements," said Jim.

"Yeah, perhaps he suddenly decided he didn't need a 'Mary' replacement anymore and decided to utilise her in with the girls," said Dave.

Mike looked across at them both. "I think that was probably the case. He put her in with them as some sort of mother figure as his visits lessened. He basically lost interest, grew tired of the effort involved traipsing back and forth from the States, and they became a nuisance to him," said Mike. "Right, guys, let's get all this back to the station and call a briefing. Dhillon's gonna want everything we've got."

Mike made his way back to the station in total bewilderment. Joseph Treville had been responsible, single-handedly, for the possible abduction of six girls, Helena, and three other women and had also ruined the lives of Nicolas and Doreen, which without a doubt had to be added to his list of victims.

Twelve

“It's Christmas Eve, Mel and I’m taking you out,” Mike said smiling.

“But I’m not really sure I’m ready to face anyone yet, Mike, I’ve only just come out of hospital,” she said, defending herself by putting up a good argument.

“Yeah, I’m fully aware of your circumstances but it’s only the guys down at the station, Mel, and the gathering is just the team in the office,” he told her.

“But I can’t walk,” said Mel, starting to worry about coming face to face with everyone.

“Ah, but I’ve sorted that, as I’ve borrowed a wheelchair from the hospital,” said Mike triumphantly.

“Really,” said Mel, knowing that when Mike was determined there was no stopping him. “And,” he said, adding some weight to his defence argument, “we will only stop for half an hour,” he told her.

“OK, OK,” said Mel, knowing that it would probably do her some good to get out there. Niko was behind bars awaiting trial, so there was nothing stopping her, she thought. She brushed her hair and pulled it up into a ponytail and stared at her reflection in the mirror. She looked pale and still had some bruising around her eyes and chin but she was alive and now needed to live her life to the full. A lot of lessons had been learned with the Gordon case, about how precious life was and that you needed to make every second count.

Mike helped her into her trainers and bomber jacket and then helped her hobble down the steps towards the van.

"So where is it then, this wheelchair thingy," said Mel, as she buckled herself into her belt.

"It's in the back, young lady, and even has some decorative tinsel," he said with a twinkle in his eye.

Mel smiled, he really did try his best, she thought, patting him on the knee. She was really nervous about seeing everyone and could feel herself trembling slightly as they approached the station car park. Mike knew that this was a big deal for her, but he also knew that if he didn't get her out and about soon, it would be detrimental to her recovery, as he knew how Mel ticked.

"You OK?" he questioned, looking her straight in the eye, after parking in his usual space.

"Yeah, a bit shaky but I'll be fine," she said reassuring him that she wasn't being tortured.

Mike opened the back of the van and revealed a slimline wheelchair with pink tinsel around the back of the chair.

"Very festive," said Mel, smiling as she clambered out from the passenger seat.

"It will make things a lot easier, Mel, so I can take you places over the next few weeks," he told her, as he helped her into the chair.

"Indeed, cos I have a hectic schedule," she said half-sarcastically, as she giggled.

"Right, we will have to go up the ramp," he said, wheeling her over to the disabled entrance.

"Oh, but I want to go up the stairs," she said, laughing again.

"Very funny," he said, steering her over to the door. He pulled open the door and wheeled her down the corridor.

"Hey, haven't you forgotten something," she said, pointing at the coffee machine."

"Very funny, you're being very humorous this afternoon," he said.

He turned the corner and everyone let out a roar. Everyone was cheering and clapping and pulling party poppers.

"Merry Christmas, everyone," shouted Dhillon, along with everyone else. Mike blushed and turned to face Mel. "I knew we were having a small celebration but I wasn't expecting this, honest," he said, accepting the beer that Paul was holding out to him. He passed one to Mel and chinked her bottle against his. "Merry Christmas, darling," he said with cheer.

"Right," said Superintendent Dhillon, clearing his throat, "I want to say a few words, if I may," he said, holding his beer up high. "Firstly, I want to thank you all for all the excellent work involved in solving the Gordon case. I understand from Mike that the girls are improving slowly but they have a long way to go, of course. Sadly, we are no further forward in identifying where the victims were buried, as we uncovered nothing at the Gordon Square address but The Sanctuary grounds are vast, so this will be our next search place," he said, raising some hope that these victims would be laid to rest respectfully. "Secondly, I would like you all to know that I have offered Mike a promotion which would involve him relocating to South Wales and as yet he hasn't given me his decision!" said Dhillon, focusing his stare on Mike.

Everyone gasped, not knowing whether to cheer or remain quiet as they concentrated their focus on him. Mike took a step backwards, totally unprepared for this sudden unveiling in front of all his colleagues. Mel started fidgeting in her chair, she really didn't want him to go, it would break her heart. She had secretly fallen in love with him and she knew her world would crumble into a million pieces if he went. She waited with bated breath for his answer as her eyes bored into his very soul.

Mike coughed to clear his throat, looked around at all his friends and then directly at Mel. He cleared his throat again and then spoke softly. "Unfortunately," he said, staring directly at Mel. Mel started to tremble, she knew he would go, he needed more than this, he needed to feel important, he needed something to get up for in the morning. "Unfortunately, you can't get rid of me that easily," he said smiling. He turned and faced Dhillon. "I'm going to have to decline your offer, I'm afraid, as I have something more pressing here to keep me busy," he said walking towards Mel. Everyone cheered and slapped him on the back.

"Good choice, Mike," said Paul, pointing over at Mel.

"Excellent choice," he responded, raising his beer.

"Where do you want to go now, young lady," said Mike, wheeling her away from all the excitement.

"Do you know where I want to go?" said Mel suddenly. "Can you take me to the cemetery?" she requested.

"I want to see their graves."

"What, Niko and Doreen's graves?" queried Mike.

"Yes, I feel I want to see them, I want to read the inscription," said Mel, suddenly feeling really curious.

"OK, your wish is my command," he said jovially. "Odd place, may I say, to spend Christmas Eve," he said, playfully.

"Just take me there, Flossy," she said, giving him that look that you couldn't refuse. They made their way back out to the van and drove the ten-minute journey across to the cemetery.

"God, you choose probably the coldest day of the year to visit a graveyard," he said shivering as he pulled the wheelchair from the back of the van.

"Yeah, I know, but I want to see them," said Mel, zipping up her jacket.

Mike looked around wondering where to start. "Well, it may take a while, Mel, until we locate them."

"Well if he was supposed to have died when he was around eighteen to twenty and he was fifteen in 1976, we are looking for graves that were dug around 1979– 81.

"Yeah but it doesn't always work like that, as some people have family plots," said Mike.

"Well we can safely say Niko didn't have a plot, Mike," she said, raising her eyebrows.

"Yeah," said Mike, feeling embarrassed. "Get in this chair, 'know-it-all', I'm freezing my bollocks off here," he said laughing.

They weaved their way up and down the foot paths until they came to an area where lots of the stones had burials which were from the seventies. "Hey Mike, what was Doreen's last name again?" questioned Mel.

"Well, she goes by the name of Johnson now but I suspect that's fictitious but Niko was called Nicholas James and they were buried side by side according to Niko," said Mike.

"Mike, look over there," said Mel, pointing, "that's it," she said, starting to shiver, "wheel me closer."

"Yeah that's it, Mel, you found them. They both stared at the inscription on the graves, lost in their own thoughts.

"Hey, Doreen's real name is Doreen Williams," said Mel, reading the wording.

"Doreen Williams, 1942 to 1979." Mike read the inscription over and over in his head and then turned to read Niko's. "Gives a whole new meaning to the saying 'Dead Man Walking' doesn't it?" he said, with an ironic tone, as he read Niko's tombstone.

"Guess it does," said Mel, thinking how awful it must be for them to be dead to the rest of the world. "You know you need to interview the priest, Mike," said Mel. "You mentioned that Joseph Treville was involved with corrupt individuals, including a priest.

Well you can't go around conducting fake funerals, Mike," she said, staring up at him.

"Yeah, we will cover that, Mel, I'm gonna leave no stone unturned not even a tombstone," he said, smiling. "Right, where can I take you now?" he said sarcastically, "Rock climbing?"

"Actually," said Mel, "can you take me to Fred and Sheila's for a Christmas coconut slice," she said smiling.

"Anything for you, princess," he said, pushing her along the pathway.

"Mike stop, stop," she repeated. "I know where all the bodies are," she said, suddenly feeling all shaky. "Mike, they're in Doreen and Niko's graves."

Mike stopped in his tracks and turned back to face the graves, the realisation suddenly dawning on him. "Oh my God, Mel, I think you're right," he said walking back over towards them.

"Mike, we need to get a team out here now to exhume the graves," she said with a look of horror unfolding on her face.

Mike turned and looked at her and then retrieved his phone from his pocket.

Acknowledgements

I would like to thank my husband, Ian, and my sister-in-law, Tina, for their support and encouragement and for taking the time to read my drafts.

Available worldwide from Amazon

www.mtp.agency

@mtp_agency

www.facebook.com/mtp.agency

Michael Terence
Publishing

Printed in Great Britain
by Amazon

66838346R00149